LEHAVRE'S UNTOLD STORIES
The Romance of the Abandoned

Marissa Conklin
Romantic Suspense; Creator of Lehavre

PUBLICATION CONSULTANTS
We Believe In The Power Of Authors

8370 Eleusis Drive, Anchorage, Alaska 99502-4630
books@publicationconsultants.com—www.publicationconsultants.com

ISBN Number: 978-1-59433-718-5
eBook ISBN Number: 978-1-59433-742-0

Library of Congress Number:

Manufactured in the United States of America

To my boyfriend Ronnie - you show me every day that romance and love can occasionally be just as sweet and healthy as a fairytale, as long as we communicate and respect each other. I am so blessed and happy that God brought us to each other!

And to my son Justin - I hope and pray that you have the best possible childhood and life, and that you always know you are whole-heartedly loved - by the Lord and by your mom!

Contents

Chapter 1
THE TRAUMA BEHIND THE GIRL

Donyelle's POV:

Ugh!! This is proper frustrating! There is nothing quite as annoying as not understanding something; and I can't for the LIFE of me figure out why a bush full of blooms that should be in the best flowering time of their life just refuses to blossom. It is simply aggravating, I had tried every trick in my botanist book, still nothing. And even more frustrating... just like my wilting flowers, I feel like I'm not able to bloom either. I am in the best season of my life to date! I am in my early twenties, more successful than I ever have been before, in large part thanks to the Queen and King a.k.a. my best friend and her husband. I am the most sought-after florist in not only the whole kingdom but in other countries as well at this point after the intricate beautiful wedding decor I created. I am in the best financial position of my life; I don't have to scrounge for pennies, I don't even have to take every job that's asked anymore, I get to pick and choose what I want to handle and which clients I don't want to work with. I've got great friends, Ahyoka and I have gotten closer, as well as the hairstylist and fashion sisters Ariana and Rita that have recently been giving me the hook up on gorgeous clothes and hair designs that I never would have had the time and patience to create for myself, and goodness knows my hair is difficult to work with. Even better than all that, I have a proper good boyfriend that dotes on me and makes me feel special all the time. *Or... at least I did. Until that went all pear-shaped.*

In an angry gesture I accidentally snipped a rose while I was pruning, making me growl. *Okay yea, I'm angry. So angry. He broke up with me because he said he wasn't getting the "full Donyelle." And I had argued, because of course I did. But deep down, I know he's right, he wasn't off his trolley. I don't want to admit it, especially to him, but I haven't blossomed, I haven't opened up and shared my life story or my feelings... and I can't for the life of me figure out why I have such a wall around my heart. I wasn't physically assaulted like Caroline was. I I was not subjected to any sexual attack. On the contrary, I really liked sex. Sex was easy. Uncomplicated. I could let my passion take over and I didn't have to try to communicate, my body did the talking with a really good shag. I am good at being physically intimate. Really good. And I only want to do things I am good at. I am not, however, good at expressing my emotions. At all. Any time I feel myself getting a little vulnerable, saying something a little too close to my heart, I get snippy. I go on the defensive, saying some snappy (maybe even rude) comment to change the subject or get the heat off me. And I don't know why. It isn't like I am trying to sack him off...*

My parents... well they weren't ideal, seeing as I had never seen them, they basically washed their hands of me when I was born. I was an only child, and they apparently wanted to empty nest much sooner than most parents did. I hadn't seen them in person ever, only a few pictures Grams had kept and shown me when I was old enough to understand that Grams was forced to 'keep an eye on me' even in the midst of Grams' condition. We were dirt-poor. Meanwhile my birth parents got to galivant across the globe to their heart's content, conveniently forgetting they ever had a daughter. I had sworn to myself that I would never be poor again, that I would work my way up and really be somebody... maybe then my family would notice me. Recognize me as their daughter for the first time, want to be around me. But apparently even being famous and successful couldn't get them to take the time. Maybe that was why I was so bitter deep down. It wasn't fair that I was taking out my issues on Flynn. But he had given up, like just about everyone else in my life did eventually, especially every man. Who needs men anyway? I can still blossom all on my own. I don't need someone telling me how I have to live, and what I should or shouldn't feel... right?

But the stabbing in my heart told a different story. I was as close to being in love with Flynn as I had ever been before. I had a lot of baggage. A lot. And I just couldn't break down and share it. I had given Caroline the cliff notes version, but even she didn't know the depths of my true pain. No one in this world did, least of all my so-called parents.

Speaking of Caroline and Ryan, that's the kind of love I aspire to have. The whole time she was pregnant, he doted on her like she was his world. Instead of being terrified, especially when it was discovered that she was carrying twins, he wept with joy, it was tremendous to see how thrilled he was, absolutely overcome with exultation and a little trepidation He tried to restrict her worries as much as possible, and when the midwives tried to tell him that it wasn't proper for people of nobility to be in the birthing room, he quickly shut that down, reminding them that as King he can and will be where he needs to be, at his wife's side. If that weren't saccharine-sweet enough, he was there for her every step of the way, and I swear if he could have pushed for her, he would have. He even deferred to Caroline when it came to baby names. They had a boy and a girl. The sweet, cooing Calista, and the feisty talkative Rigel, both named based on the parents' first letter, and because they sound like (and are) stars or constellations. Supposedly Rigel is one of the brightest stars in the sky. King Ryan was so moved by her tribute, even more so when the children had middle names based on his mom (Grace) and our impactful friend (Robbie). Somehow in a miracle of miracles, even knowing all she knows, Caroline entrusted me with godmother status of her baby son Rigel. Flynn and I got the honor of godparents of Rigel, the more rambunctious of the two, at least so far. While Sebastian and Ahyoka were named godparents of the little angelic soft-sounding easy-temperament Calista. *Astounding that we were put in such a lofty role in a baby's life. I made a promise to be kind to Flynn around the babies, and I intend to keep it.* But anyway, back to Ryan:

My friend hit the jackpot with him. Even with his aversion to tears, which I do reinforce often, can't help but cry in front of him just for his faces alone... he is a dream of a man. Proper chuffed to bits for my Care. Physicality wise, he's not my cup of tea... Flynn is much more my speed, especially when it comes to attraction. *Mm. Flynn. Those bulging muscles, both his six pack, and biceps big enough to sleep on. And those eyes... everything really, made him the tastiest chocolate in town. It has been a little bit shy of a year since he dumped me. Unceremoniously, and without warning.*

My mood significantly worsened as I checked the mail and found one lone postcard. *For the life of me, I just want to chuck it in the rubbish bin, but blimey I am weak...* I checked. Another picture. "Wish you were here" scrawled hastily right next to their smug, selfish faces. *Really? You wish I were there? Then why don't you offer to have me come join you? Or come here, for that matter. In my twenty-four years of life, you haven't made any effort; why start now?* But the thing that made me extra bitter was that I *did* know why my absentee parents all of a sudden started sending me postcards. For the first time in my life, once a month, starting with the day Caroline had her coronation. *That had been a crazy day. I'm not stupid. I get the pattern. They wanted nothing to do with me, pretending I didn't exist, right up until they realized my best friend was Queen. Now I get these false 'miss you' cards. Almost wish they hadn't started sending them... but the tiny part of me that still yearns for their acceptance and approval continues to read them, almost hopes for one to finally say that they were going to come see me after all these years. Apologize for abandoning me; tell me they loved me... even empty words would help fill the aching void that is my heart.*

It wasn't like I wasn't self-sufficient. You kind of have to be, life like I had. The day I was born was the only day I had contact with my mother and father. Apparently, they had gotten pregnant young and were still determined to see the world and chase their dreams. And whatever other cliché idiotic phrases they could come up with to explain to dementia (or whatever it was)-ridden Grams that they needed her to take me 'for a little while.' It is laughable that anyone would believe they would ever come back. But my Grams, at the time, was extremely sick. She raised me on her own even amidst the amnesia for six years. In those six years, I grew up soberingly fast. Had to; Grams couldn't work. So, I worked my fingers to the bone for both of us. Until one day, she passed away in her sleep. I didn't understand, not fully, that she had died. I thought she was sleeping for the longest time, she'd been zonked for a good portion of her last year on this earth, after all. I wasn't a wazzock or anything, but I was a young child.

When I eventually figured out that she wasn't going to wake up this time, I tried to do the best I could. I had a little dosh from cleaning houses and mucking stables. Going to the store on my own was routine, Grams hadn't been able to leave the house for years, so no one questioned it, or me working, as that was all normal. Eventually, when I was skint, I confided in Caroline, my only friend, that Grams had died. She did everything she could to try to convince her mother to let me live with her, but Susan was cold then, and she wouldn't hear of another mouth to feed.

Yet Susan must have had at least a bit of a heart because she didn't like the idea of me living alone, so she ratted me out to child protective services, who forced me into an orphanage. I was bullied daily, and it was miserable. While I wasn't assaulted, I was beaten, and the words were about as bad as the beatings. The only positive was that I saved dosh to eventually escape, I was hoping for a few dozen quid at least, but any money was useful when you were broke. The few times families tried to foster me, I quickly found out that they were using it as a scam to gain a good check and free manual labor. And so, at only eleven years old, I had as much as I could stomach. Between my savings and everything Caroline had managed to store up for me as well, I ran away from the people cashing checks for my room and board who had been hitting and shoving me around, and I found a little barn that I stayed in. I froze my butt off there, still surprised to this day that I didn't get pneumonia or worse, it was dead nippy.

I spent a year in that old barn, until someone bought the land, and I had to leg it from there too. That's when I found what now is my flower shop. It was old, rotting wood, the paint was peeling, but it was a roof over my head, and no one seemed interested in it. So, I continued to work and scrape by, until I was old enough to buy the place for real. I like to think that anyway, but I am aware no bank, or realtor, would have worked with me at the tender age of twelve unless Caroline's mom hadn't co-signed on the loan and used all the money she had received from the sale of Gram's property as a down payment. Apparently, Caroline had shown her articles of the orphanage she had dumped me at being shut down due to neglect and child abuse. She must have felt some level of guilt for not taking me in or not doing her research on the place she shipped me off to.

But anyway, I digress... I'm a waffler, to be sure. As I realized I had a passion for flowers, that gave me a purpose. Flowers and Caroline are the only reasons I'm alive to this day. Anytime I get one of these postcards with these hollow well-wishes from those wankers, I can't help but be bitter, and honestly really pissed off. Each fake-cheery rectangle in the mail was a constant reminder that my life didn't have to be that awful. That my parents chose to abandon me at birth and didn't care enough to see me, speak to me, send money- none of it. I could have had a good life. A much better childhood. Might have even been allowed to be a kid. Not stressing about where my next meal would come from or if someone would catch me hiding out somewhere to try to get some sleep before working myself to exhaustion again. I learned how to cook when I was just a toddler: (though to be honest I was never a great chef) Grams couldn't do it; she'd forget the stove was on, and she was proper knackered all the time. As the amnesia got more intense, sometimes she'd completely forget about me altogether. And that abandonment and those feelings of being forgotten and unloved have carried into my adult years, instilled deep within me like a cancer, by my birthparents and even Grams. Susan too, though I'd never tell her she played a role in my trauma.

Thanks to the part I was bestowed in the royal wedding, I am a household name. If people didn't know me before, they certainly do now. And that was both a delight and a hindrance. Surely impeded my nightly escapades.

To explain what I was about to do, my nightly routine, I need to preface this by saying I am not some mental stalker chick. At least... I'd like to think I'm not. I *might* have lost the plot. It all started when Flynn moved out of the castle. He had wanted to be with his mom, to protect her and make her happy, but over the past year she had been dating a guy in earnest, and Flynn realized shortly after completing Basic that he was too underfoot. Plus, there's only so many times you want to be present for some guy kissing your mom. Even as respectful a guy as what's-his-face was. Marko, I think.

And when Dante had hooked him up with a small two bedroom he could afford, without borrowing, off just his guard salary, he gladly jumped at the opportunity. And since then, a couple times a month, Flynn asked me over. Not to have a meaningless shag, like I had hoped and anticipated, but to try to get me to change my mind about opening up. Fat chance, I told him to sod off with that poppycock. But he started to get tired of my firm "no" to each of his inquiries, and he'd been inviting me over less and less over the past three months. When I used to go, I never once parked in the driveway. Because I was weirdly at this level of celebrity where I had people sometimes follow me around to try to get a 'scoop'. Not nearly as hounded as Caroline and Ryan, but it did happen. And so, I found places I could park my car: gas stations, abandoned parking lots, strip malls, all about a mile or a bit more from his new place,

I'd parked then walked. Was it a little excessive? Sure. But I didn't want Flynn and I to get linked in the press.

But now here I am... about to do the least sane thing I've ever done. It's become a nightly ritual. Before my head hits the pillow, I simply have to go on a drive. With a very specific destination in mind. It started three months ago when I noticed Flynn was talking with Cordelia Zebedee at the castle gate. He'd looked so carefree, smiling, and laughing and who knows what. And even though she was a bigwig wedding planner to the stars, (seriously, she's on the telly doing interviews and everything) who kept me inundated with all the work I could want... I didn't like her around my man. Even if he technically wasn't mine. And so, my head had run wild that night, picturing them together, sitting on his tiny couch, talking, and playing games like we had.... And maybe far less-innocent activities. I couldn't get the images out of my mind, of them snogging... his tongue down her throat.

Therefore, I took my car, drove it to his place, feeling like a tosser as I dimmed the headlights as I turned onto his street, just so he was less likely to notice I was there... no car was in the driveway but his. And yet I didn't feel any better. I drove around to each of the places I had parked to hide my car before. Perhaps Flynn had encouraged her to hide her car and walk. I didn't feel enough peace of mind to fall asleep until I'd exhausted every option, but once I had, I felt a sense of relief that exhausted me. And so, each night, for the past almost three months, I had repeated the pattern. Had it down to a science, sadly enough. The route was memorized, I knew the full circuit I had to check before my paranoia eased. He surely didn't know. But it gave me so much peace to know he wasn't with the company of another woman. And yes, most times as I checked his driveway and each empty lot and space, I did feel psychotic. This wasn't normal behavior. We weren't even dating anymore; it'd been more than a year. But the idea of him moving on crushed my soul.

And yes, the more I think about it, I sound proper deranged, fully wonky. There's a reason I'd taken steps to ensure no one knew what I was doing. I knew exactly what Caroline would say if she found out about my nightly drive: 'If you're that bothered by the thought of him with another woman, you know how to fix that.' And did I ever. Flynn had been proper clear that his only condition was me bearing my soul, then he'd give me his whole heart without reservations. *But it's not that simple!! I would have to tell him everything. How no one cared enough to stick around. That I was so hard to love that my parents decided the best course of action was to pretend I'd never been born. Grams once told me during one of her episodes that my birth mother would have gotten an abortion if she had enough money at the time. I could never have been born at all. And yet he thought that if I told him every trauma, sharing everything that made me feel so bitter and unlovable, he would welcome me with open arms. Not bloody likely. No, if I were to get that raw, he would find out immediately what everyone else that had gotten close already knew; that I was not worth the trouble. I was like my difficult flower, refusing to bloom, even with all the perfect conditions.* And so, I drove my circuit. And just like always, there were no cars in his driveway or any of my other haunts. Normally that makes me feel better. Tonight, I just feel hollow.

I tried to turn my thoughts to the positive: *I do have one person who loves me unconditionally no matter how much of a beastly bitch I am to her; Caroline. She's ace, Care has seen me at my worst. She saw me with my dead Grams. She knows my deepest shame. Even though I've never confided everything to her, she has the best picture of what it was like growing up. And even knowing she somehow saw through all that regardless, even loving me when I explode... I can't confide in her about this. Not only is Flynn her friend, but basically Ryan's chosen brother. And much as I wouldn't blame her, I don't think she'd be able to look at me the same if I explained my nighttime behavior. I can try to justify it all I like, and trust me, I will, but it's stalking. Pure and simple. And it's irrational, dodgy... psychotic. She'd think I was pathologically insane. And though she'd handle it in her sweet voice, kid gloved in her kind Care way... she would probably encourage me to check into a looney bin. Nope. Can't ever let anyone know what I'm doing. Ever.* Though now that I think about it; it'd be better to find a way to shake this need to know. Because that's what it was. I get sick down in my gut each night. I used to love the nighttime; lived for it. Now it makes me physically ill, at times I even chunder. I didn't *want* to make sure Flynn was alone. I felt an urge; like I absolutely *had* to get in my car and do the drive.

"I'm certifiable. And I'm talking to myself, and this is a complete faff. That's healthy." I shook my head, driving back home as I ensured my headlights had turned on. I used to love how peaceful everything was as it was bathed in moonlight. But my mind hasn't let me rest in months. I'm knackered, my peace is shattered, and if that wasn't bad enough, the beauty of the moon has lost its appeal.

Three months ago, only a couple days after I had started that stupid, daft venture, I had determined I wouldn't drive. I wouldn't check on him. It was stalker behavior and I, Donyelle, was above that petty, obsessive behavior. I learned my lesson. I moved into every position you could imagine on my otherwise comfortable mattress... sleep just wouldn't come. Behind my eyelids was a barrage of images, like watching a movie, of Flynn and Cordelia. And in my waking nightmares, they were both incredibly flexible. But what really pissed me off was the fact that I was more scared that he might be falling in love with another woman than boning her. Because that meant he was falling out of love with me. And for some reason, that was too big a pill to swallow. And so, since that night of no sleep, I have gone back each night to take a gander, feeling like a crazy person. Certifiable. Proper mental. I sighed as I turned onto my street. *Thank goodness; now I can sleep.*

Chapter 2
NIGHTLY DATE

Flynn's POV:

I had just poured my glass of wine, I only ever allowed myself one. I checked the clock - a little after 11 p.m. *won't be long now.* And just like clockwork; there she was: the woman of my dreams. It had become a bit of a ritual to sip my glass of wine as I watched her attempt to sneak outside my house. I have no idea when she originally started this little nightly jaunt, but it'd been at least three months, because, on November 2nd, I had been up later than normal, usually tried to sleep around nine or so, but it was closer to eleven, and I was staring up at the sky, marveling at the bright moon, a full one; my favorite.

Whenever I looked up at the sky I thought of Ryan, my brother and most genuine friend. He and his missus had so much love for each other, they constantly acted like they were still in the honeymoon phase, even with the tiny twins. One of them being my godson. What a privilege that is! 'Course on that day, the twins hadn't been born yet. But back to that day: while watching the moon and pondering love, something odd occurred on my street. A flash. My eyes were drawn to the source, and to my astonishment, I could just barely make out the make and model of the car by the dim streetlamp near it. *No doubt in my mind, that's Doni's. But... why are her headlights off?* I watched with fascination as her car crawled at a snail's pace around the little cul-de-sac, no headlights, then as she turned back off my street, suddenly they turned back on. My mouth quirked. *Fascinating. I thought she was coming to finally make the move and see me. Why drive by my place without knocking or texting? Especially all incognito?*

Three months later, I still don't have an answer. But I found out that I could rely on her driving by. Out of the three months, there was only one random night that she didn't drive over, and I know she didn't, because that night I stayed up waiting for her. But other than that one occurrence, I could set my watch by her coming right around 11:15 p.m. - it had become second nature to wait to sleep until she came by. Drink my one glass of wine while I watched her inch by my window. I have a desire to just randomly step out into my driveway and invite her in. But I am worried I might spook her. *Who knows why she does this, or what started it, but it feels kind of... special? I mean, it is a little odd. I keep my phone close each time, in the off chance that this is her way of warming up to eventually try to talk to me. But I had vowed, over three months ago at this point, that I wouldn't push her anymore. She would have to take the steps to be vulnerable with me on her own. No amount of prodding on my end is going to work. And I don't think that is fair to either of us. I stopped inviting her over. It was tempting fate anyway. It was too hard to keep resisting her offers of sex. She just wants only physical; I need more. But I can't move on, not when I see her so often at work since she comes to the palace pretty much daily, our godson time we share together, plus our nightly dates. Well, that's what I call them in my head. I understand fully it's not a real date. In an attempt to not scare her off, I always keep my house lights off and the windows only barely cracked so I can just make out her car, but she probably can't see me. Much as I'd love to show her I'm still here, ready and waiting, I don't want to scare her by being too eager. Plus, she might never do this again if she knew, and I so look forward to her little drive-by. Does that make me weird? Possibly. No one knew about this situation; it was our little secret. And it gives me that sliver of hope I need not to attempt to move on. I know eventually I'll have to, but I can't help but pray that someday she'll just start spilling everything. I know whatever it is; I could love her regardless. I just know it. But I can't prove it without a little bit of faith and trust on her end.* "It's up to you, Doni. My heart is in your hands." I felt compelled to whisper out loud as I watched her putter back off my road, flashing her headlights back on, presumably going home. *Time for me to hit the hay. Tomorrow's another day. Opportunities abound.*

*****

I woke up at five, as I did every morning, to get in a good run before I was meant to staff the gate. The crisp fresh air usually gave me a pep in my step and boosted my mood. But I wasn't feeling so cheery this morning. *As much as I look forward to our nightly moment... I am greedy. I want so much more. And it's cutting into my sleep as well.*

As I jogged, hearing my exercise playlist in one ear, while listening to nature with the other, my mind was once again distracted. Not by the chirping of the birds, not the squirrels skittering about, not even the gentle breeze lifting the leaves in their lovely little dance... all things I usually took delight in. *This has gotten out of hand. It's so hard to be present in the moment when her image flitters through my mind at every possible second. So inconvenient. And worse; before Donyelle, I had never been this invested in someone before, other than my mom. At least mom has finally found a decent man in Marko.*

As I wrapped up my run and followed the path to the palace kitchen, it was pretty much second nature at this point to find Marko on a nearby stool helping her prep ingredients. And there he was - handsome for an older guy; though when mom calls him a "silver fox", I want to shudder. His hair was grey, but his dark skin, just a shade or two darker than my own, helped him look much younger.

What I liked most about him was that he was respectful. Not just to my mom, but he cared about me and my feelings as well. It was rare that a man treated me so well. Then again, I hadn't had the best role models when it comes to adult men. Grew up in a hurry once my father split when my younger brother Micah was born. I quickly took on the role of mom's helper, raising Micah as best I could, even being so young myself.

I will never understand how anyone could just abandon their family like he did. Never. No matter what happens in my life, I will never follow in his footsteps. And the only other guy around as I grew up was Henry! It would not be an exaggeration to say he was the absolute worst of the worst. He demeaned me for everything imaginable, tried to get me to hate myself for not being white or rich. Despised me for being from Langley, but mostly that his son had taken such a shine to me. He hated our friendship with such passion. He only allowed me around because he couldn't deny how good mom's food was.

But anyway, my mind is all over the place today. The point is I've had bad adult male role models. But Marko is different. Mom has been dating him... like six months? It's been a little over three months since I realized it was serious enough that my mom needed her own space; and I was only too happy to give it to her. Even as good a guy as Marko was; seeing my mom suck his face... left an unpleasant feeling in my stomach. I can be happy for her and feel a little disgusted at the same time.

I smiled at Marko as he waved. "Ah, Flynn! Just in time my boy. Your lovely mother was just explaining how she was going to make her world-famous pies for my birthday next week."

Mom gave him a look, and I chuckled. "Really? Seems she disagrees."

Marko belly laughed, something I really enjoyed about him, as he responded, "I may have been wheedling her a bit. She won't tell me what she has planned. Just that she has something in the works. I thought you may use your disarming charm, get the 4-1-1."

Mom grinned. "Aw. Disarming charm. Hear that Flynn my sweet? Marko knows you so well. But no honey buns; you're sadly misinformed. My mind is a steel trap; no one can pry it open unless I want to divulge my master plan."

I grimaced, because even though mom was joking, her words were too reminiscent of the evil mad King Henry... a little too close a reminder of that man that had made me feel so small. Not to mention how he made my best friend feel growing up. "Right, well, you two will have to sort that out, I need to head to my post. The first day paired up with Romero; apparently his training with Mr. Ren has been going well."

Mom gave me a knowing look. "You don't want to miss seeing her. I understand. How is Donyelle?"

There she goes; that's the issue with having such a close relationship with your mother. Can't hide anything from her. That is my plan. I know Donyelle's routine. Though it's not set in stone, she does tend to show up around eight in the morning the past couple months. Funny that, since she used to be lovingly known as the woman who could and would sleep the day away. Perhaps I flit across her mind occasionally. I'd like to think our time together has made some kind of impact. "We haven't talked much, but from what I gather, Cordelia is keeping her very busy."

Mom raised her eyebrows. "Cordelia, is it? Not Miss Zebedee? Have you gotten that close?"

I blushed. "Nothing like that. We don't talk much either, she had just asked that I call her by name."

Marko grinned, pausing his task of washing carrots to state, "Careful with those two; I've seen the way the three of you interact. There's tension there. Not sure who it's originating from, but I've felt it."

I nodded as I grabbed a quick plate, mom always made me a nice breakfast as long as I made it before my shift. "It's coming from me. Those two stress me out, something awful. I can't tell if they like or hate each other. And Doni is either really nice to me when Cordelia is around... or even more feisty."

Marko finished chopping the newly cleaned carrots, as I wondered what mom was going to use them for. After he gave the cutting board filled with carrots to mom, he wiped his hands, then came over and hugged me. I hugged him back, eyes open to catch mom's happy smile. Marko whispered, "Keep your chin up son; the Lord has a plan."

I nodded, even though I wanted to say that it'd be nice if I could be let in on His divine plan sooner rather than later. *But my mom's boyfriend is right; I need to stay positive. Must be the lack of sleep that's getting me down. Gotta stop obsessing over things I have no control over. I've done everything I can when it comes to trying to win Doni over. It isn't healthy to worry this much over something I really just need to give to God. Everything has worked out for Ryan; and my friend is more in his head than I have ever been. Therefore, I will follow his example and focus on being present rather than overthinking. And mmm, banana bread! This is an incredibly good moment to be in.*

I thanked Marko, then went to kiss my mom's cheek as I exclaimed, "The banana bread turned out better than ever! Thanks mom. Have a good day."

She gave me a smile with all the love in her heart as she told me, "Same to you, beautiful boy. Go make the world better and keep us safe."

Even though she said about the same thing every morning, I never tired of her compliments. Or her great food. I took an extra slice, not for me though; I imagine Caroline's former student, recently graduated before he started training in earnest, would enjoy a sweet treat. Start this mentorship off on the right foot.

With banana bread in hand, I followed the path back to my gate. As I turned the final corner, I noticed Romero doing some jumping jacks. I smiled at his overabundance of enthusiasm, but then rearranged my facial features as I approached so he wouldn't know that I saw his exercises. As I suspected, as I allowed myself to make excessive noise by purposefully snapping a couple branches under my normally soft feet, he rapidly stopped exercising and tried to adopt a look of polite disinterest.

I gave him a friendly wave with my free hand as I held out the plate with the other. "Good morning, Romero. Welcome to your first day. Pro tip: if you get here early enough, you can snag a great breakfast from the palace kitchen. Greta, my mom, always has a full spread prepared by 7:30 a.m. her banana bread is especially good."

He took the offered plate, looking surprised but pleased as he bit into my offering. "Thanks, Sir. This is really good!" He wiped his mouth as he asked, "So... uh... what exactly do you do at the gate all day? Just let people through?"

I grinned. *Poor Romero looks like he really doesn't want this assignment. Truth is, I know who he'd been hoping to shadow. He'd hero worshiped Robbie basically since laying eyes on him. Everything about Robbie had screamed 'bad boy' from his looks to his carefree demeanor. It had been a huge shake up to everyone when he suddenly died... And though I had been offered Robbie's position after a long grieving period, I had refused. And the new guy, Javi, is much more like Dante than Robbie had been. I guess he's okay; if you like a rock-like face that doesn't show a hint of emotion. He may be great, appearances can be deceiving after all, but his job as head bodyguard to the King sounds far more exciting to a young guy than guarding a gate all day, even if Robbie was originally the one that had inspired Romero in the first place.* "Not exactly. Let me show you." I placed my headset on just in case anyone needed me, then I turned.

With a flourish, simply because I wanted to make a good impression on the kid, I motioned for him to move with me a little to the left of the gate, near where the key shed was. I unlocked the area that held all the secrets that my job entailed as I stated, "These are all the keys to the castle. Ryan, Caroline, and I are the only three with the key to this shed."

Romero didn't look overly impressed. But I didn't expect him to be. The place was tiny. Unassuming. Just a small shed with a row of keys on a wall.

I smiled, knowing he was about to be as shocked as I was the first time Ryan showed me. I quickly typed in my access code, tapped three areas in the shed, then things started to shake. "Whoa! That was a big earthquake! We don't get many of those." Romero half-yelled in surprise.

I shook my head in amusement. *About the same as what I'd thought when I was about ten. Ryan had been so excited to show me what he'd discovered. Apparently one of the old guards who was not loyal to Henry let Ryan in on the secret way Henry spies on us all, so Ryan could protect himself as best he could as a child.*

I pointed behind Romero, and as he turned to look, he gasped in open-mouthed disbelief. "Was... was that there the whole time?"

I shook my head in response, as I placed my hand on the palm reader. "What I'm about to show you needs to stay secret. If I hear you leaked this, not only will you jeopardize your position as a guard in training, but I will not be able to trust you with the many other facets of my job that only the privileged few know about. Do you understand?"

Romero's eyes were shining with unbridled excitement for the first time since realizing he was stuck with me. "I understand. I won't breathe a word."

I nodded, typed in my code, which combined with my hand-print, opened the hidden door. I stepped through it, then said, "Good, then come with me." He and I walked down the circular staircase, very ornate, Victorian, but of course it was. Henry always had to have the most lavish and most expensive of everything, even in his secret forbidden areas. *Make it make sense... but whatever.* We descended into the bottom, revealing a luxury mahogany brown-and-orange room surrounded by a full wall of video monitors; seventy small ones all around two much larger ones. Both of those were blank, as was expected. But all the smaller cameras were showing the main corridors and communal areas all throughout the castle. Romero looked mind blown.

"There's a camera in the school! I never noticed! Whoa... why are those large monitors blank though?"

"Those cover the more intimate areas of the castle. This is why they remain unused unless there is an emergency. For example, when Caroline was abducted, I checked those feeds, to see if she were anywhere on the castle grounds. It's a huge invasion of privacy, so only myself and Ryan have access to those. Robbie did as well... before... well, you know."

The kid perked up at the mention of his idol, even though he was devastated, he would never fail to be happy to have a reminder of his fallen hero. Then his eyes swept the room as he asked, "So why even stand at the gate, since you can see the entrance from here?"

"We need to keep up appearances." I answered. "This room is a secret from the public, and from just about everyone else. We changed the security when Ryan took the crown, and yet again since we figured out *Gavin and Sons* isn't as secure as they advertised."

Romero nodded solemnly. "I'm glad... I really thought you just guard a gate all day."

"Speaking of which..." I said as I noticed on the monitor that Donyelle was pulling up, which meant we only had five minutes before she reached the gate. "Run!" I knew firsthand how cranky Doni could get if she wasn't immediately let through. I sprinted back up the stairs with a stunned Romero on my heels. The second we both cleared the stairs and were back in the shed, I quickly placed my hand on the palm reader and typed my code in order to put things back to normal as the building shook again as it returned to the small space. I didn't wait for it to change to rush out the door, locked it quickly as I saw her car parked.

She looks so annoyed, God love her. This is how I know I have a problem. Even with that patented scowl on her gorgeous face, I feel my heart skipping a beat. "Finally!" She exclaimed, then registered who was beside me. "Oh. Romero. Good to see you. Right, the mentorship. How's the first day?"

Romero smiled wider than I'd seen in a while, and I felt some concern that he may spill the beans at this very moment. *Shortest mentorship in the history of the world, if so.* "It's been good. Flynn is pretty cool."

Donyelle raised an eyebrow. "Is he?" She looked me over, a tiny smile taking over the scowl. "He is at that. I'm a little surprised to hear you're enjoying yourself watching a gate; but good for you."

My lip quirked. Just about everyone thought I had one of the least glamorous jobs at the palace. Donyelle had even asked with Ryan and I being so close, why was I stuck with such a dull job. I wanted to tell her that my job was much more meaningful than she knew, but it was better that she just thought I guarded a gate.

Romero answered, "I think Flynn has great instincts. I'm proud to learn under his mentorship."

I gave Romero a surprised but happy look as Donyelle looked taken aback. She whispered to Romero, as she looked into my eyes. "He's pretty incredible. You'll do well under his tutelage." Then she shook herself from what appeared to be a daze as she said with frustration, "Now if you'd be so kind as to let me pass, I'm supposed to be Caroline's assistant today."

I buzzed her in, but before she went back to her car, she asked, "Are you still going to be able to get baby time with your mentorship?"

I nodded easily. "Ryan told me for my lunch break he is having Dante take over the gate, then they are going to discuss more expansions. He wants to make sure you and I both get our time with Rigel."

She smiled prettily, as she always did when our godson was mentioned. "That's ace. I'll see you around noon then."

I again nodded. It wasn't as easy to talk to her with my internal struggle to keep my innermost thoughts and desires strictly my own since our breakup. After Donyelle went through, I shifted gears to showing Romero the ropes. "Here's your headset. I am going to warn you; you're going to hear a lot of chatter throughout the day. This is the power button at the bottom. At the top is this slider that changes the frequency; you can broadcast to everyone with an intercom or a headset, or just one person."

As he began to try out his new toy, using my mom's frequency to request what he wanted for lunch, my mind began to wander, as it was prone to do. Donyelle's words echoed in my mind. *Just guarding a gate... if only she knew. I'm basically the lead bodyguard masquerading as a lowly gate-watcher. After all, I was trained by the military and SWAT after the coronation incident. Nothing held a candle to Basic training.* My mind flashed back to that day, over nine months ago, directly after the wedding, before the coronation debacle. Ryan had been looking particularly upset. *For good reason – his wife had been threatened by my... brother. Though I definitely don't claim him as family, even nine months ago I'd already realized how evil he truly was; his heart, whatever he possessed, was rotten all the way through. The last thing I wanted to do was claim that psychopath as family. And while Henry was a formidable foe, something about Micah's betrayal just hit harder.*

*****

Before the impromptu war centered around Queen Caroline's coronation, before they had even gone on their honeymoon in fact, Ryan and Robbie had approached me with the issue. "My friend, I'm at my wit's end. I feel like so much has happened that has left me feeling powerless. I hate being out of control. I want Care to always feel safe with me. I was thinking... Ren is going to train the guards in training, and I have asked him to teach me as well. I want to make sure I am prepared for any future attacks. I know you and Robbie only received the most rudimentary of training... but I am afraid that won't suffice anymore..." He gave us both an apologetic look as he continued, "Sebastian gave me the number of his contact at SWAT. He has agreed to take you and Robbie and the rest of the guards I select under his wing... but first he requested you both receive military training."

I wasn't too surprised to hear it at the time, all the guards, including myself, had been woefully unprepared for the many attacks on Caroline and Ryan throughout their short romance, now that they are married and officially King and Queen, he had needed to ensure we all received the necessary training. Ryan's shoulders had been up to his ears, obviously incredibly stressed to broach this topic with us. I had offered, "I am glad to hear we will receive more training. We could use all the help we can get."

Ryan had smiled with so much relief as his shoulders immediately eased. He was always so careful not to upset me, or anyone he cared for, for that matter. "Brilliant! I knew you'd understand! Naturally, we can forgo Basic training, I have the influence to set each of my guards up with a Martial, or Captain or someone of similar status."

I had shaken my head, respectfully disagreeing. "I believe a lot of good could come of being treated as any other recruit or volunteer. We need to start from the ground up, earn our places and learn all we can. We only received our positions due to friendship and lack of qualified options. That's certainly not how we should keep our jobs, especially considering what you and Caroline have already been through."

Robbie had made a face, but in the end, he had said, "Much as Basic doesn't appeal to me... especially losing my awesome head of hair... Flynn has a good point. We can never be too prepared in this line of work. And Ariana will kill me if I don't do well. She is looking for new challenges, for us both." Ryan was thrilled to hear that his two main branches of security were on board, though being his close friends did help. I really believe that if Robbie hadn't passed away before we were supposed to be shipped off to Basic that Ryan would have interceded with the Captain for Robbie to be allowed to keep his mane of hair.

*****

Back to the present, I watched Romero as I allowed him to check a maid's ID and wave her through. Since I wasn't really needed, my mind flashed forward a little over a week later from my last memory to yet another moment that was etched in my mind. When

I had attempted to say goodbye to Doni. I had informed her that I was going to leave for Basic for at least two months, she had snapped, "Seriously?! You're going to get yourself killed! And for what?! To guard a gate? You don't need to enlist in the military to guard a glorified fence! You're putting yourself in unnecessary turmoil for no reason you knob! I know you're not a melt, you don't need to prove anything. Not to me or anyone else. We just lost Robbie, what; you want us to lose you too?!"

I had allowed her to rage because I had possessed a feeling of peace; she was showing, in her angry way, that she cared about me. She was worried about my safety, and didn't want me to get hurt. That gave me an odd surge of happiness, though I wasn't totally sure why. After she'd calmed, I had said, "Goodbye for now, Doni. We will meet again." She had moved into my arms, hugging me, looking torn between angry concern and genuine care. She had been perfumed, as she always was, in flowers, adding to her appeal. We were on the brink of kissing when she withdrew slightly. I was again overwhelmed by her great beauty. *She had and still has such magnetism. Not just because of her profound sense of style, of course that helped. She always dressed in the brightest colors, sometimes florals. And since she spent most of her time in her gigantic greenhouse, she always smelled so lovely.* Everything about Donyelle Cox drew me to her, made me feel crazy that I knew so little. I didn't even know her middle name, (still don't), but when we were close, like that memory, I could almost pretend we were. That she'd finally let down her walls and let me in.

But then, I'd gone to basic training with over fifty of Ryan's other guards, that's actually where I met Javi, Robbie's future replacement. My life drastically changed, just as abruptly as when Ryan and I had befriended each other as boys. I hadn't wanted to cut corners. I wanted equal treatment, as it would prepare me for the physical and emotional challenges of protecting the Royal Matthews' family. I learned so much in those ten weeks... Just two months and ten days... and it shaped my whole life going forward. Before that point, there had been many days that I had felt woefully unprepared to be a guard, much less the crucial component Ryan wanted me to be with regards to everyone's safety. From the very first day of Basic, I learned quickly that it wasn't what I was expecting. *If I thought Henry was tough... he was nothing compared to the harsh and demeaning Drill Sergeants. Most of them tore me down, calling me an insect, worthless, just about every insult under the sun. But I figured out the tactic pretty easily; tear us down to have somewhere to grow from; supposedly to build us up. Nothing was more nerve wracking than when we were commanded to line up for random inspections. If everything wasn't perfectly in place; outfit, weapon, the way I was standing, even the amount of water in our canteens... we would be punished. Extra laps, no chow hall; if at all feasible, I had wanted to avoid all that and try to be as receptive to the experience as possible.*

The first two weeks I think were the most brutal, at least in Basic, if I had to pick which phase was the hardest. Everything changed in an instant; gone was the luxury of sleeping in or having any free time for yourself. Bright and early took on a new meaning at 4:30 a.m. and then we were worked hard with very little breaks until lights out at 9:00 p.m. In between that time was a very strict schedule. They were very clear from day dot that this was not meant to be fun. It was the most challenging couple of months of my life, with the only exception being SWAT training. During Basic, I was shown that I was in nowhere near as decent shape as I had thought I'd been, and muscular or not, this wasn't something you could fake your way through. I took a little comfort in realizing that Javi, who was much more buff than I, was panting hard beside me. I could tell that our main Drill Sergeant was a kind man, but he could bark orders just as well as the rest of them. Some of the ruder officers set my teeth on edge, but I followed every command. It was foreign not to be given choices. Halfway through, in between the red and white phases where I was completing obstacle courses, training with assigned weapons (guns, swords, and knives, as Ryan had requested) and I was prepping for an intense field exercise known only as 'the Anvil' I began to realize I sort of liked that I wasn't allowed to think for myself. My body alarm had been set at this point; I was always awake at least ten minutes before that annoying bugle lets out its trumpet sound.

By the time we'd reached the blue phase, the last two weeks, I felt like a new man. My marksmanship had vastly improved, my skills were far more on par with my important responsibilities once I was shipped back to Lehavre. I think if Robbie had been there, he would have been more upset at the loss of his great mane of hair than the brutal endurance training and constant barrages of insults. My hair had always been short, though it was tough when they had shaved my small afro curls, made me feel like I was abandoning my African American roots. But I took heart that so many of my brothers and sisters were in the same boat. Women were afforded a little more leniency with regard to their appearance, but still, the rules were strict.

It was nice that each Sunday we were allotted an hour to fellowship with others whose religious beliefs reflected our own. Even though Javi wasn't technically Christian, I'd say he was a bit curious, he did tag along during our weekly service.

Anyway, once Basic training had been completed, we were immediately shipped to SWAT Basic training, a whole 'nother can of worms. We were included in an extensive and intensive two-week course. During that period, we went through every screening known to man. Medical, physical, psychological, tactical... you name it. Again, my level of physical and mental capacities was drastically challenged. After those two weeks, we were evaluated like every qualifying SWAT officer had been. Fifty pushups – that I could handle, I'd done my fair share in Basic. Then sit ups... eighty were required with only a two-minute time frame. I confess, I struggled, but I completed that event as well. About half of the original fifty from the palace guards attempting those tests got that far. I only had to do twenty pull-ups, but that is so much easier said than done! Every single muscle in my body ached by that point, and only fourteen of us passed that third hurdle. One last one to go; and I had felt so wiped at that point that I had doubted I could run the way I needed to. But as the timer started, and I knew I only had eighteen minutes allotted to run three miles... I used every little bit of my strength to propel myself forward. And I held on to that moment Doni and I had shared, the almost-kiss, as my mental escape as I pushed my body to its limits. I honestly think, even now, almost seven months later, that if I hadn't had that mental snapshot of a better time, I wouldn't have been able to summon the strength to pass that final test. Which is why when someone, particularly Donyelle, makes a comment about me being 'just a gate guard' or something along those lines, I can't help but smile. *If only you knew. I am part of the top two percent of people who passed not only Basic but then intense SWAT training tests as well.*

Sebastian's contact had even been brazen enough to try to poach me, said if I ever wanted a more glamourous career, I was welcome on his team. But that prestige came with personal sacrifices I couldn't make. I wouldn't see my mom's smiling face every day, taste the fruits of her labor as she made delicious things in the kitchen, or watch her proudly show me whatever she had designed in yet another suite of the palace. I wouldn't have the opportunity for my daily dose of godson cuddles, and I had been extremely surprised how healing holding a baby could be; even a fussy one like Rigel. Not to mention my best friend Ryan and his kind wife Caroline were in Lehavre waiting eagerly for my return. I would have felt like such a leech if I did all this training and used these opportunities that were funded by the King and Queen, then turned around and abandoned them.

And then... there was Donyelle. Truthfully, her presence was the biggest factor on whether I should return to Lehavre or not. Try as I might, I can't imagine a life without getting to stare into those feisty eyes. Even when she is angry, at least I am able to be around her. Even during that almost three-month stint, she never left my thoughts, or my dreams. When I closed my eyes, she was there, greeting me in soft bright lace, hot chocolate in hand. Other times, she was only in my oversized hoodie, no makeup, hair in a ponytail. Still others, she had on a long flowing dress, and her hair was done up with all these majestic braids. The dreams were all the same. Not sex dreams, like Micah, my estranged brother had described to me at random when he was bored, mine were more about... longing. In mine, she appeared vulnerable and achingly beautiful, no matter how she looked. She always said the same thing. She told me she wanted to talk; that she'd tell me everything she'd kept buried all her life. That she trusted me implicitly, and I was the only person she wanted to share her soul with. And right as she makes that heartfelt passionate speech... the floor collapses from under her, and no matter how quick I am to try to grab her, she's just... gone. Even though the end of each reverie is chilling... I can't bring myself to classify them as nightmares. They start so well! But anyway, with Donyelle, my mom, little Rigel and all the Matthews family on my mind, I had politely declined his very generous offer.

I was well received at home, though I had been shocked to discover mom had grown remarkably close to a man in my absence. I gave it a couple of months, but it became clear that he was there to stay, and though they were kind and respectful with their romance, I felt like I had overstayed my welcome. Mom deserved love, the best love the world had to offer, especially after how shitty dear old dad had been to her. So, I'd hit up Dante for a small place. Once I had that, I'd begun earnestly to have Donyelle over, trying to recreate the beginnings of those lovely dreams. But try as I might, I never broke through that impenetrable fortress around her heart. And as she not-so-subtly tried to turn our conversations to sex... I had rejected her. I could see the pain and confusion in those eyes I'd been dying to see for months... and I couldn't stand that I'd been the one to taint those haunting eyes. But I couldn't just have sex. It wasn't enough. My heart was far too invested to try to attempt a mere fling. And so, after a handful of attempts at dating her, I had stopped inviting Donyelle over. Mostly, I stopped myself from hoping that out of the blue she was going to wake up and realize how happy I could make her. Which is yet another reason I cherished those nightly drive-bys. *Who knows, perhaps one of these days she'll actually come in. I can't help but hope.*

*****

As I forced myself back to the present yet again, my apprentice was still busy fiddling with his headset, but a movement to my right caused me to come to attention. Dante sauntered up, hugging me (which I was still getting used to; he used to be so very robotic, and now he was initiating hugs), then hi-fiving Romero.

"Logan mentioned you were starting today. He's so jealous. Try to do well here, Logan is only one of like a dozen kids that are looking up to you, hoping to follow in your footsteps. The palace has never opened up guard in training positions before, so you and those other boys are trailblazers. Please show my girlfriend's kid a good example." Dante finished encouraging/challenging Romero, then paused for the boy's answer.

Romero nodded solemnly. "I will, Mr. Dante. I am happy to learn. Flynn is making my first day good."

Dante gave a tiny smile, which was still a little jarring, since he used to be so good at presenting an emotionless expression. Dante took my headset, then I waved as I rushed to the nursery. Caroline had insisted that no one but Ryan and her would raise their twins. Even though royals and governors of the surrounding lands tended to go the nanny route, she wouldn't hear of it. *It makes total sense though. Not only because she and Ryan are very hands-on rulers, but she is the ultimate lover of children, after all. Her days are spent teaching, tending to her son and daughter, while also somehow summoning the energy to advise Ryan with a gentle but wise word or look. She is incredible. I can see why Donyelle and Caroline are so close. While it is true that Doni comes off prickly, she is fiercely loyal, and she has a sweet streak that not everyone gets to see under the barbed sarcasm and British phrases. I think some of it is a defense mechanism, perhaps she is trying to scare people away that are fickle, leaving only the profoundly good influences. Some thought she liked her solitude and freedom, but I know better. I see how lonely she truly is. For all her bravado, she very much doesn't want to be alone. I can only surmise that she's been abandoned by someone with an eminent position in her life. I wish I knew more about her...*

Forcing myself out of my thoughts yet again, I thanked Dante for taking over; told Romero I'd be back in an hour. "Feel free to take your break now, just make sure to be back after the hour; we try to stick to our allotted break time unless something important comes up."

The kid didn't need to be told twice; he immediately skipped off, probably to find lunch. Luckily, my mom was such a gem, she always had a meal waiting for me in the nursery, normally with extra to share with Donyelle. It had become second nature to spend my whole break there, whether little Rigel was asleep or awake, while also giving me the chance to sit for a bit and eat. It was one of my favorite times of the day; mostly because I loved those babies, we did get to play with sweet Calista as well, but the added bonus that Donyelle always seemed to be there when I was made my time so much better. We always talked about the most random things, which I really enjoyed. She kept me on my toes, romantically and platonically. It was so nice to get to see her in this unique way, this new environment we've been in for the past couple weeks really did my heart good.

As I turned the corner, I heard humming, so I slowed and listened. It wasn't Caroline; she was a songbird and everything she sang or hummed sounded like it came from the heavens. It wasn't so completely off-pitch and hair-raising that it could be Ryan. I inched forward and tilted my head to get a look; and I saw Donyelle smiling brightly at Rigel, who looked fast asleep. She continued to hum, then said, "Blimey, it must be nice to be a baby. Not a care in the world. You don't have to worry 'bout where your next meal is coming from, how to pay the bills... who does or doesn't love you... you're so lucky bruv. What I wouldn't give to be a baby again, I'd be buzzin'. Before my life went all pear shaped - before I found out my parents were prats who willingly sacked me off. Must be nice to have parents like yours." She stroked Rigel's hand as he made a soft cooing noise in his sleep. She giggled, a musical sound, as she continued sadly, "You're proper cute. But you're also a right cheeky sort. Yet I know for a fact no matter how cheeky and naughty you might get; your parents will love you regardless. They'll sweetly show you right from wrong. And your godfather Flynn and I will too." She smiled again, as I felt a rollercoaster of emotions at simply hearing her say my name. She looked up, as heart in my throat, I rushed to duck out of her eye line. But she merely peered at the clock. "It's not like him to be so late. Where is that lad? Don't get me wrong little babe, I do like alone time with you. But he's supposed to share these moments. And it's not really a chin wag if only one of us can speak, is it?" She shifted positions, holding Rigel closer to her left hip as she said a little anxiously, "He said he was going to be here... it's not like him not to follow through... I wonder if he's okay? Does he not realize I budget my very precious free time in order to make sure we see you together, Rigel? It's rude to be late, innit? He'd better be here in a jiffy. Hmm... maybe he's in the loo. Let's give him five more minutes Rigel, and if he doesn't show up, we can be proper miffed together. Deal?"

I had planned on slowly walking out, revealing my position without embarrassing her, but I paused as she mused about my well being. She continued, as I stayed very still: "Really, what could happen to a gate guard, anyway?" She sounded like she was trying to convince herself, but then her voice raised a couple octaves as she said in a rapidly panicked tone, "Then again... lots of unsavory people try to force their way through the gate. What if someone's trying to nick something from the palace! I've never even seen him armed. What if someone has a gun? A knife?! If anything happens, his first instincts will be to protect Romero and ensure no one gets through that gate. *Ugh*! Why does he vex me so?! Should I text him? Would I look like a right nutter?" She stopped talking, as Rigel started making fussy noises as he began to wake. I peered through the gap in the walls as she patted his back. "Sorry to wake you babe; I'm not going to shush you; you go ahead and cry if that's what you need. We can both cry together. Ah, I'm so pathetic. Can't let him fully in but can't stand it when I don't know where he is... how he is... oh Rigel, I've gone all pear shaped. I feel like a sandwich short of a picnic! This is just beastly. Look baby, I know I'm loquacious, but a conversation takes two, and you're not holding up your end of the deal." Rigel made a cooing noise, and Donyelle's face morphed from worry and frustration to the most beautiful moment of awe. "Can I tell you a secret, little Rigel?"

She paused, and I couldn't help but lean forward, waiting for whatever she was going to reveal. It seemed wrong to let her keep talking, not realizing she had an adult audience... but I felt compelled to stay and learn what I could. I'd already gleaned that she cared for me far more than she'd ever let on in the past. *Though it may be wrong, I feel like I'll never learn these hidden truths unless I stay put... a moral quandary, for certain.*

"Here's my secret: I want a baby. Just like you: a bird or a bloke; full of spirit and curiosity; life." There was an eagerness in her tone that was a stark contrast to her sad demeanor, and I found myself aching with longing to be able to help her create the wonderful baby she and I both wished for. She lowered her voice even more as she sighed, a single tear rolling down her lovely cheek. "But it's not to be. I can't be a mother. Not one a baby deserves. I have too many issues. Too stroppy. I want so badly to curse... but I shouldn't say that in front of you. Let's just... pretend I didn't say I wanted to, okay? But Rigel, I can't even get a guy to stay. Not a guy... the right guy... but it's no matter. As much as I want a baby, I can't be selfish. I refuse to be like... them."

So much malice in that last word. She really and truly hates whoever 'them' is referring to. I checked my watch; I only had about twenty minutes left of my break; I'd really let observing eat into my time. I checked, made sure she looked like she hadn't been crying, then started whistling to alert her that I was coming. I watched her quickly use her right arm to wipe at her eyes, cleared her throat quietly, then I moved back and around the other side of the nursery, so hopefully it wouldn't look like I'd been there for any period of time.

Her face broadcasted her relief, until the second we locked eyes, when she quickly showed her frustration, lifting Rigel a bit as she snapped, "Nice of you to finally join us! You're extremely late!"

I just barely stopped the grin that threatened to overtake my face, as I kept my expression blank. "My apologies, I lost track of the time. But I'm here now, for the next fifteen minutes. How is Rigel?"

Her face softened as she looked down at our godson. "He had a good nap in my arms. A little fussy, but he wouldn't be Rigel without feeling those emotions. Loudly. Not slagging him off, just... an observation."

I chuckled at that; it was a great summation of our godson. His personality was far different than his sister's, but truthfully both Doni and I loved him just as he was. While Calista was sweet, calm, and angelic, mirroring her mother and father, Rigel was far more like Doni and I; wild. Rambunctious. Feisty and full of energy. He would not be a follower in life with such a vibrant personality. That stubborn streak, though it might make things a tad more difficult as he grew up, would surely make him a leader. And I loved that his strong personality was evident even at just a few months old. Donyelle offered him to me, as I eagerly took him, being sure to prop up his head. The first time I'd forgotten, Doni waited until the baby was out of my arms to smack me for my improper care. A bit unnecessary, but it did help me remember to always hold him correctly from then on, and she had threatened to give me a 'shiner' if I ever did it again.

I said softly, "Since I was late, I definitely need help eating my lunch. If you wouldn't mind picking what you'd like from that bag on the table while I play with him a bit, then we can switch before I need to head back."

She nodded easily; the first dozen times she had argued, protested that she didn't need me to feed her, and she was an independent woman who could take care of herself. But I had pointed out that my mother made the delicious meals and treats in those bags, she always made way too much for just me, so it was only going to go to waste if I didn't share. I had looked her in the eyes as I kissed her hand that first time, shocking her protests into silence as I had told her, "I am well aware that you are a strong and capable independent woman. But you can still be all that and allow people to help every once in a while." After that first time, her protests had diminished the next eleven occurrences to something like 'if you aren't going to eat it' and after that, she eventually just eagerly went for the bag, sometimes not even needing to be asked. It was yet another tradition we shared, and I treasured it.

When I'd explained the situation to Ryan, he'd given me a bemused look as he put his hand on my shoulder in a comforting gesture. "Flynn... I don't want to hurt your feelings. But I worry about you. You seem to be... well, how do I say this... it's possible that you like her more than she likes you. I just don't want you even more heart broken than you've been in the past. It seems the longer you pine for her, the more your heart is entangled. It's been... well, it's been close to a year since you guys were actually doing well as a couple. Isn't it time for you to move on?"

I had smiled at the man that was more like a brother to me than my blood relation as I had reminded him, "Clearly Caroline doesn't feel the same, or she wouldn't have decided for Doni and me to be co-godparents. At least that's my thought."

Ryan had a good chuckle at that, before he admitted, "My dear wife will never stop matchmaking. It's in her blood. You're right; Care is rooting for you and Donyelle. But as much as I like Donyelle, and I really do; I care more about you and your feelings. And since she's made it pretty clear that she isn't willing to take that next step with you... I just feel that you're stuck in this limbo where you can't move forward, can't move on... I want more for you, Flynn. You're the best guy I know. Well, you and Sebastian. He's a pretty good guy too."

I had laughingly agreed with him at the time. Even though Sebastian was an actor by trade, he was the most genuinely kind person. He and Ahyoka were incredible together and extremely dedicated to their long-distance romance.

I was rudely interrupted from my musing by a harsh alarm. Donyelle was struggling to use her one free hand to fish out her offending phone from her left pocket, but Rigel's fidgeting and screaming was making the task difficult.

"Want my help?" I offered, and to my surprise, she nodded. She continued to rock Rigel as I quickly moved close, squatting down, giving her an apologetic look as I fished her phone out of her jacket pocket. I expected it to be some kind of reminder alarm, something I could easily turn off... but that wasn't the case.

"Doni, this is an alert for your shop's basement window."

Panic took over her features as she gave Rigel to me. Somehow Calista was still asleep, which was even more crazy considering how loud Rigel was being. I heard rushed footsteps approaching, and then Caroline was there. "What's going on? Is everyone okay?" Even in the midst of a crisis, Queen Caroline looked and acted with a regal, sweet confidence.

Donyelle answered, "Soz Care, I was just trying to figure out how to turn off this god-awful winding up alarm-" she pushed a button, and it finally stopped blaring. She was still tense as she continued, "One of my shop alarms is going off, might be nothing... but I need to go check anyway."

Caroline grimaced before smiling at her two children, scooping up Rigel as she soothed him. "I don't like the idea of you going and checking on your own..." Caroline gave me a look, and I immediately picked up on her hidden question.

I volunteered easily with a wave of my hand, "I could go with Donyelle, help her make sure everything's okay at her shop? My lunch is almost over though."

"You don't need to come; I'll be fine-" Donyelle insisted, even backing up physically, but as Caroline gave her a very pointed mom look, Donyelle stopped everything - moving and talking. *Wow. I guess that's the power of being friends so long.*

"Oh Flynn, thank you. I'll feel *so* much better knowing my best friend is safe. Dante is watching the gate, right? He'd be fine to stay longer, especially since Whit will be here soon to get Logan and Bobby-Jean. Speaking of the kids, I should get back to class. Ahyoka took over when I heard the alarm on the monitor. Lily is coming to get grandkid time. Love you both!"

And just like that, she kissed her now-calm son, placed him softly in his crib, then swept out of the room, leaving both Donyelle and I no time to argue. Donyelle in particular looked pretty shocked by how that interaction went down as she mused out loud, "...She's getting better at using that look. I pity Calista and Rigel; they aren't going to be able to get away with much if she looks at them like that."

I chuckled a bit, as both Donyelle and I blew a kiss to our god-son and then left the room, Doni two steps ahead of me. "Yeah, I was just thinking that she's really got that mom-stare down pat already. So different from her ever-present smile. I would like to help; let me just tell Dante and Romero what I'm doing. I imagine you won't let me give you a ride."

She looked behind her to give me a raised eyebrow. "You assumed correctly. I don't need to be chauffeured around. Having you there to check things out with me is the wise choice. But no need for a ride." She paused, then raised her head a bit to look me straight in my eyes. "Soz Flynn, Thanks... I do appreciate you coming."

I smiled at her, temporarily taken aback by those eyes of Her's locking onto mine, then following as she went out to the parking lot. *If I didn't go with Doni, I'd be worried about her the rest of the day. Thank goodness Caroline stepped in when she did.* I got into my car and turned the key on Old Faithful... and after about three or four times, it turned over and eventually started.

Dante greeted me as I made it to the gate. I opened my mouth to explain, but Romero was standing there with Dante, holding an almost-eaten sandwich, saying between chomps, "Queen Caroline let us know you need to help Miss Donyelle. Mr. Dante is going ta' stay with me til' you get back."

I nodded. *Should have known she'd have already gotten things under control.* They waved me through - Donyelle's car right ahead of me, as we both traveled toward her shop. I stayed on high alert; I always seem to be a little bit on edge when Donyelle was. That feeling increased exponentially when we reached her property and quickly figured out the source of the alarm: a broken window. Shattered, glass everywhere, but the vast majority of it was on the inside. Blood was visible on the left side of the wide-open window frame, with fairly large blood splatter leading down into Donyelle's shop basement. The alarm was distractingly loud, touching the window triggered it on her phone while the blasting alarm still went off on the premises, but thankfully she noticed, and turned off both alarms, immediately creating silence.

I surveyed the scene as I suggested, "We don't know who did this, but it's obvious that if they are still here, they are wounded. Please unlock the shop and call the cops, I'll go check everything out. Once it's safe to come inside, I'll let you know." I stopped for a second, then asked, "Where is the feed to those security cameras I set up for you after the fire? Isn't it on your phone?"

She frowned immediately, and I knew I was in for an argument. "You mean the cameras you strong-armed me into letting you set up? What was it you said..." She trailed off, puffing her chest and scowling as she deepened her voice in imitation of me. "I am installing sur-veillance cameras and an alarm system. I won't hear any arguments on this matter. I know I normally don't butt it, but not where safety is concerned." She stopped scowling and added in her regular tone, "Anyway, short answer is no – I do not have the cameras or alarm set up for my phone. It's in the basement where I store the hardiest flowers. I don't want you going in there alone. Whoever it is may be dangerous..." she bit her lip and leaned back with crossed arms, broadcasting without trying that she was concerned for my safety. That bolstered my confidence as I stepped toward her, arms outstretched. *I don't want to force a hug, but she seems out of sorts, and the contact might help her relax a bit.*

After a beat, right as I was about to put my arms down and shrug off the attempt, she stepped into my embrace. Her heady floral scent filled my nose and caused me to smile despite the circumstance. She took a few deep shuddery breaths, her heart was beating really fast, but whether that was due to high anxiety or my sudden nearness I couldn't determine, then she held up her phone, so I moved back a step to allow her the space she needed to make the call. She fished out her key as she answered the person who picked up the call. "My name is Donyelle Cox, my flower shop, Dazzling Dreams by Donyelle, has been broken into. The address? It's 604 Beraguse Blvd in Langley Province. No, it was not left unlocked; there is a broken basement window. And blood." She paused, listening. "One of the palace guards is here with me, he's offered to check it out... okay... yes, just try to come soon, yeah?"

She hung up with an exasperated sigh. "I am so frustrated! She doesn't have any officers she can send at the moment; said I should take you up on your offer and report back, or we can wait until a cop can come by, but the closest one is at least forty-five minutes away..." she trailed off, a pinched, frustrated look taking over her bold features. She sighed. "Well, let's go. I'll cover your back. I've got some self-defense stuff in this cupboard." Intrigued by that, I watched her open the latch and reveal a hammer which she gave to me, and a bottle of mace, which she grabbed for herself.

"Smart." I commented, as she gave me a raised eyebrow. I asked, "What's that look for?"

Donyelle grinned cheekily. "I don't know, I guess I thought you'd chew me out for having a cupboard of weapons at my disposal at my place of business."

I shook my head, stating, "If it keeps you safe, I'm all for it. Since you refuse to stay outside, at least please stay behind me."

She didn't put up a fight at that, so I twisted the doorknob leading down to the basement. It was dimly lit, the broken window very bright in comparison to the rest of the space. But then she flipped on the lights, and I was treated to what looked like a wild indoor garden. It was obvious Donyelle, with Dante's help, had transformed the basement into a sort of greenhouse.

It was filled to the brim with every kind of flower I could have imagined, many I had never seen before. She was cross-pollinating quite a few, obviously experimenting with seeing what other colors and types she could nurture. *So many planters, trellises, ivy, it would have been chaotic if it weren't so beautiful. I love getting a peak into Donyelle's head, and being here in her space, it really feels like I am very privileged.*

Chapter 3
THE INTRUDER

Donyelle's POV:

I felt a large amount of pride well up inside of me as I watched Flynn take in my little indoor paradise. *He and I might argue about some things, but he appreciates what's truly important, and that says a lot about him. He's so bloody attractive. Doesn't help that his arms are so toned, so peng, having him wrap around me like that to calm me down... well, let's just say it had the opposite effect. For those brief moments where I tried to force my breathing to regulate and my heart not to explode, I almost found myself blurting out everything. That I was an unwanted and unloved orphan whose parents were very much alive, but would never deign to act like parents, so they were dead to me. Almost told him that if he could really actually love me despite my past and lack of family; not to mention my deep-seated insecurities I mask with bravado and humor, that I'd be willing to try. But then I found myself shattering the moment, raising my phone to my eyeline, and because Flynn is respectful, he allowed me to call 9-1-1.* Down in my hidden slice of heaven, watching those enticing eyes survey all I had accomplished since the fire, I felt something warm in my chest. Pride, certainly, but there was more to it.

I heard a faint sound, so I zeroed in on the far right, where the little sniffling noise had originated from. My eyes quickly went to him, and he nodded slightly, so thankfully he'd heard it too. I raised my mace but waited until Flynn advanced before taking any steps myself. *He does have the hammer after all. And he's in better shape than me.* As we both approached the sound, I couldn't see around his broad shoulders, but I was more focused on making sure I was right behind him. So, when he suddenly stopped moving, I slammed into his back.

I let out a grunt, but he didn't look my way. After I got my bearings, I peered around behind Flynn. I don't know what I was expecting the intruder to look like... but it wasn't this. It was a small girl, couldn't have been older than ten. Her hazel eyes flashed with defiance, but as I got a better look, it seemed those eyes were filled more with a deep sadness than anger. It was hard to tell from the dirty white rags clinging to her frail body and covering her hair, but I think she was a redhead. Flynn said softly, "Are you alright child? What's your name?"

The little girl sucked in a breath, raising a little hand dripping with blood. She was holding on to a large particularly pointy shard of glass like it was her lifeline, but it was cutting into her fingers, making her wince. That's when I saw it; she reminded me so painfully of me as a child. That lost, scared look masked by aggression and false bravery. *This little one has been through hell; and she isn't taking it anymore.*

I stepped around Flynn, who very obviously didn't like that I was approaching a child with a jagged piece of glass, but something instinctive told me I could reach this girl better than Flynn could. *But how?* Thinking of what Caroline would do in this situation, I took a few steps forward, picked a few white Daisies, dropping the mace softly, then I sat down on the floor, bringing them to my nose.

My actions had the desired effect; she very slightly lowered her glass weapon, casting large hazel eyes on me as I sniffed my flowers appreciatively. "Do you like Daisies?" I asked, using a very friendly tone of voice I hardly ever used except with Caroline and Ahyoka.

"I... I guess. Purple are better." *Her speech is a bit broken. There is a hint of some kind of accent.* I stood up slowly, leaning over several planters as I selected the ones I wanted. Picking a couple of the best blooms, I combined those flowers with the Daisies into a small bouquet as I held them out to the child.

"I agree with you; purple flowers are pretty special. These are called Night Sky Petunias. See how this dark purple looks a bit like the sky? And what do you think the white parts looks like?"

She peered at my flowers before answering with a ghost of a smile, "Stars!"

I smiled back encouragingly, "Exactly! Would you like these flowers? I think they'd look lovely in your hair." She looked torn, so many conflicting emotions taking over her youthful face, but eventually, she nodded.

I eased closer to her, until I was near enough to notice that her hair wasn't red at all... it was blonde but caked in blood. *Oh my gosh...* I gave Flynn a worried glance, causing him to take a few steps toward us. In response to his approach, she raised her glass like a dagger, pointing it toward him. He raised his hands, moving slower, as I said in as soothing a voice as I could, "This is Flynn, my friend. He's very kind, I promise."

The little girl looked at me, silently communicating that her newfound trust in me was tenuous and easily broken. I asked, "Could I lift this fabric off your head, to see where I can place the flowers?"

"Owie up there." She answered, sounding noticeably young in her vulnerability.

I nodded solemnly as I swore, "I will be very gentle." She allowed me to lift the veil-like fabric slowly off her head. At first it was hard to tell where the source of all the dried blood had come from, since her blonde hair was such a tangled mess caked in dark red. Eventually, as I pretended to be looking for the best place to set the flowers, I noticed it; a huge area in the back of her skull was caved in, right where her hairline began at the nape of her neck. Even with my feather-soft touch as my fingers moved across the area, she winced and groaned. Flynn looked pained by the sound, and I felt a stab in my heart at her strangled moan as well. *I don't want to make the girl even more uncomfortable, but it looks like there are some kind of marks on her shoulders, and there are assorted color bruises along her jaw line. Now that I'm getting a good look, it's as if they are in various stages of healing. My earlier thought was correct; she has been through it. What 'it' is though is anyone's guess.*

"What's your name sweetie?" Flynn asked softly, as she looked at him with fear.

"Lydia." She answered, her big eyes darting between Flynn and me. *What a coincidence!*

I smiled when her eyes landed on me. "Can I tell you a secret Lydia? Something I've never told anyone before?"

Her blonde hair shook as she nodded, before wincing at the movement. I slowly stretched out my hand, palm down so if she wanted to, she could hold my hand. No longer was I emulating Caroline, instead I was thinking of what I would have desperately wanted someone to do for me at that age. "I always loved the name Lydia. I used to dream I'd have a daughter I'd name Lydia Grace."

Lydia grinned a little despite herself at my share, and Flynn gave me a warm smile as well. She had again lowered her glass shard, though she still held it with her right hand, her left slightly grazed my hand as she hovered it above mine. "I don't know what you've gone through, Lydia-" I placed one of the purple Petunias behind her left ear as I continued, "But I do want you to know that I want to help. Did you come in here because you need a place to stay?"

The small amount of headway we made was instantly shattered as she shut down; eyes darting toward the door. Flynn noticed the change as well as he crouched down and said abundantly softly, "We aren't upset with you Lydia. You're safe."

She seemed to be measuring his words. "I've heard that before." She scoffed, with a tone that was far too jaded for her years.

Poor sweet girl, what happened to you? What have you been through, and how do I navigate this so we can help?

Sighing, I twirled my flower bouquet with my free hand, catching her attention. "I know it doesn't feel like it right now, but you are safe. Flynn and I will make sure nothing else happens to you. If you don't let us take you to a hospital, you could get infection or worse. Please let us help."

"No... no I can't go hospital. They might find me! 'Specially big hat man. No- no!" She started violently shaking, causing me to feel like a cold shadow took over my body.

Flynn offered, "What about the palace? Doctor Cornelius is a kind old man who can help you and you won't be by anyone that can find you. Unless big hat man works at the palace...?"

Lydia stilled as she answered, "No. Big hat man and them live Monic."

Monic. Hours away. Did she walk all that way to my shop? In this condition? Flynn nodded. "Will you let me pick you up?"

She hesitated. Flynn added, "I know you don't know me. How about this; I will give you this hammer-" he held it out to her, and Lydia grabbed it with the hand that had been hovering over mine. She now held the glass in one hand and the hammer in the other. Flynn asked, "Now that you have a hammer, a way to defend yourself, let's drop the glass. It's cutting your fingers."

The kid hesitated again, so I interjected, "Flynn's right, if you don't feel safe you can clobber him with the hammer." Flynn rolled his eyes at me, and suddenly I heard the last sound I expected to; she giggled. With a snort in the middle. It was a very welcome sound, and it made her seem much more her age before fear overtook her face.

"I didn't mean to; promise I didn't. Please don't smack me!" She ducked her head and made herself small as I rushed to ease her fear, but Flynn started talking before I could figure out what to say.

"Dear Lydia, no one is going to smack you! Why would you say that?" Flynn asked, concern lacing his voice.

She ducked her head slightly, and I didn't miss the jolt of her body as she felt the pain of the movement. "They didn't like me laugh. I's in-so-lent. Not 'llowed ta' laugh. 'Specially not at people."

The twisting in my heart physically hurt as the picture I was getting of this poor child became clearer. *The abuse she must have gone through...* "You laugh whenever you want with us, Lydia. Are you ready to go?"

Once she said a soft yes, Flynn scooped her up in his arms, and Lydia let the glass shard clatter to the floor. I followed as he carried her up the stairs, but when we heard a siren in the distance, she started wailing and kicking her legs as she cried, "You called police! No, they bring me them! You bad!!"

"We called the police because of the broken window; we didn't know who broke it. Flynn, please hide her in your car while I tell the cops we didn't find anyone. Bring her to the palace, I'll join you when I'm able."

Flynn raised an eyebrow at that, but he didn't argue, as the girl calmed at my words. He power-walked to his car, buckled her in, though of course not in the booster seat she probably needed, still don't know how old she is, and then they took off as I awaited the patrol car's approach. A kindly looking man I just happened to know ambled out. Well into retirement age, Hank was probably the best cop I could have dealt with at this moment. He had been courting my Grams back when she was losing herself, and he'd always been exceedingly kind to me, treating me like a surrogate granddaughter. I gave him one of my brightest smiles as I said, "Hank! It's been a while!"

He returned my smile with a toothless one of his own as he sighed, "Sure 'nough has been. So, what happened to ya' winder? Broken by hooligans?"

I summoned an innocent expression as I sighed, "Seems that way. Flynn and I searched the place, seems like whoever did it didn't nick anything."

He frowned a bit, leaning down to inspect the window frame. "There's visible blood, I should be able to run it for DNA, maybe we'll get lucky, and the perp will be in the system."

"No!" I exclaimed, causing Hank to startle at my harsh tone. I tried to cover my blunder as I said, "Don't want to put you to all that trouble. Flynn offered to fix the window this weekend for free; no need to press charges if they didn't take anything. If I figure out anything is stolen, I'll grass up so they can get nicked."

Hank looked entirely confused, so I interpreted myself, "I just mean I'll let the authorities know if I find anything has been stolen so they can be arrested."

Hank nodded after my clarification, looking down into the basement as he fixed me with a stare. "That Flynn feller sure is sweet on you. Have you cut the kid a break and told him you like him yet?"

I smiled despite myself at Hank's bluntness. *Probably the closest thing I have to a grandfather figure, and he isn't one to sugarcoat.* "I've told him before. I like to keep my air of mystery, remember?"

Hank scoffed as he slowly went upright. He placed a loving hand on my shoulder as he let loose a world-weary sigh. "Oh Don, you'll never keep a man if mystery is your first thought. How is he supposed to prove he worthy if ya' don't trust him?"

I grimaced, because his words hit a little too close to home. But then, I grasped my opportunity as I smiled brightly again. "You know; you're right Hank. Maybe I should go see him; thank him for coming with me and checking out the break in at least. Yes, I think I'll go do that right now."

I gave him a quick hug, then turned on my heel, as Hank gave me a suspicious look. "You're hiding something from me." *Crap.* "Whatever it is; if you're in any trouble, you can come to old man Hank. You hear?"

"I hear." I answered, grinning a little. *What a sweet man. Crotchety and blunt, but sweet.* "Thanks Hank."

Once he got back in his car, I made myself slowly go towards my own, not wanting to appear too eager. *If Hank wasn't extremely busy it wouldn't be too far-fetched for him to follow me to satisfy his curiosity, and I'd basically promised the kid I wouldn't bring unwanted attention towards her or the break in.* I made my way towards the castle again, thoughts consumed by those hauntingly sad hazel eyes. *Should I get Caroline? Late afternoon... class would be getting out soon. She's far better with kids than me. But then again... maybe adding more people would be too much for Lydia. What a beautiful name. Quite the coincidence that she just happened to have a name I'd long awaited bestowing to a future daughter. I wonder how bad her injuries truly are...*

A very confused-looking Dante let me through, asking, "What's going on?? Flynn basically flew past here, there was someone in his car that he was hiding in the back, wouldn't tell me anything..."

I wanted to grumble with frustration, but I said quickly as I drove past, "We'll explain later; emergency!" I stopped in a random parking lot and legged it toward what I knew to be the Doctor's private hospital. Been there enough times for Caroline and even for myself over the past year. I apparently wasn't far behind Flynn, because he was still holding Lydia when the guard opened the waiting room doors for me; she was lying very limp, barely grasping the hammer, and her breathing sounded raspy and shallow. I approached quickly, as Flynn mouthed, 'You okay'?

I nodded quickly, because Cornelius, who had been running his hand through his grey and white hair entered and ushered us back. "Who is this?" He washed his hands immediately as he waited for our answer.

Flynn opened his mouth, but I beat him to it. "My cousin. Please help her; she's got a pretty big dent in the back of her head, and her hand got cut. Not sure what else at the moment."

Cornelius gave me a cursory glance, causing me to feel like shifting in place, but I willed myself to remain still and look truthful. *He knows us well, and he is far too good at picking up body language, can't give anything away.* He asked Flynn to lay her down on the exam table, but as Flynn started to ease her down, she grabbed onto his back, clinging desperately.

"We'll be right next to you, sweetie." I said, being careful not to say her name. *Better to keep her anonymous right now.* She stopped clawing onto Flynn's back, and allowed him to lay her down, still clutching onto the hammer for dear life. The Doctor noticed this immediately, giving her a kindly smile.

"I like your hammer. You can hold it, I'm going to check the back of your head, okay?"

She whispered that it was alright, then the Doctor began his examination, explaining as he did that he was putting on gloves and was just going to take a look at everything that might be hurting her. Massive worry lines took over his whole face the more he examined her, especially the back of her head, shining lights in her eyes, ears, and throat until he asked, "Child, would you like to watch a movie? Nurse Brenda can put on anything you'd like to watch. Flynn, Donyelle, and I are just going to be out in the hall for a little bit."

Lydia didn't seem enthused by us not being next to her, but apparently a movie was exciting enough that she acquiesced. As soon as we were all in the hallway, Cornelius immediately inquired, "Who is that child really?"

I mumbled, "My... my cousin. Is she going to be okay?"

Doctor Cornelius pinned me with a formidable stare. "If you're telling the truth; that means you probably know the god-awful humans who have been abusing that kid. It's obvious even without further tests that she has an extensive TBI - traumatic brain injury. She has bruises and burn marks like someone used her as a punching bag and an ash tray for many years. Whoever did this needs to go to jail. Immediately."

I agree... but I don't know who did this. "We don't actually know who she is or who did this to her. But she's under our protection now. What can be done to help her?" Flynn asked quickly.

"She is severally malnourished. Her vitals show she has a fever, extremely dehydrated, and hasn't eaten in far too long. I need to thoroughly examine her to take stock of all her injuries and make sure there are no other pressing concerns, but her hair and body are coated in blood, mud and who knows what else. First, I need X rays and a CAT scan to determine if there's bleeding in the brain, any tumors or other possible internal damage. Then, she needs a shower and a hearty meal. Since she seems the most comfortable with you two, we can keep up the family charade for now; but I do have to inform the King and Queen, I'm sure you understand. I will run every test I can to try to obtain as much information as I am able. And I will document and photograph each injury as it is discovered, in an effort to put whoever abused her away for life."

Is this what a parent feels like? This clenching under my chest that makes me feel like I'm about to collapse? The full-blown anxiety I feel for someone I didn't know what, an hour ago? If so, how does Caroline stand it? Especially for two tiny babies?? I didn't feel this pain when I snuggled Rigel... but then again, I knew Rigel was safe and cared for by the two kindest people I knew. This girl: she was abused. Horrifically. Imagine being evil enough to want to hurt a child. Someone punched and burned her... hit her hard in the back of the head... how can a person like that really exist?? I felt Flynn trembling with rage beside me, and as the Doctor walked away, seemingly to order the tests or inform Caroline and Ryan, Flynn whispered, "That poor girl..." he looked down at his arms, coated in blood and dirt, and it made me want to throw up. *I think I chundered a bit in my gob. Disgusting!*

I put a hand on one of his shaking arms as I announced, "I have no idea what we can do for this girl, but we need to do everything we can." *I said 'we'. Twice. Not 'I'. 'We'. Would he notice? Do I care if he notices?*

"Yes. Of course." He answered quickly. "I'm going to text mom to make a tray of her best snacks. Maybe you could help with the shower part? I shouldn't be around for anything... uh, you know, girly. Private. Happy to assist with anything else."

I chuckled silently. *Sweet Flynn.* I nodded, then jolted to attention as I heard Lydia screaming. Both Flynn and I rushed into the room as we saw the nurse had turned on the tv, and the monitor was playing the news. She was even whiter than before, pale as death as her eyes were locked on the screen. Something about the unnatural fear in her eyes made me look at the screen too. It was showing some kind of press conference; the banner at the bottom stating 'nominees for Mayor of Monic' my eyes immediately went to one man specifically. One with a very tall black hat and a particularly cruel demeanor. Something about the way his eyes shifted or the sneering domineering smile. I wanted to turn it off, Lydia was obviously distressed, she had hopped off the exam table and was curled in a ball on the floor holding her knees and rocking chanting over and over "I'm just clumsy, I'm just clumsy."

My heart broke as she hid underneath the table, but I turned back to the screen as the man that turned my stomach started to speak, the banner announcing it was Senator Ziddim Strawfeld. "As Senator, I have brought Monic peace and prosperity tenfold. Now I humbly request that you consider me for Mayor. You don't need someone old, senile, and too soft; you need someone who's going to get the job done. Who's with me?!" Many at the conference shouted out their support, and I changed the channel. *Senator Ziddim Strawfeld. Public enemy number one, if that's the guy who hurt Lydia. One thing is for sure, he will not be Mayor if he's the piece of shit who laid hands on her. I won't allow that!*

I got down on the ground as Lydia continued to rock and mumble her sad little chant. Softly, I placed a hand near her, hovering above her again. *When I was hit as a kid, the last thing I wanted was to be touched, not even by a gentle hand. But I would have liked to know that someone kind was there, and if I chose to grab their hand, I could.* So, I stayed stock still like that, until eventually Lydia lifted her trembling hand to mine. I closed my fingers around her hand, using my other hand to gently rub circles onto her palm. I waited until she met my eyes to say, "I am so sorry he scared you, Lydia. But he can't hurt you anymore. We won't let him."

Flynn, who had also crouched down beside me, added, "Right now what matters most is taking some pictures of your head, the

Doctor needs to see everything. After that Donyelle is going to help you take a shower, and my mom is bringing some delicious food."

Surprise and confusion clouded her pretty eyes. "Me... me shower? Me get clean?"

I nodded, feeling very sad. *Who knows when she last was cleaned or fed, but I have a bad feeling it's been an exceedingly long time.* Eventually between Flynn and I, we were able to coach her off the floor and back onto the bed. Cornelius performed the necessary X Rays and such, then brought us to a medical area where she could shower in privacy. I heard Ryan, the King and Flynn's best friend, outside the locked door. I was actually grateful to hear his voice, knowing that meant I didn't have to explain, especially in front of the kid. I set about giving her a swimsuit, because if she was like me, she wouldn't want to be naked around strangers. I turned my back as she changed into it, then I focused my attention on gently cleaning her hair. The Doctor had explained that soft touches to the dented area were okay, provided they were minor, as gentle as possible, and that I should use most my cleaning efforts everywhere else, but that cleaning extensively was preferred. I was surprised how much Lydia was already trusting me. She didn't close her eyes, so she didn't fully trust me, but she did allow me to go behind her back, even though she flinched as I explained what I was going to do, she allowed me to do it. *Better than I would have acted at her age. That reminds me...* "How old are you, Lydia?"

She hunched over at my question, reminding me of how much I hated (and still hate) personal probing questions. But I needed to know at least the basics about this girl. "Six... I think. I have a birthday February 9th, but I don't know what day it is."

"It's February 7th, so happy birthday in two days!" I said cheerfully, but I felt anything but. *She's so young to have such a haunted look, so little to be covered in bruises and scorch marks.* There was also some kind of gash on her left hip, it was partially covered by the swimsuit, but it looked like someone had sloppily sewn it together in a way that caused a scar. Uneven and jagged, and it made me feel even worse for this little trooper. *No one should have to experience any of what she's gone through. It makes me feel like my life was a picnic by comparison. Sure, I was abandoned, and kids beat me at the orphanage... but this all looks to be from at least one adult. Maybe more. The amount of trauma and distrust that would breed in a person... especially a child...* I continued to massage the shampoo into her hair as she sniffed.

"That smells yummy." Her stomach was making plenty of noise, and she looked down, seemingly ashamed.

I smiled gently stating, "I'm hungry too. We'll get some good food after we're all clean. Let me finish with your pretty hair, then I'll let you get out of that suit and you can scrub your body on your own. I'll be right outside the door."

"You promise?" She squeaked, staring at me very intently, not blinking even though water was still pouring down her head.

"Yes Lydia, I promise. I won't go anywhere. Not without you." She visibly relaxed, and I swore internally that I would make sure never to break a promise to this girl in my lifetime. *Never.* I finished the gentle massage, got all the caked blood, and after a good rinse applied the conditioner. *Her hair is actually really lovely under the gunk. Like wavy waterfalls of shimmering gold. She is a stunning little girl, with very cherubic features. Again, how could anyone hurt someone so vulnerable?? I will never understand the brutality of others.* I posted myself outside the door, joining Flynn.

"How is she doing?" He asked softly as he turned towards me.

"A little better." I answered as I looked into his dark worried eyes. "I was able to get all that dark blood out of her scalp and what was clinging to her hair. Flynn, she looks like a beautiful angel. But those marks... they are everywhere. I noticed a gash of some kind on her left hip, from what I could tell it looked like someone didn't do a respectable job fixing it up. She has had a lot of abuse. I thought I had it bad..." I trailed off, kicking myself for bringing my experiences into this. *It's not okay to compare. And I don't want Flynn to ask...*

But he didn't. Instead, his face twisted. "I let Ryan know that I need some time off. I feel bad, since I'm supposed to be mentoring Romero, but we can't leave her alone like this."

"We won't be. But that doesn't mean you have to take time off work. She might even enjoy going to work with you sometimes, and other times she could come hang out with me; she seems to like flowers well enough."

Realization dawned across Flynn's handsome face. "Yeah, I need to fix that window of yours soon too. Don't want your plants to suffer. Are you really saying you're okay to tag team nursing her to health?"

"Of course!" I bristled, a little offended he'd even asked. "She's just like me at that age. I can't abandon her." *It's the most I've opened up to him about my past. Hopefully that'll show I really mean it.*

He held out his arms, and I moved into his embrace, as he kissed the top of my head. *Somehow all the petty stuff about keeping him at arm's length just doesn't hold the same amount of weight anymore. The truth is, I'm more worried about that almost-seven-year-old than I am about how Flynn sees me, which used to be the most important motivation I had. Crazy that so much changed in mere moments.*

The door opened behind us, but I didn't move away from Flynn. Whoever was watching could; I don't care anymore. I need some cuddles. I heard a tiny giggle/snort that I knew belonged to Lydia, so I moved away from Flynn and looked at her. "You huggin'. You married?"

I felt the warmth flush my cheeks, and Flynn looked pretty red as well. "Uh no. Friends; remember?"

Lydia did not look convinced. *But who cares if a kid thinks we're married?* She was wrapped in two towels, but shaking, so we quickly ushered her back to her room. I texted Caroline that I needed clothes for a six-and seven-year-old girl, she always had extra for her students of all ages. *Who knows if Ryan had told her yet, but it can't be helped.* I asked Caroline to take them to the Doctor's office. She responded back that she was on her way. *Leave it to Caroline not to task a maid or someone with the job but to do it herself.* Only minutes later, Caroline arrived. I saw her outside the door, motioning to me, so I told Lydia I would be right back, and that Flynn was there with her. I swept out of the room and into the hall where my friend was waiting with bags of clothes.

"Care thanks. Did Ryan get a chance to tell you what's going on?"

Caroline gave me a worried look. "Yes, what little he knew anyway. Poor sweet girl; is she alright? I heard there was extensive abuse. She must be terrified. How did you and Flynn come across her?"

Right, we didn't tell anyone that story. Not even Flynn to Ryan, apparently. "You know that alarm on my phone?"

She nodded easily. "Your shop security."

"Right. Well, the kid broke the window, I think she fell into the basement, or jumped down, either way, she hurt herself. But it's obvious she was already very hurt before that."

Caroline's face twisted with pity and a sad expression. "Goodness; she's been through a lot. The nurse told Ryan some press conference news bulletin seemed to really set her off. One minute she was fine, the next shaking, muttering and rocking in complete fear. Do you know who elicited that reaction?"

Might as well tell her. I trust my best friend. And she has power as a Queen I don't have as a commoner. "Senator Ziddim Strawfeld."

Caroline's eyes narrowed. "I never liked the look of that one. Ziddim Strawfeld. Slimy and shifty. Met him at one political dinner... it was enough to make my skin crawl being in his vicinity. So full of himself, and far too forward. If he hurt her... Ry and I will do everything in our power to demand justice. For now, I hear Cornelius is treating what he can. Where is she going to stay? At the palace?"

I shook my head. "She's going to stay with Flynn and I."

Caroline raised an eyebrow at that and gave me a sweet, hopeful smile. "Flynn and you hmm?"

I playfully shoved her shoulder as I lowered my voice. "It's not like that and you know it; don't be daft. But she has bonded to us. We are going to help her heal."

"And then what?" Caroline asked, in a blunter fashion than I was used to from her. It took me aback.

"Excuse me?"

Caroline was not deterred. "You and Flynn are going to help her heal. And then what? She's a young girl. One who probably ran away from home. I am sure you know the law isn't exactly on our side with this one, even if it should be an open-and-shut case. I can pull strings as much as possible to find a child advocate who will listen to the girl, hear her story, and try to appeal to a judge, but most cases unfortunately tend to go to OCS and those rulings not only may take a while, but often take the child into foster care. I just want you to be aware that unless you are only thinking temporary care, you both would have quite the uphill battle."

"So be it." I snapped, without even thinking of the ramifications. "Flynn and I could be better foster parents to that child than whoever allowed her to be so mistreated. Either her family are abusers, or they are so neglectful they allowed it to happen. Either way; they are scum who don't deserve Lydia."

Caroline blinked, "I know you wanted to name your daughter Lydia, and it's a sweet sentiment to call her that, but I'm sure she has her own name-"

I chuckled. "No, Lydia is her name."

"Oh. Wow. Really? That's like... a God thing." I smiled at that, and she added, "Ryan and I want to help any way we can. Is there anything we can do right now?"

I shook my head, taking her outstretched hand. "Being here and bringing the clothes; that helped. Would you like to meet her?"

"I would, but I don't want to overwhelm her."

I opened the door to see Lydia having some kind of under-the-blankets swab. My heart twisted again as I asked Flynn, "Is he...?"

Flynn nodded solemnly, whispering, "He recommended a r-a-p-e kit. Hopefully it's not necessary, but every test gives a little more insight into her plight." *Oh man, I have to remember to spell things out now, she's almost seven and obviously much more able to repeat things than infants...*

We waited until Cornelius withdrew, then I said softly, "Lydia, this is Caroline. My best friend."

Lydia's hazel eyes assessed the new intruder, distrust clear. Caroline gave her a warm smile, moving very slowly and gracefully toward her bed, bringing the bags with her. "It's so lovely to meet you, Lydia. You've already become someone Donyelle cares about, and we care about you too. Would you like a present?"

She shook her head, vigorously, looking like she was about to bolt. Caroline's eyes widened at the intense reaction, but she quickly set down the bags and lifted her hands. "No problem; you don't have to. I just brought you some clothes."

Lydia stopped her movements toward escaping at Caroline's words, fixing her with a stare. Trying to help, I took the first bag from the floor and pulled out the clothes. Lydia's large eyes fixated on what I was holding, as an equal mixture of delight and fear took over her expression. *Something about the word 'present' set her off. Noted.* I pulled out a couple more outfits, laying them flat at the foot of the bed for her to inspect. Her hand that wasn't treated and bandaged ran over a pair of soft black pants, a matching long sleeve shirt, and a plaid brown and white jacket.

"Good choice Lydia. That brown will look great with your eyes." Caroline said softly in a friendly teacher voice.

Lydia is thawing towards Caroline a little, I can tell. The little girl asked, "Are you going to take me to the big hat man?"

Caroline quickly shook her head. "No sweetie. No one is if we can help it. You can either stay with Flynn and Donyelle, or with my husband and I while we sort out how to make sure you're comfortable and safe. What would you like?"

I resent Caroline for offering the option, but maybe the kid would do better with actual tried and true parents... the lurch in my stomach didn't get any better at the thought though.

Lydia pointed two little wobbly fingers at Flynn and me. "They."

I felt a smile overtake my face, and Flynn was just as happy. *Surprising that she didn't automatically bond better with Caroline, the ultimate lover of children, but maybe she just felt closer to people who have gone through similar experiences. That'd be my guess at least.* Caroline gave her another equally warm smile, completely unfazed by her choice. "Wonderful; then Flynn and Donyelle will care for you. Flynn's mother, Miss Greta, will be coming shortly with some yummy food, I would be very hungry if I hadn't eaten today. And she's such a nice lady."

Lydia relaxed a little as Caroline went back towards the door, dipping her head in goodbye. Care gave me a quick squeeze on her way out, then we were left to wait. Before long, Greta arrived with a large steaming tray. Lydia didn't look as nervous at her entrance, though if it was because of the motherly look or the presence of scrummy grand food was anyone's guess.

"Honey-child, you just take a gander at all this good eatin'. You'll feel better in no time." Lydia cracked a small smile, and I could see why. *Greta is probably the least scary kindest woman I know. And her tray smells divine - scrummy is the word!* She rested it on the counter beside the bed as she explained, "I made a couple more trays, so I'll be right back." Flynn gave his mother a loving look that made my heart beat up tempo, then he lifted the lid. A full cheeseburger, mashed potatoes in some kind of red sauce gravy, an orange, some sweet corn, a bag of crisps, and a small salad with a spoon and fork. She darted a quick glance between both of us, as if waiting for permission to eat.

"Go ahead Lydia, this is all for you." I heard her stomach rumbling painfully loudly, but instead of eating ravenously as I'm sure she wanted to... she daintily nibbled at the burger and had little sips of water, and the fruit punch Greta had provided. Before long, Greta was back with a second tray, filled-to-overflowing with all different types of fruit. Strawberries, melons, grapes, berries, oranges, apples, bananas, kiwi, pineapple; just about all the fruits I would have thought of if I'd taken the time to name them. She tried a few, making noises of joy as she seemed to try things she'd never experienced before. *I wonder what she has eaten before, since apparently it wasn't fruit.* Greta smiled happily watching Lydia consume her offerings before she left again. When she came back, she had a huge veggie, cheese and cracker tray that she had shaped into a jolly looking Santa Clause. Sugar snap peas, olives, cauliflower, cucumbers, celery, red peppers, saltine crackers and sliced cheese and meat.

I said softly, "That's a lot of food."

Greta chuckled merrily. "Yes, you three will have leftovers for several days I imagine. And whenever you need more or different options, you just come back to my kitchen, I'm always happy to feed the child. And two of my favorite people, of course."

"Thank you, so much." I said, barely above a whisper, so it wouldn't make Lydia feel uncomfortable.

Greta blushed with pleasure and Flynn smiled gratefully before his mom asked, "Changing the subject... where is she going to live? At my son's? Or at yours? And... since she seems to want you both, are you folks going to do the reasonable thing and live together for the time being?"

I felt my jaw opening with shock. *What is it with the generation above me being so blunt all of a sudden? First Hank, now Greta. Not to mention Caroline. Why is everyone I care about pushing me to be close to Flynn? Including my own treacherous heart...*

"We haven't discussed it yet; but I think having the ladies both move in with me while we sort out a longer-term plan would probably be easiest." Flynn answered after taking a beat to think about it.

"Why not my place?" I asked, surprised that he was actually humoring this thought.

"For one thing, location; my place is closer to the palace being centrally located. Second, I have empty rooms, while yours is... well, filled from floor to ceiling with plants. Beautiful plants, for sure, but might make the living conditions kinda... tricky."

"Oh. Right." I deflated a bit at his sound logic. *He made good points. And it wouldn't be forever. Plus, this was more for Lydia than for either of us. It wasn't like I wanted to be his roommate... so why was I feeling excited deep down at the prospect?*

Unable to answer that internal question in a way that satisfied my rapidly pounding heart, I mentally shook myself for allowing myself to get so caught up in what I may-or-may-not feel when a real human child was suffering and needed to be my main priority. I added, "Then we'll need to swing by my place on the way to yours so I can at least pack a suitcase."

Flynn nodded easily, "That's fine; we also need to drop by your shop. For now, I will board it up until we find a replacement window. At the very least you'll need double-pane glass, but I think the frame was pretty warped too."

I shrugged. "You do what you think is best when it comes to that, it's not my expertise, but I trust you'll make it good as new."

He smiled warmly, and for a minute, it was just him and I; everything and everyone faded away; even his mom who was looking at us with a knowing smile. It was something about his eyes on mine; they arrested me, holding me hostage with his loving intensity. As quickly as everything faded away, it all came back into focus as I realized we needed to make sure Lydia was safe. "Enough dilly-dallying." I announced as I put my hand on the doorknob leading back into Lydia's room. "We need to get everything set up and start making a plan. Caroline is going to look into child advocates, but for now, Lydia needs to remain out of sight and safe. So, let's get her ready to go with us. We could always board up the window tomorrow and get the suitcase then too."

Flynn shook his head though, stopping my movement to open the door. "We want things to look as normal as possible. You wouldn't just leave that window alone. The cops may come back and be overly curious if we haven't even cleaned up the glass and blood, not to mention taking care of the window. Plus, I know it would kill you a little bit if any of your flowers or plants were affected."

My goodness, he knows me far too well. I don't know how I feel about being read so thoroughly and precisely... "You're right... that would be hard on me." I admitted grudgingly. I paused one more second to make sure he didn't have anything else to add, but when neither of them did, I turned the door handle. Lydia had changed into that adorable plaid outfit, causing her to look much more her age. *Well, until you look into those big hazel eyes. Trauma is apparent in those irises, and more than anything, I long for the day when only joy and excitement stare back at me. A difficult wish, but one I think might just be possible to achieve... something to strive for.*

Lydia regarded us as we came back in saying, "You didn't leave me." *Oh, my heart... Such a simple statement, but so much power and pain in those words. How many times had I thought that, but never been brave enough to speak it?* I sat down at the edge of the bed near her while still giving her space before I answered,

"We will never leave you without first telling you where we are going and when we are coming back." I promised. I looked at Flynn for a brief second, but he didn't seem opposed to being lumped into my oath; thank goodness.

Cornelius came back in, motioning for us, so while our patient was distracted with all the food, we huddled up with the Doctor. "My exam and the kit provided conclusive evidence that the child is still a virgin. So even though she has sustained extensive physical abuse, she has not been sexually abused. As I'm sure you both know, I'm a mandated reporter. I'm under oath to file a child abuse report. However, the King explained that this is an even more delicate situation than I had suspected. Therefore, I have filed the claim with him, he and the Queen have assured me they are looking for a child advocate, lawyers and the like to give that child a fighting chance. They also informed me the two of you are taking temporary guardianship. Is that right?"

Flynn and I shared a look. It was heated for a minute, with an intensity that scared me just a bit. I responded, "That's right. She's coming home with us."

Cornelius, both a medical professional and personal friend of ours, appraised us both for a minute, and I felt this weird fear that we might not pass whatever inspection checklist was going on in that man's head. But his smile became friendly as he nodded, told us he was going to get a couple over-the-counter pain meds for Lydia, then we would be free to go. "But I do want to see her every week. Need to keep an eye on her healing progress."

We agreed, then turned back to the child. She is still eating dainty bites. *It makes me think that someone forced her to eat like that for so long it's been ingrained in her. Thank goodness the level of abuse is just a hair better than I'd originally feared... but seriously, that guy is evil. I could never imagine hurting a child, not for any reason. And to use her to put out cigarettes?!?! Who knows what else... Flynn and I have a lot of damage to undo. I sure hope we are up for the task.*

Lydia was looking at us guiltily with actual tears in her eyes, so I quickly asked, "What's wrong sweetie?"

She kept her eyes down as she said softly, "I sorry, I try eat all food, my belly hurtin'."

Oh no... Flynn sat down beside her and smiled as he spoke softly and sweetly. "My mom made all this food for all three of us to last us a couple days. No one is saying you have to eat it all. Are you ready to see your new home?"

She peeked up from between her legs as her little face showed just a tiny bit of hope. "You mean it? I get home with they?"

I almost winced at her grammar but stopped myself in time. *Obviously, she's been deprived of a lot. There's plenty of time to help her, now wasn't the time to be correcting English mistakes.* "Exactly right sweetie. You're coming home with us." I added, and her sweet eyes went to me. I held out my hand, and this time Lydia took it; hesitantly at first, but then more confidently as she slipped off the hospital bed and onto the floor. She shivered as her bare feet touched down, but not for long. Flynn fished through the bag Caroline had brought; pulling out socks and shoes of various sizes. He held a couple shoes up to her feet until he figured out her size, then he eased her into the socks and footwear while I did the same with a nice coat.

Flynn grinned again in a way I think he reserved especially for kids. "There. Comfy cozy?"

Lydia blinked, then smiled a bit as she nodded and repeated his words as if they were foreign. "Comfy cozy."

The interaction was so sweet, and as he helped Lydia to his car and I got mine so we'd both drive to his place, I evaluated how difficult this was going to be. Not just raising a child for the foreseeable future who seemed to be either related to or at least knew a very public prominent figure in Monic but being in such close proximity to the charmer that was Flynn. *How am I supposed to keep the stone wall of protection up when he is so sweet and thoughtful, and I am going to have to live with him for who knows how long?? It was hard enough to get him out of my brain before... now it'll be physically impossible.*

The trip was fairly short; it felt far too familiar from all those late-night drive-by moments that I would surely take to the grave. *I will never tell Flynn I had gotten that deranged. Not even if we've been married for fifty plus years. Never. It's so embarrassing... he'd either be repulsed and creeped out... or flattered. Either way; it cannot happen. I guess now I won't feel the compulsion to head around his place every night at least. There's a positive. But the child; that's what needs to be our focus. Ugh! Stop thinking in 'our' and 'we'. I am not in a couple. I am single. I am an individual. That's the way this needs to stay. And as individuals, both Flynn and I need to do whatever's best for Lydia.*

Not sure exactly where to park, his driveway (and house) wasn't exactly very big, and I didn't want to block him in, I parked on the side of his lawn by the mailbox. Hopefully that will be ok. *It is so odd second-guessing everything I am doing. That isn't like how I'd be at home at all. But I guess I am going to have a lot of adapting to do in the days and weeks to come. Hopefully far longer, if we win the legal battle we are about to start... so even though I am very set in my ways and hate change... I have no choice right now. Lydia comes first.*

I locked my car, noticing that Flynn and Lydia were waiting for me outside his car. Hastily I scanned the nearby houses and road, before taking long strides toward Flynn hissing under my breath, "Get her inside! We don't know who's watching!" *Paranoid? Maybe. But I'm not taking any chances. A man campaigning for what... Governor? Mayor? Whatever it was surely had friends everywhere. Even slimy ones. We can't be too careful in this situation.* Flynn seemed to understand my fear, gave a swift nod then invited Lydia inside. Once we were all in and the door was closed and locked, I surveyed the surroundings.

Flynn watched with a hint of a smile curving his lips. "You've been here before, Doni."

I couldn't help but smile back. "Technically true. But those were short visits. This is more... permanent."

Flynn's face showed how happy he was at that concept, keeping it hard not to show that I too was intrigued as well. *Terrified, but intrigued.* "Then please, browse your new home at your leisure. Lydia, I'm going to go take care of a few things, then I'll be back. You'll be with Donyelle, you two can start setting up your room; it'll be this one over here on the right."

I watched him point to one of the three doors, and something dawned on me. Going to the middle door to check, I flung it open to reveal... a bathroom. I turned around and asked Flynn, "There's only two rooms?" *I'll have to call bagsy on the bed...*

Flynn nodded, not smiling for once. "Yeah, sorry about that. I didn't think I needed a large place. But you can have the room on the left, this couch will be fine."

The couch in question was assuredly not fine. Not only was it ridiculously small; barely a two-seater so there's no way his tall frame could lay comfortably... it was obviously worn out and even from this vantage point I could see a couple spots where the leather had cracked pretty drastically. My eyebrow raised as I said, "Absolutely out of the question. You'd be barmy to even consider it. You'll never get more than an hour's sleep on that thing. How big is the bedroom?"

Wordlessly, he moved past me toward the left door, opening it gently. As it swung open, I realized a couple things; the bedroom was very small. It was impeccably clean. And the bed, that took up most of the room, was a queen size. There was no other furniture in the room other than a dresser and a small set of shelves bolted into the wall with picture frames. Unable to help myself, I snooped, moving toward the shelf to check out the pictures he had displayed. There was a scattering of him and Ryan, the Queen Mother Lily (I never knew what to call her now that she wasn't considered the Queen, royalty titles are just too confusing). There were two more prominently displayed in the middle in larger frames than the others; one with him, his mother and a younger looking Micah... and one with him and I. It was from the Paris trip our friends had taken us on, back when we weren't really a couple, but the feelings were still there. That was very evident in this photo; we looked so in love it hurt my heart to see it. *Reminds me how good it felt to be with him... before he started asking all those pesky questions.* My eyes traveled from the picture frame to Flynn, who was studying me with an unreadable expression. I expected him to say something, but he stayed silent. It was impossible to know what he was thinking at that moment, but I desperately wanted to know. After a minute of charged eye contact, he said softly, "I should probably get going. If you text me a list of things you need, and are okay with giving me a key, I can stop by your house on the way back after fixing the shop window, get you whatever is necessary for the short term until you can go yourself and pack up?"

I nodded, still not able to get over my picture being so large in such a small space. I fiddled with my keyring until the house key came off. He held out his hand, and I lightly dropped it into his palm, trying to avoid physical contact. Gesturing to the picture I couldn't get my mind off of, I asked, "Forgot that was there?"

He chuckled, lightly, but I heard it, before he answered as he played with the key I gave him, "No, I know it's there. I see it every night before I close my eyes, and first thing when I open them."

Oh. What do I say to that?? Is he admitting he still has feelings for me?? Turns out, I didn't need to come up with a reply, because he turned on his heel, pivoted, then said a quick goodbye to Lydia, who was still exploring the guest room, her new space. He mouthed "text me" waving his phone near his head, then he was gone. *Guess it was a good thing I didn't park behind him.* My mind swam with dangerous thoughts, so I cleared it by shaking my head like a crazy person, then headed into the other room to see how Lydia was doing.

She was just standing there, eyes taking in her surroundings. She still looked so skittish, eyes darting all over the place, and her body language was scared and frazzled.

It makes me sad, seeing such an accurate representation of me at her age. My trauma was different than Her's, that much I know, but to this day I still feel like a scared little girl, eyes darting around, paranoid about every possible danger. How do I help her feel at ease when even I myself don't feel that calm to this day? Truthfully, the closest I've come to that feeling was when Flynn and I were at our best. Before the arguments... before I started pushing him away to protect my secret shame, I was genuinely happy. It was a beautiful feeling, and something I could sometimes tap in to if I closed my eyes. But did this child have any happy memories to steady her? A secret carefree place to retreat to? The way she is looking and acting... I doubt it. Flynn and I... we must create that for her.

I stepped out of the bedroom and explored the living room a bit, and again I was surprised by what I found. Lots of pictures of his family, several more included me. Two things really stood for me though:

First, a large bundle of well taken care of magazines. *Hmm. Interesting.* I took a couple out, taking care to be gentle, then I brought them to Lydia, laying them on the bed. "I figure we could decorate your room in a bit, maybe look through the magazines to give you an idea of what kinds of things you would like in your room, plus colors and all that." Lydia's eyes darted to the small pile, nodding silently, so I backed away to give her some space.

I went back to the living room, to examine that second area of curiosity. His whole place was fairly sparsely furnished, save for a large rectangular box that was impossible to ignore. I ran my hands along the cherry wood, but when I tried to lift the lid, I finally noticed the lock kept it firmly in place. *What could he have locked up in there? He was such an open honest person... right?*

My mind flashed to the craziest possible scenarios. *It wasn't big enough for a body. Not that he'd have a literal skeleton but crossing that off the list did help my rabid curiosity.* The lock just added to the intrigue. *A gun safe? No... probably not. Should I ask him? Wait and hope he mentions it? Ugh!! I hate not knowing! I have to figure this out! This is going to cause sleepless nights; I just know it.*

I heard my phone beep, so I checked the screen; Flynn said:

Window is boarded up for now, glass debris is clear. I measured & ordered another, but it's going to take a couple months.

I pressed his text, liked it, then responded:

Thanks! Much appreciated!

I didn't know what else to say, so I pressed send. I could have said Lydia was looking through his magazines. Really wanted to causally mention the locked box... but there was no way to hide how much I wanted to know, so saying as little as possible was important in this moment.

The rest of the hour I tried to make myself at home. But even more importantly, I tried to help put the little girl at ease. After asking a few questions, I was able to determine that she was hungry, and that soup was something she really liked. *Now, me and cooking... we aren't friends. People who know me well enough know I'm no chef. Or baker lady. Or whatever. But I figure I can make a basic soup. How difficult can it be?*

*****

... about a half hour later I found out just how difficult. I raided the fridge and pantry; *he had said to make ourselves at home after all, and who was I to turn that offer down. But I... I don't know what I am doing. Not even the basics, honestly. Now that I no longer needed to cook for survival, I was rubbish at it, thought all soups need a good base. Could have sworn I'd heard Flynn's dear mother swear by that many a time.* So, I fished around in the fridge until I found the milk. I stared at the jug for a good long time as I internally willed the inanimate object to tell me what the base of a good soup consisted of. Alas... it didn't answer. Therefore, I was left to my own devices. I sighed, as I started pouring in a rather generous amount. Then I got nervous it wasn't enough, so I dumped a bunch more in. *Okay... now what?* I turned on the burner, about halfway. As I pondered, something weird happened. There was like... smoke coming from the little pot with the milk. *Surely milk can't burn... right?* To be safe, I doused the pot in even more milk. "What am I missing?" I pondered out loud. My eyes frantically searched the kitchen as more smoke... or steam... or whatever was emanating from my pot dangerously bubbled near the surface, precariously close to making a mess. That's when I remembered it; *I forgot you're supposed to stir milk; surely that is where it is all going wrong!* I grabbed the nearest scooping thing-a-ma-bob. *Don't ask me what it's called; I can't tell you. It is metal, and heavy, that's about all I know.* I started vigorously stirring, expecting the milk to calm down.

...It didn't. If anything, it became more problematic. Somehow the pretty creamy white milk was looking... brown. Chestnut brown. And the bubbles of steam were shooting out of the pot and hitting the burner, causing small explosions of flame. I let out a shriek, my hands flying instinctively to protect my beautiful face. But suddenly... I was nowhere near the volcanic eruption. Nowhere in the kitchen, even. In the time it took to blink, Flynn had somehow ushered me away from the kitchen, protected me by shielding me with his body, then jumped into action. He turned off the burner immediately, grabbed a nearby potholder, carefully but with deft speed rushing the pot of what looked like molten sadness in the sink. He barely turned the water on, just enough to cause even more smoke. I expected the smoke detector to go off, but he instantly touched a couple buttons on a remote he grabbed, and the windows swung open. My mouth gaped with shock and awe.

"I'm sorry- I don't know what I did wrong, I-" In the midst of my very rare apology, he pulled me into his arms, making me forget what I was going to say. He pulled back just long enough to cup my face with his hands as he asked,

"Are you hurt? Did you get burned?" His voice dripped with sincere concern. *Here I am thinking he'd be more worried about the travesty of trashing his kitchen... but he is focused entirely on my well-being. Why is he still so good, even after the breakup? He's supposed to be angry. An entitled pissed off jerk. Like all my exes. I know how to deal with those kinds of guys. But Flynn... he is a different breed. I am so good with my words and my womanly wiles with just about anyone else... why is Flynn so different?* His eyes narrowed with even more concern as I forgot to answer him. He pulled away, his hands going from my face to my arms as he lifted them close to his face as he inspected them. His breath hitched, and my eyes locked on his as he whispered sadly, "You burnt your fingers."

What? This is news to me. In the chaos, my adrenaline spiked. Now that things were calm, I felt a sharp pain in my ring and pinky fingers. Sure enough, there was a nasty welt-like bruise forming on the two. *Probably a second-degree burn. How beastly.* Flynn must have noticed my grimace as the pain hit me, because he motioned for me to sit on the couch. Normally, I would have argued. Said I was a tough girl. I could do it myself. But I didn't feel like it. It did actually really hurt. And it was one of those times where it was wiser to accept the help than to prove the point that I was a strong independent woman. So, I kept my mouth shut, sunk onto the nearby couch, and followed the handsome man with my eyes as he grabbed his first aid kit.

One thing I'll say for the lad; he certainly is prepared. Figures he'd be a boy-scout. I expected he'd just put a band aid on the two fingers. But as he cradled the injured hand in one of his large ones, he softly cleaned the two fingers. Then he applied some white liquid that both stung and cooled the area. His eyebrows furrowed as he saw me squirm. "I know it stings Doni, but I'm afraid you have to bear it. You need these beautiful fingers for botany, so we have to do it right."

I felt my cheeks warm at the surprising compliment. Also, his gaze was so... loving. So sweet and caring. *Remind me... why did I break up with him? Why didn't I cherish him when I had him? He would make any girl lucky and happy... why did I bodge it up and push such a man away? Bollocks: he is incredible.*

My internal scolding ceased as I heard a small voice say, "You got owies?"

I turned my body partway so I could see the sweet child. I nodded, forcing a smile. "Just small ones. But Uncle Flynn is fixing me right up, I'm going to be just fine."

Lydia's grave look didn't soften. Flynn looked startled at my use of 'Uncle' but then his face relaxed into an easy smile. "Yes Lydia, Aunt Donyelle is going to be alright very soon. Would you like to help me apply this bandage?"

Much faster than I expected, she had rushed over to our position, her hands outstretched, seemingly very eager to help. My heart got a little erratic as I watched him include Lydia in helping him wrap the bandage around my two fingers. He showed her how to hold it, so it wasn't too loose or tight, and she lapped up the attention and information. *She's very bright.* I noted internally. It wasn't long before my hand looked like a mummy, at least about half of it, but Lydia was having too much fun, with a genuine smile that even reached her eyes. *I would rather my whole body be bandaged than ruin her fun and destroy that happy look. I feel at this moment I'll do just about anything to make that little girl happy. In this second, she doesn't look like a ghost of a child, the haunted look is gone from her eyes that makes her appear much older and world-weary. This is how a child should look.* And so, I said with a small fake wince, "Lydia, I think my other hand could use a bandage too; could you help me?"

She immediately nodded her head and lept up to grab another one from the kit. Flynn's expression was a mix of surprise and respect. *He knows what I am doing.* He gave me a smile that conveyed how proud he was that I had played along and prolonged the fun. After about a half hour of this, Lydia's belly started to rumble, loud enough to echo throughout the house. She blanched with embarrassment, so I quickly said to Flynn, "You know what? I'm very hungry. Could you possibly make us some soup?"

Flynn's all-knowing eyes danced as he said a little louder than his normal, "Man, soup sounds great. What sounds better; tomato basil or chicken noodle?"

Lydia immediately picked the first, so of course we went with that. I took note of how Flynn expertly chopped the ingredients, how he made the soup free hand, no recipe in sight. And yet I was never concerned. *He certainly looks at home in the kitchen in his cute little apron. I am willing to bet his mom made it for him.* As his soup began to simmer, I was even more sure that it was going to be exceptionally good. He held out a spoon to me, one hand underneath to catch any stray drops, and I eagerly took a taste as he held it to my mouth. *Let's just say... it isn't anything like my debacle.* I praised him, he smiled happily, going back to his task. And it wasn't long before a sensational smell filled the entire place.

I noted that as soon as he had scooped our bowls, he set to work cleaning the very caked-on burnt milk that had scorched the surrounding burners. Somehow the goop had trailed down almost the entirety of his oven and had trickled into a deep brown puddle of nastiness on the floor. He didn't look even a little frustrated, not one word about my mess was uttered. *If it had been me; I doubt I'd have the restraint to keep my mouth shut. At the very least I'd want to find out what he'd done to cause such a mess, maybe tease him a bit. He is a far better person than I. This just confirms it.* I grabbed another green sponge, hunching down to clean beside him. "Thanks for... well, not blowing up at me."

He swiveled his head, and I think we were both startled at our sudden nearness. Quite by accident, our faces were less than an inch away; and I just couldn't resist a soft, gentle kiss. I drew back, almost immediately, realizing that even though I wanted the physical side of the relationship and Flynn would almost certainly not complain about a kiss... nothing had changed on his end. He needed more... craved more. And I... I just couldn't. "I... I have to go back to the shop. My uh- the flowers. They need – fertil... water. Something. They need something. Bye Lydia; bye Flynn." I rushed to my car, snapping the door so hard I almost broke the handle, realizing it was locked. I fumbled for my keys, noticing out of my peripheral vision that Flynn was watching from the window. I didn't acknowledge this, I simply rushed to my car and sped to my shop.

The first thing I noticed was that the window damage was indeed cleaned and boarded up neatly. I sighed. "Why are you so good to me, Flynn." Of course, he wasn't there to answer. I took quick strides to my greenhouse, but instead of going inside, I skirted around toward the back, to the area no one knew about. *Only three extra-special species of flowers are back here, and they were meant for two of the best individuals I know.*

Only two were flowering, Greta's absolute favorites, the Chocolate Cosmos, and The Middlemist Red. Flynn had mentioned after we'd been together only a short time, that when Greta was very young, not more than five, her mother slowly began to pass away. Greta's mother had married much older, given birth to Greta's younger brother David days before, and she was not healing like she had been meant to; she was losing too much blood. And so, her mother took little Greta into her arms, kissed her soundly on the top of her head, telling her softly that she was very, very loved. That her mother couldn't stay, that God was calling her home, but that there would be reminders of her mother watching over her from heaven.

Greta had told Flynn, "Mom told me 'Greta, my dear one; you watch over your brother. I want David to be big and strong. And take this; always remember, whenever you read this book; and each time you see flowers; your mother loves you! And I'm going to be cheering you on from heaven'." Her mother gave her a book of a huge collection filled with flowers; some that were extremely rare, the rest a vast assortment of what was attributed to the most beautiful of plants.

Greta had asked her dying mother which ones were her favorites. Her mother had replied fairly weakly that she liked the rarest flowers of all for two reasons; because they were her favorite color (red), and because the rarer the flower, the more they reminded her of her lovely one-of-a-kind daughter. So, both mother and daughter picked out two favorite flowers; and to this day, Greta not only had pictures of those flowers up, she also still had the book her mother gave her; it was her most cherished possession. And so of course, it only made sense that I should plant it. *Right when Flynn and I had begun our dalliance, almost immediately after Caroline and His Highness had played matchmaker, I had heard that story when I'd asked him what I always ask: everyone's favorite flowers. The answer says a lot about a person, and I always used it to pick my partners. His answer though... it was special. It was filled with cherished memories. And that he shared his mother's with me was so special. But then he had to go and ruin it; telling me he couldn't choose between Sunflowers and Dandelions for his favorite. Bollocks!*

I smiled at the memory. Another time, far later into our relationship, I had tried to encourage him to change his favorite flower. I had snapped, "Dandelions are weeds! Sunflowers are basic, but at least they are flowers! How could you like Dandelions? Why?!" *Never in my life had someone infuriated me so much answering one of my most important questions. He's lucky he just shared that memory about his mother, or I would have shoved him out of my house then and there.*

Calmly, and with a ghost of a smile, he had answered, "I see you're passionate about this topic. Dandelions get a lot of flak. Yes, they are weeds; you're right. I tend to like things that other people find bothersome. But it has a lot of uses. It's one of those childhood rites of passage to blow them when they're in pussywillow form. Making a wish and blowing them out, watching each one dance in the wind; Micah and I used to bust up laughing as we raced to try to catch as many as we could before they hit the ground." He grimaced, obviously thinking about his younger brother.

I found myself uncharacteristically putting my hand on his, slipping my fingers through his, and applying just a slight amount of pressure in order to comfort him. Flynn's eyes widened, but instead of shooing me away, he used his other hand to run his fingers over mine, still interlocked with his. It made me shiver, just slightly, hopefully it wasn't noticeable. I said softly, "It must be difficult to remember who he used to be, trying to make sense of what he's turned into. Flynn: I know you feel guilty."

He said as halfheartedly as I've ever heard, "I don't..." But he couldn't even lie properly. I saw the beginnings of a tear mar his beautiful dark eyes.

My voice became even more gentle as I replied, "You don't have to lie. Maybe some people would believe you. But it's me. And I know, even though recently I haven't done much to earn your trust, you still trust me. Please listen when I say this: you are not to blame. Your mom's not to blame either. Micah is old enough to be accountable for his own actions. When he was a child, he was probably very sweet. I'm sure you have plenty of good memories. Those aren't just wiped away because he's now in jail for life. He was groomed by Henry, but no one knew that; especially to what extent. You try to take on so many people's burdens. It's not healthy. I don't want you to get sick or worse because you're so caught up in things that have no easy answer."

Flynn unashamedly let the tears fall. *I've never seen a man like him before. Ever. The few times I recall seeing a lad cry, they weren't men, and they were so quick to wipe their faces and make excuses like allergies or whatever bs they could come up with. But Flynn, he just lets them out. He doesn't look embarrassed about it either. He sounds like he is in control of his emotions even as the tears continue to run down his face.* "I do trust you, Doni. And your words... they help. A lot. But if you're going to keep being there for me, it's going to give me too much hope. To be extremely honest; you are already so engrained in my heart that unless you are willing to be with me as a genuine couple working towards marriage and forever... I need to take a step back. Has something changed on your end?"

And I vividly remember that I had immediately unclasped his hand. *Physically answering him, because I was too much of a coward to voice my concerns. My deepest fears. Rejection was the ugliest of words. I loved him; I loved him then, and I loved him now. But admitting feelings equates to giving him the control. The power to smite my already injured heart into even more pieces. To be honest, I didn't feel I was worthy of his unconditional love then. And I feel even less worthy now, almost two years later. But he has my heart; what pieces of it remained, and even though he didn't know that his mother was the closest thing to a parent I'd ever had. So, ensuring that his mother experienced two of the rarest flowers in her book; not only Greta's favorites but Greta's deceased mothers' as well... that would set things a bit more right. There's no easy way to explain that I loved Flynn, just about as soon as I met him. He was a real gentleman, the kind only women authors seemed to be able to create. In fact, it had taken quite a lot of seduction on my part to get him to share any kind of intimacy with me. And even though I had told all my friends that we'd had sex... we hadn't. Because Flynn said he respected me too much. But when I told him that I was going to tell everyone we did anyway, because that's what you do with a boyfriend, he said that was fine. He didn't care about his reputation. But Flynn was a virgin, at least back then. And from my sort of crazy stalker-like drive-bys, it had never appeared that he'd dated anyone since me. But who knows for sure. Either way, his mother will be delighted to have these.* The Chocolate Cosmos is velvety soft, a rich maroon, and received the first part of their name for their dark brown center, and of course, because they actually somehow smell like chocolate. Getting this plant to flower is very tough; everything had to be just right; the temperature, the ground had to be not only fertilized but almost slightly acidic. More sunlight was required, the water specificity was also a challenge. But I had done it; for the woman who had become such a mother figure;

it was the least I could do. The Middlemist red flower was slightly easier but also had multiple important conditions that had to be attained. *Both a challenge, but then again so is what I am attempting to create for Flynn too.* Sunflowers are easy, of course. And you'd think Dandelions would be too; right? Well, the answer would be yes, except I don't want just plain hum-drum Dandelions. I want Flynn's to be special.

Flynn had told me what his mother and his favorite flowers were when I had asked, but I doubt he realized I not only retained that information, but I also had immediately gone about outsourcing for those particular tubers.

If all of Flynn's secret flowers blossom, all at the same time... perhaps that will be God's sign that I'm meant to confess my feelings... maybe. I heard from afar the sound of that bloody awful doorbell bird call, so I hastened toward it. To my surprise, there were three guys, I didn't pay even a passing glance to the other two though as I gave Flynn a death glare. *How can he even think of leaving such a fragile girl alone?!* He seemed to read my murderous expression as he spoke. "My mom is watching her, I need to head to work, but I wanted to let you know. Your shop was on the way anyway."

After a moment of silence, one of the two other guys said softly, "Don, I wanted to introduce you to someone. Sorry if it's an inconvenient time!" Sebastian said with the signature grin that had won him so much fame.

"It's been a long time coming; it's lovely to meet you, Don." The stranger's voice was honey lipped, but I kept my gaze with Flynn, who looked like he needed a little reassurance.

I snapped to the stranger, "My nickname is only used by my closest friends." Flynn looked pleased at my cool approach. But then, Flynn's eyes actually widened as he looked behind me, in the direction of that guy's voice.

Curiosity won over, and I let my eyes spare the new guy a glance... I got weak in my knees. Literally, my legs buckled. I had never had such a physical reaction before. To anyone. *But no wonder; he's a chocolate wonder. The words I normally use to call a guy handsome just do not do him justice.* My tone immediately shifted into a soft lilting melody as I couldn't help but flirt. "And you can definitely call me Don. Or... anything, really, and I'll come."

I heard Flynn make a little noise of disapproval; *but really, how else do you address someone that attractive? He looks like a movie star. Every inch of him that I can see is utter perfection. His skin is like dark rich melted chocolate, it glistens in the midday sun like I could just lick it right off. And oh, it's tempting. His eyes are this fascinating shade of hazel, more yellow than green, like twin orbs of unlimited beauty. They are just so bright, so appealing. His face looks sculpted, with cheekbones that could cut anything, I am certain of it. He has just a hint of a five o'clock shadow, only adding to his allure; and while normally bald doesn't do it for me; this man has it shaved so flawlessly; it just suits him.* As he smiled at me; obviously picking up the change in my tone, his teeth were so brilliantly white, it was almost blinding.

"Well now; I'm flattered; thank you Don. You're as lovely as your pictures."

To my dismay, I felt myself flush. I cursed my body for yet another reaction to this man. To stop myself from doing anything embarrassing, I turned my attention to my friend.

"How do you know each other? And to what pictures is he referring?" I asked Sebastian, wondering how this guy could know anything about me.

Sebastian looked embarrassed, about the same as when Ahyoka complimented him for any reason. Something about how his ears got all red, and he went from city-slicker movie star guy to a cute puppy dog. "I might have been bragging about my friends here; and I may have shown Jabari our pictures from our trips... and when he showed interest in you specifically, I might have then proceeded to show him your session with the photographer... pretty snazzy by the way!" It was obvious he was complimenting me using one of my words in an effort to lessen my level of upset for him showing off the pictures. *But a guy as hot as this was interested enough in me to want to see more? Why would I be upset by that?!*

"I'm flattered!" I said with a grin, keeping my voice flirty and melodic. "That answers my second question, but how about the first?"

The big-shot actor looked confused, so Jabari answered, "Allow me, my friend. We're both in the entertainment business. Though while Sebastian does top ten movies and films, winning more Oscars than I can count, I am just one of the side characters in each movie and tv show he gets signed on. The benefits of having a brother so beloved in the industry!"

Sebastian scoffed as he rolled his eyes, patting Jabari on the back. "J is as humble as ever. He tends to leave out the fact that he is a big-time star, and that his plays and productions are all on Broadway. He writes the scripts, produces and teaches how to produce, and also somehow has the time to act and win Tony awards as well. We actually met because he was the screenwriter and producer on a handful of my movies; Jabari here is the one who gave me my big break when so many had turned me down for lack of experience. It can be so hard to break into the biz, but he took a chance and mentored me; felt that we were kindred spirits the way people underestimated us back then. He's as close to a brother as I have! Sisters I have in spades, but it would have been nice to have a brother."

Jabari gave him a wide grin. "And look at us now!" To me he said with plenty of charm, "I stick with plays and productions for my actual fame; it's my own niche; and it's wildly fun." His eyes trained back on Sebastian. There was a strange sort of... something in his eyes that was impossible to pinpoint as he continued, "Everyone likes to say they always knew we were going to be sensations in our respective fields... but most wouldn't give us the time of day. We remember who our true friends and allies are. But enough about that; we could sing each other's praises all day. I never did get your name, brother."

Jabari stuck his hand out to Flynn, who answered, with a bit of a forced smile, but a pleasant enough tone. *Good on him; I imagine*

Flynn feels Jabari is competition, but yet he is civil. If the tables were turned, and I had a goddess of a woman standing before me, and Flynn suddenly shifted from acting cold to flirting and being all forward... yes, the double standard isn't right. I adjusted my tone again, to be less flirty and more friendly, as I tried to make up for my earlier blunder and win points with my sort-of-ex kind-of-want-him-back boyfriend. "Flynn is the one who made those poses and pictures turn out so well; weren't they wonderful? He's so handy with his hands too, he boarded up my window after a break in..." *Oh shoot; me and my big mouth. Bringing up the break in will lead to questions!* "Plus, he's a fantastic cook, and the King's right-hand man. Seriously, I doubt Ryan could fully function without him."

Flynn looked pleased as punch over my effusive praise. Jabari raised an eyebrow as he responded, "That is quite impressive, my man. And Don; you are on first name basis with the King himself?"

"Well sure; he's married to one of my two besties. Plus, he's basically a brother the way he tries to look after me and help where he can."

Jabari looked thoughtful, his piercing eyes casually moving between Flynn and I before he answered, in a somewhat lazy voice, like he didn't really care about the answer. "Is that how you are as well; you two? A sibling-like relationship?"

Sebastian let out a laugh, though when I sent a deadly glare in his direction, he had the decency to cover it with a loud fake-coughing fit. *Why are you so good at acting but in real life when you attempt to act... you suck?*

I opened my mouth to answer Jabari, but Flynn beat me to it, "No." His voice was very resolute, as was his posture as he stepped closer to me, wrapping my waist in his arms from behind so I was gently pulled against his firm chest. "I most definitely do not think of Doni as a sister." I felt my body react to his nearness. That plus his words were enough to make me melt. *What is wrong with me today?? Why is everything causing such intense physical reactions? And why haven't I moved out of Flynn's feather-light grip? It's obvious he wouldn't have forced me to stay; he isn't that kind of a man. Flynn is showing that he still has interest, but he is allowing me to decide how I want to handle the question from another potential admirer. And how had I responded? Like a kitten, curling into the arms of her favorite person; I am two seconds away from purring at this point! Bonkers.*

I didn't move as I smiled up at Flynn, rubbing his arm affectionately, then I looked at the other two guys. Sebastian's face showed shock and pleasure; he hadn't seen us this couple-y in who knows how long. Jabari continued to smile as if he was unfazed, but his eyes never wavered from my face. "Flynn and I are very close." I left it at that. *I don't honestly know myself what to categorize our relationship as. On-again-off-again doesn't seem to do it justice, and isn't fair to Flynn. He had never wanted to break up; I was the one that had pushed him away each time. He is an incredible guy. No matter how stunningly handsome another guy is; that doesn't change the depth of Flynn's character and patience. Plus, Flynn is also very, very attractive. And he doesn't deserve to feel insecure.* I snuggled in closer into Flynn's muscular chest as Jabari merely smiled.

"That's nice. Well, as long as there's a little wiggle room, I'd like to offer my number; but only if you two aren't closed off."

I thought about that for a moment. *We certainly aren't closed off; we aren't even currently together. Surely, I'd gave Flynn enough reassurance that I can take the number; that is harmless enough a gesture... right?* Before my mind ran away from me, I said, "Sure, I'll take it. But no promises it'll get used."

I felt Flynn's gentle hands loosen even further, as if he felt defeated. I felt bad, but it would be rude to change my mind and decline the number... right? *Ugh, why is being single more difficult to navigate than being in a relationship? I used to be so good at this. The casual hook up. The easy-breezy flirting without consequences. No one got hurt. But that was all before... Flynn. But I can't bring myself to cut ties with Flynn. He is my constant. My go-to for all things... well, everything honestly. He is such a good listener; so easy to talk to. He so rarely gets angry; he possesses the patience of a saint. So why am I always testing that patience? Maybe... maybe I am checking to see if something I do, something I say, will make him abandon me like my... parents. Perhaps. My family issues might be at fault. I don't know.* I fished in my jeans pocket for my phone, giving it to Jabari, averting my eyes from Flynn, but not before I saw the ghost of hurt that appeared in Flynn's chocolate eyes. *Gosh darnit. I had tried so hard to talk him up so he wouldn't feel bad by this interaction... and then I go and ruin it.*

I fought the urge to lunge for my phone before Jabari could finish inputting his contact, continuing to rub Flynn's arm. I felt him stiffen under me, but he didn't pull away. *The mood has shifted though. That much I know for sure.* I quickly took my phone back, nestling back into Flynn yet again. *He feels a little less tense; but the damage is done. I am going to have to do some serious groveling to fix this blunder. Ugh. Why did Jabari have to be so drop-dead gorgeous? A lesser man wouldn't have caused these waves. How am I going to make it up to Flynn?* I decided to change the subject, hoping that might cover my blunder. "Jabari, have you met Ahyoka yet? Ahyoka Little Feather?"

Whoa... that's odd. The handsome face that had been so full of charm and ease hardened, as if a literal cloud had darkened his features and ruined his good mood. The man that caused such an upset between myself and Flynn, and who had looked so intensely angry not a moment ago, he flashed me a brilliant smile as he turned on the charm. "It was lovely to meet you both. If you'll excuse us; Bastian and I need to get back to planning for our pitch to their majesties."

My curiosity was peaked, as that was the first caution sign I'd seen in that guy, and only when Sebastian's girlfriend, one of my friends, was brought up. *Weird. But I don't want to make things more awkward, and I figure prolonging the conversation will just rock the boat further.* I waved as they walked away. I didn't move from my comfortable position, other than to bring my hand to cup his face, tilting my head to lock eyes with his. He did his best imitation of a carefree smile, but it didn't quite reach his eyes. "I need you to know how important you are to me."

The edges of his lips twitched as he gave me a sad half smile. "I know I am."

I internally sighed, trying again as I dug deeper. "Before meeting you, I would have jumped on that opportunity without a second thought. He's hot as hell, famous, and charming."

Flynn's smile faltered, threatening to turn into a frown. I hurriedly finished my thoughts. "You know I'm bollocks at cheering people up. I meant that... that you're different. You've made me different. I flirted a bit; sure. And I took his number. I shouldn't have; I know that. While I'm technically single... I still care about you far too much to disrespect you the way I just did. I just... ugh I'm so rubbish at this. I care... that's all." My finish was lame, but for the first time since Jabari was introduced, he had a genuine smile gracing his handsome face.

"You're not rubbish at cheering me up. Thanks for the effort, Doni." He whispered my nickname, right against my right ear, and I shivered involuntarily. *He has such an effect on me. Different than that Broadway star or anyone else for that matter.*

What am I doing? Everything in my body screams when Flynn is near. My heart most of all. I feel like I'm trying to get my idiotic head to understand that Flynn is my person. Who else could put up with me? Who else has stuck around this long, honestly?

I heard my phone blasting one of my favorite songs, *You Don't Own Me* alerting me that Cordelia had more clients to send my way. Flynn mouthed a goodbye, walking toward the door while looking over his shoulder a bit forlornly at me. Feeling uncomfortable with his emotions, I turned my back and answered the call, flinching slightly as I heard that bird noise alert me that Flynn had left, and the closing door making everything feel far too final. *I just made a huge mistake. Is it too late to fix it??*

"Is now a good time to stop by? If so, I can be there in about five minutes." I straightened up, taking the small trek to the front of my shop, telling her that now was fine. True to her word, five minutes later, she breezed through the door. Cordelia gave me a fresh batch of two dozen upcoming clients, then at the end, instead of leaving, she instead asked, "Do you have time for a non-business-related question? Something a bit more girl-to-girl?"

I blinked, surprised. *This woman is all business, all the time. Perfectly cordial, professional, but always right to what needs to be accomplished when. What could she want to ask?* "Sure, I've got a bit; go ahead.

She smiled, and it was radiant. *She is an unbelievably beautiful woman. If I was insecure, I'd feel inferior. And while I am pretty proud of my curvy body, it's still a bit tough to see someone who looks like they are meant to be on some catwalk or magazine.* "I was just wondering... and feel free to tell me it's none of my business... but about Flynn. He's been hung up on you for quite a while now. Do you ever think you two will give it a real go?"

I felt something grip my heart. Panic. *She likes Flynn. Why else would she ask me such a question!* "I honestly don't know. Why do you ask?"

Cordelia flashed a confident smile as she ran her hands along several of my Carnation bouquets. "To be direct; he's exactly the type of man I want to get to know. I don't love him or anything; I don't know him well. But he's as hot as they come, very sincere and thoughtful; and he is so respectful to you, I feel like he'd make a good boyfriend, and an even better husband. But it's obvious you two have a history. I don't want to discuss it with him without speaking with you first. I value our business relationship. So, if you tell me you want to be with him; I won't bring it up again. But if you're unsure, I'd like to ask him out."

My throat closed up like I was having an allergic reaction. But I hadn't been stung by a bee... this was only plain old jealousy. *Who would have thought I could be bitten by the big green monster? I thought I was above such petty feelings. I can't be with Flynn without opening up. Which I just can't bring myself to do. Flynn deserves to be with someone that will open up to him. This supermodel of a woman will probably have no issues with that. It's not fair to say he's mine while telling Flynn no...* I fixed my eyes on Cordelia who was waiting patiently. *She is allowing me time and space to think. Come to think of it, I have never seen any kind of red flag out of her. She is great.* "I have no claim on Flynn." Six words, but they pierced me the second they came out of my mouth. I wanted to scream, but no sound would come out.

Her already large eyes widened, seemingly not expecting that answer. "Thank you for letting me know. To clarify; when I speak with Flynn, no matter what he says; it won't affect our business relationship?"

I wanted to say 'of course it will! I love him! Flynn is my lad.' But fear caused me to say instead, "It won't."

She gave me a cheerful smile, leaving the notebook of clients to meet with to discuss preferences over the next month, and then sauntered over to the door. I watched as I felt myself pull a face. *Even her walk is sexy. And I just gave her the okay to ask the man I love out to dinner. There's no doubt now; I am certifiable. Completely and totally.*

I paced my shop continuously, out of sorts, I put the closed sign on the door. About half an hour later, Cordelia texted me, asking if we could chat again, that she could come back to the shop. I immediately replied that yes, I'm available. I rushed to change the sign back to open and tried to look as unbothered as possible.

When Cordelia came back into my shop, her sunny smile made the knot in my stomach grow even wider. I was on pins and needles wanting to blurt out asking what Flynn had said. But business first, as usual. I somehow made it through the sketches and PowerPoint presentation. I would be showing these to three sets of future couples next Saturday, and she went over each, making some minor revisions and giving me her input. It was all so very normal; I wanted to grab her by her perfectly proportioned shoulders and shake her until she spilled about the encounter. After we had gone through everything for the upcoming meetings, she said, "As I suspected, Flynn is just as invested in you as he ever was. Since I suspect you are far more interested in him than you are letting on;

I'll give you this advice, as I feel we are becoming friends: either confess your feelings and show him you want him or find a way to gently set him free. While I won't go into what he said exactly, as that's for the two of you to discuss, he is willing to wait far longer than I could, for you, in the off chance you decide being a couple is what you want. We both know how incredible and rare he is. If I were you, well, I'd do just about anything to make it work. But that's just my thoughts; take or leave them as you will; and I will see you next week!"

She breezed out of the store, while I, on the other hand, forgot how to breathe. I was so wrapped up in what she'd said, I started to feel the rush to my brain at the lack of oxygen. I inhaled a huge gust of air, making me cough like a mad woman. *Did I hear her right? He said no? Because of me? He made some kind of comment about waiting... for me? He really cares, so much more than I thought. I had been so worried about him wanting Cordelia. I shouldn't be surprised; Flynn is the most loyal person I know. The only other guys that were that devoted are the King and Sebastian. Ryan and Caroline are basically made for each other; Sebastian and Ahyoka are making the long-distance thing work far better than most, he flies to her and flies her to him as much as they possibly can. And Flynn... he's always been there. Especially when I needed him. Every single time. He's the first to comfort me. To offer me a kind word. To fix things. To make my life easier. And the way he dotes over that little girl... melts my ice-cold heart. That may be the culprit. Because we've randomly been thrown into a pseudo co-parent situation, it's brought us closer. But is that actual love, or is that manufactured by our nearness? If I went back to my apartment or my shop..., would I feel the same? Ugh. I know I would. Who am I trying to fool? I've admired the guy since the first glance. I tried to make myself believe it was lust. But we've never done anything more than kissing and heavy petting; it's more than lust. A lot more. I respect him. I trust him. I tried so hard to keep my heart hard... but everything he does thaws another shattered piece. If he thaws the whole thing... I'm scared of what the results will be.*

My door chirped, alerting me that more potential customers had arrived. I frowned at the annoying robot bird. Ryan's contribution when Dante had recreated my shop, they had made plenty of improvements and generous addons, but Ryan's obsession with birds made him think that it was genius to have a bird call each time the door opens or shuts. He had been such a kind benefactor; I had only slightly grumped about the bird call. *But ugh Caroline needs to tell her lad to take it down. Asap.* I slammed the vase I was holding, and it shattered into several large pieces, and a couple tiny ones. I wanted to curse, but since obviously some people were just entering the store, I absentmindedly welcomed the people in, not really feeling in the mood to chat. While they were preoccupied with looking around, I hurriedly slipped on a pair of gardening gloves and picked up the pieces. I put them in the back, near the coat rack, on a nearby counter. A couple of small pieces fell on the floor; because that was the kind of day I was having. *Whatever. I'll sweep that up later.*

I returned to the front of the store, where some couples happily chose several make-your-own bouquets, which usually delighted me. *Usually, I love watching others create with my beauties. But today is different. It makes me sick. How dare others openly show their affection on such a gloomy day!*

I forced a smile as I reached the front counter. *I can get through these customers, then go home. Go to bed extra early. Forget this day ever existed.* But as I was prepping them, multiple times my experienced hands were scratched and torn by errant thorns. *No self-respecting florist with as much experience as I would ever make such a mistake. But my mind is elsewhere.* Thankfully, the small group didn't notice, they were all too busy looking at my flower installations on the ceiling. *Another moment that usually energizes me, but I feel even more exhausted instead.* Once they were gone, thankfully I had remembered to ask how they wanted to pay, I felt in such a funk it was a miracle I had gotten the payment sorted. I then switched the sign to closed; I was not fit to work the rest of the afternoon.

I almost walked out, but it was raining. *Ugh. Of course it is. I hate it when my hair gets wet! What a minging day! Such a pain.* I half-ran to the back to fish out my coat, juggling with my purse, my phone, and my keys as well. The stupid coat wouldn't cooperate, so angrily I threw my stuff to the floor. I chucked my shoes somewhere, kicking them off with far too much force, but I was angry. I couldn't see my rain boots, something else I'd have to find before I could go home, so I continued to fight with my coat, not understanding why I couldn't get my hand through it. I yanked and yanked; then I heard a *riiiip** noise. I collapsed to the floor, feeling completely done with this day. I inspected the jacket; I had apparently been trying to force my hand through the pocket. *What a numpty move!* Why I hadn't realized that wasn't a sleeve, I really don't know. But now I had a gigantic hole in the fabric. I stood up again, pulling on the coat the right way; and the hole landed right where my stomach was. Bloody fabulous. I waved my arms in exasperation, screaming, "What else you got?!" to no one in particular. I was given a resounding answer as I started screaming for an entirely different reason. My right arm had found that broken vase from earlier... and it hurt like crazy. I gingerly lifted my arm, seeing that the vase had made quite the cut, through the sleeve of an obviously flimsily-designed coat and through my arm. *I bet Giovanni or Rita would have made something much better quality.* It was a stupid thought, but that's what came to mind. There was too much blood to see how bad the cut actually was. I blinked back tears, torn between wanting to call Flynn and not wanting him to see me like this, especially with him probably still annoyed from earlier. I looked around the dimly lit room, until I noticed my rain boots. *Thank goodness. I may be a bloody mess, but at least I can get out of here.* I took a couple steps toward them, then felt a sharp pain in my feet. "Ahh!!" I screamed, I tried to step back, but instead, no clue how, I fully lost my balance, feeling very doddery, and landed hard on my knees. Right onto the source of the pain in my feet – the sharp little shards of glass on the floor. *There is seriously nothing* *going right for me today. At all.* Giving up every shred of my dignity, I crawled backwards, in an odd crabwalk sort of way, trying to lift my feet so I was only on my heels, and trying not to put as much pressure on the bleeding arm. I reached for my phone, and I didn't hesitate. Instead of calling 911, I pushed the first number in my favorites: Flynn. I felt an awful head rush, but this time not from lack of oxygen, maybe it was lack of blood, maybe it was adrenaline, all I know is I couldn't fight the feeling that I had to sleep. I was utterly knackered. At least a kip; immediately.

Chapter 4
REVISITING TRAUMA

Flynn's POV:

I was still so thrown because of that quick kiss. I had asked my mother to watch Lydia for a little while so I could take a bit to breathe and overthink. But that didn't happen. Suddenly the wedding planner showed up, and instead of any kind of small talk, she immediately said, "I like you; I'd like us to go out to dinner. What do you think?"

I blinked, totally confused. I said after a second, "I... you know I care about Doni. I can't do that. I'm sorry, Cordelia."

Cordelia's expression saddened. She didn't look angry, just hurt. "But what if she never gives you a real chance? Will you wait around forever?"

I thought about her question. *How long will I wait? Can I love anyone as much as I love Donyelle? Is it possible? That would mean falling out of love with Doni... I don't think I could ever make myself do that.* "I would rather pine for Doni and have an epic one-sided love, contentedly single and available to at least be her friend, than to love another. You are a lovely, kind girl, Cordelia. It's an honor you think I'm someone worth knowing. But I'm afraid Donyelle Cox just burns too brightly, everyone else pales in comparison. There's nothing I can do about how I feel. It wouldn't be fair to either of us to go to dinner together knowing that I can't give you my heart or the attention you deserve. If I may; Queen Caroline has had some great success matching others in the past; perhaps you might consider turning to her expertise."

I wasn't sure how she would react. She was, in a way, a big part of Donyelle's client base. Though Donyelle was technically her own boss, if Cordelia decided not to pass on her information to all her rich fancy clients, Donyelle's business would suffer another huge blow. *I hope I was kind and respectful enough... I didn't even consider that. Should I have agreed just to keep Donyelle from bankruptcy?*

"Donyelle should count herself blessed. Not only is she the most talented florist I've beheld, but she's got the most loyal love interest as well."

I let out a soft sigh of relief, which made the woman smile. *She's beautiful, even more so when she smiles. Someone else will find her just as amazing as I find Doni; I'm sure of it.* I ventured to ask, "Does that mean that you'll still work with Donyelle?"

She let out a tinkling laugh. "Goodness yes. I'm a grown woman; it would have been lovely if we could have seen if we were compatible, but not even your pretty face would cause me the loss of her expertise. As far as I'm concerned, as long as she wants to do business with me, she will always be the first choice for each of my clients' events. Always. And I do appreciate that although you were rejecting me, it was done in a classy, respectful way." She turned, as if she was about to leave, but then slightly turned on her heel with another dazzling smile. "However, if you ever change your mind and decide you may be up to giving me a chance; look me up." And with that, she walked swiftly away, with another tinkling laugh echoing through the halls in her wake.

I shook myself from yet another wild encounter. *I need to have baby time. My godson always helped me get out of my head; that's exactly what I need at this moment.* I picked up the pace, now on a mission. *It's like... twelve thirty. Around the time that Caroline has been handing her class to Ahyoka for an hour to spend with her children.*

Sure enough, Caroline was in the nursery singing to both her babies. She looked blissfully happy as she sang angelically about how she'd always be there for her children. *This is a very touching moment.* Calista was cooing along as if she was attempting to sing as well, while Rigel was all over the place, rolling around and making the silliest noises, like a pterodactyl screech, but like... a happy one.

I smirked as Rigel was anything but calm. Caroline let out a musical laugh as she bent over, picking up her son and cradling him in her arms. "Always so busy, my little babe." She kissed him softly on his head as Rigel wriggled around in her arms. Caroline smiled, stooping down. "Alright little love; where are you wanting to go?" She laid down her son gently on the tummy time mat, tracking with her eyes as he immediately swerved into a sitting position and started his funny little scoot towards me. Rigel hadn't mastered crawling yet, not like his twin sister, but he had this hilarious butt-scoot thing that got him from point a to point b just as well.

"Oh, Flynn! A nice surprise. What is it this time?"

I blinked, wondering what Caroline could mean by that question. "Good to see you too, your Majesty." She shook her head, and I corrected, "Right. Caroline. That will be tough to correct in my head. But I'll get it."

She chuckled, as her look encompassed her sleeping daughter and her son who had almost reached me already. "I'll say this; you'll get back to using my name far faster than Dante, I'm sure. Now back to my question. You look pensive; you normally come for baby cuddles when you need to unwind. Want to talk about it with me? Or I can get Ryan if what you need is more of a boy-chat."

I grinned sheepishly. "I wasn't aware I was that transparent. Since it mostly revolves around one of your best friends, I'm not sure if talking with you about it would be wise, or... I don't know."

She gave me a sweet smile. "I'm here if you need me. No pressure either way." She moved closer to me, taking care not to step on her son. I sat down as Rigel made it to my legs, so he could explore my shirt and my face.

I unburdened myself as I began, "Ryan has been encouraging me to protect my heart. But it's just far too late for that. I was about at the point of giving up hope that we would have any forward momentum ever again, and I was going to have to be okay with acting like acquaintances, not even really friends, the way she avoids my gaze. But then we found Lydia, and she has bonded us like we never have been before. As you well know as both a teacher and a parent, kids have a way of melting even the coldest heart."

She smiled easily. "True for most people."

I nodded. "But I feel like I'm taking advantage of the situation. For now, they are both living in my house. I don't want Donyelle to get confused; sometimes proximity is enough to be misconstrued as love. I want Donyelle to love me, but not because she and I are caring for a child. And not because she feels pressured too. Like she gave me a quick kiss, a peck really, and I don't know what it means; so, I'm really in my head."

"Kissed you?!" Caroline exclaimed excitedly in a much louder volume than before. Rigel made some screeching noises, apparently attempting to out-perform his mother's loud outburst. Somehow Calista slept through it all, just as she often did, smiling in her sleep. *What an easy baby.* Rigel pulled on my ear as I chuckled softly,

"It wasn't a huge deal to her, I think. Of course it was for me. I thought maybe she was trying to tell me something. But next thing I know, the wedding planner is showing up here asking to go out to dinner-". Caroline raised an eyebrow at that, but she didn't comment. "It just solidified that much more that Doni is it for me. I'd rather be single than settle for someone I don't love. That's not fair to either party. In the off-chance Doni changes her mind in the future... I always keep her ring in my safe at home. Just in case."

She made a near silent "aww" that made my lip quirk. "Sorry. I just adore love." Caroline put her hand on my shoulder as she gracefully sat on the floor opposite me. "You're an incredibly good man, Flynn. Everyone around you can see it. Your loyalty is admirable. But I..." she trailed off as a tear rolled down her normally happy face, she didn't wipe it, instead looked me directly in the eyes. "I don't want you to be alone just because you want to stay loyal to someone you're not in a relationship with. If you want to give Doni some more time, that's great; but you and I both know it will take a miracle from God to get her to open up the way you both need to grow together. If I had known the love story between you two would be so tumultuous... I might not have set you up in the first place. At the very least, I could have given you a disclaimer. I always assumed my girl just needed the right guy, and then she'd feel comfortable to be vulnerable in a way she never had before. So far though, I seem to be proven wrong."

I shook my head, pulling a tissue from the nearby box on the rug beside me, handing it to the Queen. She took it with a grateful smile, dabbing her eyes. "I don't regret meeting Doni. Not for a second. Before her things were monotonous. Being around her and loving her may be a rollercoaster, but it's not boring. It's not toxic either; as that's something I wouldn't want, obviously. She's not abusive, she's not mean; she's simply scared. Like... like a grown-up version of Lydia - it's not as pronounced, you have to look far deeper to see it, but it's there. They share that haunted look in their eyes. And Doni is similar to Ryan in some ways too. Both have trauma. Deep trauma. The difference is Ryan speaks about his experiences; with you, me, and his therapist. Donyelle tells only you what's going on in her head."

Caroline looked down sadly. "And even then, I doubt she's sharing more than about ten percent of what she's going or gone through."

I shrugged as Rigel put the string from my hoodie into his mouth. I smiled despite myself at my godson's antics. "I've asked so many times, I decided I'm going to back off. Especially with us sharing a place for who knows how long, I don't want her to feel pressured."

I scooped Rigel into my arms as I put my head to the baby's. "You are so loved Rigel Robbie. So very loved." His tiny appendages squeezed around my pointer finger, so I tilted my head down and kissed his little fingers, then blew on his face causing him to giggle hysterically. *Babies have the cutest laughs.* I turned my attention to Rigel's mother, who was giving her son an expression of pride and joy. "You and Ryan are doing great; the twins, the kingdom, still just as love as when you were dating. How do you do it?"

She smiled brightly, all traces of sadness gone. She blew a stray hair out of her face then answered, "God, really. I pray, often, for His will to be done. And I intercede specifically for my loved ones and everyone in our Kingdom. Lehavre is a special place; Langley especially, but all of the provinces. Thanks for saying that; it means a lot. As for marriage, it's all about each day choosing to love my person. I tell him honestly when he does something I don't like, and vice versa. We challenge each other respectfully and with love, to grow and become better. For ourselves, for us as a couple, for our children, and for our people. Love is a funny thing. People act like they know all about love. Some think it comes on first meeting. Others think it takes time to mature and blossom. Still others think that you can love many romantically at the same time. What I have learned the most about love is that it is a choice. You choose to love a person, you choose not to love a person. Honestly, I think Doni needs to be challenged. I love her so incredibly much, but she's gotten extremely comfortable flitting through life without setting down actual roots or family ties. While she's lived in Langley her whole life, other than her store and home, she doesn't have much to show for it. Ahyoka and I are her friends, because we decided to love her knowing we may never truly get all of our questions answered. Others that weren't okay with her level of secrecy just gave up. While it's not my place to share what little she was willing to speak on with me... I think just having you around is a soothing balm for her. But if I were you... I'd sit her down and be extremely honest. You've already given her so much time, space; you've been very respectful. I know I sort of said the opposite earlier in this conversation... but I'm becoming more convinced she needs a good honest talk. Perhaps... maybe if you shared; something you don't tell others?"

I rubbed my forehead, feeling a bit of a stress-headache coming on. "Donyelle and I both have that issue. Sharing those things... it's really tough. It's like going back to that place. Being reminded of what I thought, how I felt... I know she'd feel the same. However, if I don't know her life story, about her inner struggles, then and especially now; how can I truly love every aspect of her? I only know a small percentage of what makes Donyelle herself."

Caroline grinned, lifting her hand from my arm and holding both arms out for her son, who went from snuggling against my chest to suddenly doing a death-drop as he flung himself back into his mother's waiting arms. My mouth hung open, and Caroline laughed, loudly. "Just like I know my son's little quirks and tells, you know at least some of Don's. More than most, I'd wager. Try not to get discouraged. And yeah; Rigel does that now. Anytime he's fighting a nap, the second he looks comfortable, he catapults himself back in order to wake up. It's only been the last day or two, but he does it often."

Whoa. Rigel's gaining so much personality so quickly. And Caroline's right. I've constantly asked Donyelle to share; but I myself haven't told her much. But I need to keep in mind there is a distinct possibility that even if I bare my soul Donyelle might not share much, if anything. I need to have the expectation that I am going to share without expecting anything in return. Can I do that?

I thanked Caroline, said a quick goodbye to my godson and his sister who was stretching adorably, making happy little noises. Rigel, by comparison, was back to screeching, though now it sounded more hungry than happy, so my timing was great, giving Caroline time to breastfeed in privacy.

Feeling more assured, less confused, I began to make my way to my mom's kitchen, where she and Lydia would surely be.

I was almost at my mom's kitchen, about to pick up the little girl. I heard them talking and laughing; they seemed to be using cutters to make shapes for cookies or pies or something. I felt my phone vibrate, so I pulled it out of my pocket. Doni. I opened it, asking, "Hey Doni, everything alright?" No answer. I double checked to see if the phone was on mute or low volume, but that wasn't it. *Weird... Donyelle has never accidently called me before. Actually, normally she doesn't call unless it's some kind of emergency...* I put the phone closer to my ear; nothing. I called her name several more times. *What's that... I could swear I hear something; but it's so faint...* Feeling like something was definitely wrong, I called dispatch and got a cheery girl's voice. I told her the situation, said it may be nothing, but it's not like Donyelle to call and not be there. She said she'd send the closest squad car and ambulance to each of the locations I gave just to be safe, and I thanked her, profusely. I texted my mom, telling her she would need to watch Lydia a bit longer, I thought if I went in there, I might confuse the little girl, she and my mom were doing just fine. I then rushed to my car, which was sounding significantly worse, but as long as it didn't catch fire, it was better than not knowing what was going on. I tried listening, as I was still connected to Donyelle's phone, but all I could hear was this faint wheezing sound, *like... labored breathing, maybe? What could have happened?* All kinds of awful scenarios came to mind. *But my brother is still in jail. And while the want-to-be mayor might be psychotic, he wouldn't have gone after Donyelle... would he?* I throttled the gas, causing my car to whine that much louder in protest. *Yeah, this car is basically garbage at this point.*

She could be one of four places. Well, she could be anywhere, but Donyelle is pretty predictable when it comes to her schedule. She'd either be at her shop, her house, Caroline's castle, or my place. Using deduction, if she was with Caroline, she or Ryan would have called if something was wrong. Considering it's only just about 1 p.m. on a Tuesday, that means she is most likely at her shop. And if she isn't... well, I won't think about that right now. I slammed the gas once more, making my hunk of junk lurch forward. Somehow, I reached her shop before anyone else. It was raining very heavily, but things didn't look too out of the norm. The window I'd patched was untouched, nothing suggested a break in of any kind. *Oh... the sign says closed, which is odd for this time of day.*

Just to try it, I turned the doorknob, and the door opened. I heard the bird's cheerful call, but no Donyelle to greet me. Everything again looked normal. No evidence of any kind of struggle. *If something had happened, wouldn't flowers be ruined or something?* "Donyelle? Donyelle, it's Flynn, you here?" I strained to listen for any faint sound, then I had an idea. I put the phone up to my ear and repeated my questions. I could hear my voice resonating from the phone's speaker, though kind of faint, so not this room. *There are only a few other places where my voice can still be heard – the basement, the backroom, and maybe the greenhouse, but that one I'm not sure of.* I rushed to the back, and then immediately stopped in my tracks.

There was blood everywhere. It was puddled all around what appeared to be Donyelle. I felt my breath catch in my throat. I immediately called 911 again, told the girl where Donyelle was and that there was a ton of blood. She redirected the ambulance to my location. When she asked me if Donyelle was still breathing, I lost it. I started sobbing. I leaned down, careful not to jostle her, and put a finger near her nose. I felt only a tiny puff of air. I relayed the information, asked if I should start CPR. Dispatch told me no, with as much blood as I'm relaying, and with her breathing, I needed to find the source of the bleed and try to apply pressure to the area until the EMT's arrive. I frantically looked around for a towel, and I found a couple. I noticed that there was glass, coated in blood, some on the floor, but a huge sharp-looking piece by the sink on the counter. *How had this happened? Was someone attacking her? I feel uneasy searching her body for bleeds, as I have been very respectful of her privacy, even when she was trying to throw herself at me. But now is the time to save her life. That is the most important.* I crouched down, barely avoiding the glass on the floor, and noticed that her stomach, right arm, knees, and feet were all exposed. A quick inspection showed her stomach was unharmed. I didn't lift her right arm, as I noticed it looked to be a source of heavy bleeding. I bit my lip, not wanting to hurt her, but I covered the arm in my towels, clamping my hands over them. *She looks so pale and frail, I've never seen her like this. I want to throw up.*

"Please God: help what I'm doing save her. I need her. Please don't take her away. Please!" I muttered my prayers under my breath. I looked around, from my crouched position, and noticed her knees had small cuts. And it was hard to tell from this angle, but I imagine her feet had them too. I felt the blood seeping through the towels and onto my fingers. I gasped as her eyes fluttered, not opening, but like she was attempting to try to open them.

"Donyelle? I'm here. It's Flynn. Try not to move. Does it hurt to talk? Can you tell me what happened? Who hurt you?"

Her whole face winced, but her eyes opened. She was in very intense pain, that much was certain. I heard the siren of the ambulance, the most welcome sound in the world. They rushed in, as I moved out of the way to allow them to do their job, telling them what little I knew. Donyelle seemed to be losing the struggle to keep her eyes open. One of the EMT's was a young-looking guy. He said, "Ma'am? I know it's hard; try not to go to sleep. You've lost too much blood."

I wanted to collapse with anguish, but I needed to keep Donyelle safe. I wracked my brain to think of what I could say that would make her fight to stay awake. "Doni, I never finished telling you why Dandelions are my favorite flower."

Donyelle's eyes snapped fully open, a look of frustration over-taking the pain on her face. The EMTs looked confused and be-mused, but then quickly and efficiently hoisted her onto the gurney and ushered her and I into the back of the ambulance, as the young guy took her vitals and wrapped her arm while the older woman sped to the nearest hospital. *It's at least ten miles away. Even speeding it will be a long time to try to keep her awake.*

I started, "Well Dandelions have plenty of health benefits. How many flowers can you say that about?"

"At least thirteen." She said slowly, but with passion.

"Really? Do you know their names?" I asked, as I tried not to let my fear show in my face or in my tone.

Donyelle knew what I was doing, but she was just stubborn enough to have to answer anyway. "Chamomile, Squash Blossom, Honeysuckle, Hibiscus, Purslane, Lavender, Lotus, Chrysanthemum, Nasturtium, Rose, Borage, and Pansy."

I had been counting in my head, so I asked, "That makes twelve, right?"

She forced a pained smile. "Dandelions make thirteen."

I want to crow that she has accepted a weed as an edible flower. But now isn't the time. And her lashes are wilting again. I whispered, "How much longer?" To the man beside her, still cleaning her smaller wounds.

"Three minutes out." He whispered back.

I cringed, but continued, "Dandelions have some great vitamins, and you know you probably have heard their leaves make good salads, you can ask my mom. Her tea is really good too, only she calls it 'Priest's Crown' so it sounds more royal. It may be a weed in some people's eyes, but it's bright, sunny, parts can be eaten, even used for wine and coffee stuff. Plus, it's used to treat a lot of medical conditions; I bet Ahyoka's tribe uses it in some form or another. Let's ask her together, what do you think?"

She made some kind of sound, her eyes dangerously close to closing.

"Donyelle Cox; I love you. Don't close your eyes!" It was the firmest my voice had ever been, but it did the trick. She showed me her tantalizing, all-encompassing eyes.

"You know... I hate my last name." Her breathing was very labored, but the ambulance stopped; we had reached the emergency room. I texted Caroline, Ryan and Ahyoka telling them to meet us at the emergency room. I waited until they had taken Donyelle, still on the gurney, into the nearest room, and I was allowed to come with her. I thought they had rules about only family; but they didn't ask, so I didn't tell.

I was grateful, extremely, that no one had bothered to see if I was related. *Truth be told, the state Donyelle is in, I am willing to fight anyone who tries to stop me from being by her side. Her eyelashes are yet again wilting. What can I say that will get her passionate or angry enough to stay awake?* I whispered, "Donyelle - you have to fight. We have to protect Lydia. And no one will know how to care for all your flowers like you do."

She was trying. But it was a failed attempt. I clasped her hand as the gurney was transformed into a bed with wheels. I kept pace as we rushed into the nearest room. When her eyes were dangerously close yet again, I pleaded, "Doni, I can't lose you." My voice cracked; I felt the tears threatening to fall. I saw the strain on her face, it was obviously exceedingly difficult to fight to stay awake. But she did it. And as the Doctor, someone I didn't know, examined her, announcing she needed surgery to remove the glass, just like that, they whisked her away. I felt my shoulders slump. *I feel unbelievably tired. Scared. If she doesn't make it off the table...*

A nearby nurse who had checked us in when we first arrived peeked her head in the doorway. "Try not to worry, handsome. You helped her stay awake, making the chance for a positive outcome far greater. She's lucky to have you." She gave me a sympathetic smile, and I tried to smile back, but I just couldn't. *There is nothing to smile about. If Donyelle doesn't make it, the world will be the worse for it. She is an incredibly special very bright light. If I lose her... all the color that has replaced the monotony will dissipate. Everything about her brought a liveliness that I had become accustomed to, and whether it was friends, lovers, or partners for life; I crave the beauty that she brings to my world. I don't want to contemplate the pallid existence I would be plunged into if she was somehow gone.*

And what about Lydia? Of the two of us, Donyelle bonded with her on a deeper level. But it was more than a trauma bond. The understanding that went across Doni's face as she had interacted with the little girl. The way she had offered her hand, hovering, but never touching. I wouldn't have known to do that. Not knowing what else to do, I turned to prayer.

"God; I need her! I want her selfishly, but she is also so needed in this world. If she were gone, the color would be sucked out of everything; You didn't mean for Your creation to be monochrome, or You wouldn't have taken the time to create each vibrant hue in the universe. You gave her a larger-than-life personality; it's too important and too needed in this world, and in my life, to be extinguished so soon!" I prayed in tongues under my breath as I paced the room. Hospitals brought bad memories, and unbidden they floated through my brain like a taunting carousel. My mother's deep guttural screams, piercing through the door of her room and enveloping the waiting room where my father and I were. I was young at the time, but old enough to remember every painful detail. I tried to blink back the memories, force them out of my brain, physically shake my head, trying to focus on something in the room to will them away. But none of my tricks that sometimes worked to stay present worked this time. I was too immersed in my pain, feeling pulled back to the day that forced me from boy to man younger than any child should ever have to grow up.

*****

Not comprehending the pain of labor, I had been anxious on my mother's behalf. The stranger that was my father; he didn't help. I'd never built any kind of bond with the guy; all he ever did was sit on his specific chair, lay back and pound beers as my mother waited on him hand and foot. He was never appreciative of her efforts either, I can recall far too many instances where she brought him what she'd just created and he either wouldn't try it, or he'd use this dismissive tone droning on about what he would have done differently to make the dish much better. That hers were barely palatable, while his was savory. The guy had never wanted to play with me, so I'd gotten used to no longer asking. He only got annoyed each time

I tried, he was happy only when he was sitting watching what he wanted drinking until he passed out, most often in his chair.

So, on the day that changed everything, I wasn't expecting any comfort or sympathy. He was a cold unfeeling man, not caring enough to belay my childish concerns, even the more important ones. I was too concerned for my mother to remember to keep a distance and not bother the man. It's not like I had pestered him either; I specifically remember only asking if mom was going to be okay.

And then he suddenly unleashed on me. Snapped about my lack of respect; about how children are to be seen and not heard. That women are meant to be in pain. And that I'm such a nuisance and a burden he couldn't fathom having another whiny bratty kid to feed and clothe. I was used to his anger; just as his words no longer surprised me. I was old enough to understand them, to be hurt by them; to know that no matter what I did, it would not please my father. Worse yet, unless I was perfectly still, silent, and acted like I didn't exist in his presence, he would beat me. Not when mom was around to take the abuse for me, shielding me with her own body, but when we were alone... he'd wail on me. Told me that disobedient disrespectful children deserve to be a punching bag for their father's righteous anger.

So, when he began to punch me in the hospital room, I was barely fazed. Something about my mom's screams of agony made me feel brave, and with courage I'd always lacked before until this moment, I tried hitting him back. I was only what; five or so? But I gave it my best attempt. And as hospital staff rushed into the fray, my father had cursed at them to mind their business. He broke free of the multiple people trying to hold him back, sneering. "You're no son of mine! And neither is that other one- you're bastards." I didn't know what the word meant at the time, but the intention behind it was clear. He ran, and with him the foul odor of stale alcohol and nasty cigarettes evaporated. I hadn't understood the ramifications of that moment. No one expects their parent to just leave; to decide not to parent. Technically he'd never been a father to me, not in any sense of the word. Yet I didn't know that he was never coming back. Nothing would have changed either way; he still hurt my mother, hurt me; I would have defended us regardless. Especially now that there was a baby to protect as well. When I was ushered into the room, my mom was wet everywhere; I didn't know why, now obviously I know she was sweating from intense labor. But at the time, it just looked like she was turning into a puddle, and I remember worrying that she was going to melt...

*****

I continued to reminisce on those not-so-good memories as I awaited Doni's triumphant return. It felt like it took ages for the surgery to be completed, but in the end, it probably took about four hours or so. She was asleep, looking more peaceful than I'd seen her outside of when she was in her greenhouse and while we had traveled in the past with our friends. It was almost eerie. I'd rather see her full of life, chattering nonstop, than this motionless version.

Someone who looked very official, and had a grave look on his face, strode right up to me. "Are you related to Donyelle Cox?"

Drat, I was hoping they wouldn't ask. The quick answer is no. But as far as I know, she doesn't have any relatives. She's never mentioned parents, siblings... frustration bubbled up inside me at how at a loss I was. *Here the love of my life is in pain, and I don't even know the most basic information about her.* I answered, "She's family." *I hope that's enough to be told what's going on. She is my family; I fully intend to be her husband... if she'll ever let me.*

Apparently, that's all the Doctor-guy needed, as he nodded, then crossed his arms behind his back, an odd way to stand, as he began. "We removed all the foreign debris on her knees, feet, and hands. For the deep laceration, the glass has been removed. I have been informed you covered and applied pressure to the wound?"

I nodded, feeling too queasy to speak.

"Well done. Your quick action helped stop the heavy loss of blood and made it unnecessary to treat with extreme antibiotics.

The other injuries are minor; they will heal in several days given the right conditions. Donyelle's arm, however, that was another matter. Due to the jagged edges and the depth of the laceration, we did some trimming to ease the healing process. We used sutures to lower the risk of scarring, and as long as the patient thoroughly washes the affected area with soap and water, applies the antibacterial ointment, then re-dresses the arm in an absorbent dressing each day for the next four-to-six weeks, it should heal properly and close completely. I recommend weekly checkups; does the patient have a family doctor?"

"Yes; and I will help with the cleaning, ointment, and bandage."

"Very good. Then I will release her into your care. She is under general anesthesia, so she should be awake in the next hour or less. Does Ms. Cox have insurance?"

I blinked, yet again unsure. Probably not, honestly. I don't want this incident to put her into the red, her business has been doing okay, but doctor bills are so expensive... "Actually, I will be paying out of pocket." I volunteered. *Old Faithful, my car, is still running. It isn't an immediate need. Paying for Doni's possibly life-saving emergency room visit - that is far more pressing.* He unclasped his hands and directed me toward the billing department. Even seeing the sign caused a tightness in my chest.

*****

I remember clearly that after my coward father had left me, mom, and brand-new baby Micah, he'd also left mom to pay for the labor, delivery, and hospital stay bills. My mother was an extraordinarily strong woman, so full of faith. But even faith can be challenged, especially under the weight of understanding that she was on her own with two children; one was five and one was not even an hour old, and she had to bear the brunt of everything, including all the bills. Mom had struggled extremely hard to not get emotional, but I saw the tears she seemed to be trying to will away as a kind nurse sympathetically hugged her, but then laid out the fact that she owes almost twenty-two thousand dollars, for a "Cesarean with complications." As so many words were at that age, those were foreign as well, but I saw the gut punch it gave my mother. But it was nothing like when my mother, in a wheelchair for healing purposes, fiddled with her wallet, her hand visibly shaking as she gave the woman her debit card. Yet that wasn't the worst of it. The woman swiped her card, then looked extremely uncomfortable, as she relayed to my mother, "Your card was declined due to insufficient funds. Do you have a credit card?"

My mother, who had been trying to stay so strong, in immense pain after having the worst labor of her life, had slumped so badly. I had rushed in front of her, so she didn't fall out of the chair. Not like my tiny kid-sized body would have helped, but at the time I thought it would. That was the first time I saw my mom fully break down. She had cried before, only hiding, as she prayed deliverance, safety, and protection over me and her each day before dad had come home, always with packs of beer and cigarettes, but this was far worse. Her whole body was shaking, head to toe. Her tears soaked her hospital gown, her hair covered part of her face, but what little I could see of her eyes; she looked more scared and hopeless than I've ever seen her.

"I... I don't have anything; all of my life savings are in that account. My Hu-husband must h-h-have-" she couldn't continue, and thankfully the nurse had understood. She crouched down, very close to me, as she had put a hand on my mother's trembling arm.

"Let's just take your information down, I'll sign you up for our payment plan. Five thousand each month for five months. That does mean you're paying over three grand in interest, but that gives you a month to determine how to pay the first installment. Does that work for you?"

My mom quickly agreed, though she looked very unsure of how she could secure those kinds of funds. At my age, I had no idea how to comfort my mom. I took her hand, cuddling it to my face. She gave me a radiant smile through her tears, and I had felt a little boost of joy, like I had done something right. I knew at that moment, even as I was barely about to be in kindergarten, that I would do everything dad never did. And I would be the best big helper mom ever had; especially with the baby, who was wailing, in the NICU. And that's when I'd realized; I remember a friend of mine, someone I'd fished with that had looked like he didn't belong in our Province, had mentioned that he lived in a castle. Every book I'd read that had a castle in it had made it sound safe. Like my momma would not cry if she was there. What was that kid's name? 'R' something. Maybe he can help?

*****

My memories jumped to almost a month later, mom had almost fully recovered from the C section, whatever that was, and she was trying her absolute best to make the five thousand for the first installment, plus some angry guy had come by and thrown out words that had made momma sad. Words like 'rent' and 'eviction' and 'streets'. I didn't want mamma to be sad. I went to the special fishing spot, waiting for my friend to come; and he did. I told him, "Mamma real sad. She wantin money - I didna help."

The boy nodded, very quiet. "I'll tell my mother." Ryan then moved to me, putting his arms around me. "Sorry." He said sadly. "I always pray my daddy leave. Not your daddy."

I hugged him back, making Ryan flinch. I said sorry, but Ryan just gave me a small smile. "I'll be okay." He said it in a way that made me think that was something he said all the time. Then, he had left. Turns out he told his mom about my mom, how she makes yummy treats, is so nice to let him and Flynn play, and is really sad about money.

The rest was history; that's how my mother was able to pay off the hospital bills; when the Queen comes to the hospital personally and speaks with the staff, your debt is wiped clean. Not just for the first month, but for all of it. I'll never forget the way mom had tried to curtsey to Ryan and his mom. The Queen quickly told her not to, and Ryan had taken my mom's hand, asking her not to cry, it makes him sad. And from then on, Ryan and I were inseparable, even more than before; and my mother and his were the best of friends. To this day, mom calls both Lily and Ryan 'answers to prayer'.

*****

The bright headlights of a passing car pulled my focus from that long ago memory back to reality. *Right, I have a bill to pay.*

A woman with a bright smile very happily took my information, relayed the bill, which almost made me have a heart attack on the spot, then with my nod of assent, swiped my card, and as she did, I could almost see the beautiful car I envisioned disappear before my eyes. *That 2025 Chevrolet Corvette Z06... the ultimate in luxury, especially for my limited budget... it will not be attainable for who knows how long now. All my savings for the past four years; gone in the time it took to swipe my card. It's worth it though. Doni will always be worth it. In four years, I'll be able to buy the car of my dreams. It'll work out. Perhaps Old Faithful (my mom's name for the car in question), will somehow hold out that long. Doubtful, but possible.*

I gave our friends the update, as Caroline, Ryan, and Ahyoka were in the waiting room. Ryan rushed faster than the girls to me, as he gave me a long, much-needed hug. Once I pulled back, he asked immediately, "How did she get cut? I understand by glass, but was someone attacking her?"

I felt my muscles drooping as I answered, "I honestly don't know, it's either an attack or an accident. She was pretty weak, so I couldn't get any answers out of her before."

"Poor Don!!" Caroline exclaimed in lament. "You must let my husband and I cover the bill."

I shook my head, firmly. "You know Donyelle wouldn't allow that if she was awake." *Truth is, she wouldn't have allowed me either; but no one needs to know I already did it.* "You're the best friends Donyelle and I could ask for, but right now I'm just waiting until she wakes up. Once she does, I'll let you guys know. But other than her arm she's mostly all right, and it sounds like with proper care in about a month that should heal nicely."

All three breathed a sigh of relief at the status of our friend's condition. "Is there anything we can do to assist either her or you?" Ahyoka asked in her soothing voice.

I was in the midst of shaking my head, when I thought of something. "Actually, maybe Ahyoka. Would you mind asking your boyfriend if he knows any good lawyers revolving around custody, abuse, and adoption?"

She opened her mouth with surprise, but then shut it again as she stated, "I will ask." I was grateful she didn't ask questions. I was suddenly feeling thoroughly exhausted.

Ryan put an arm around me as he said, "We'll let you go; go back to bed. Get some rest."

Caroline nodded. "If we can help you, Don, or..." she looked at Ahyoka quickly then finished, "Anyone, in any way, just tell us. We'll be right here."

Ahyoka nodded, seemingly not upset that she was out of the loop about something. "I'll go outside to call Sebastian, and I'll let you know what he says. I'll stay too."

Thank goodness for loyal friends. Especially Ahyoka for being so kind without asking what Caroline and I are alluding to.

I hurried back to Donyelle's room, using the last of my strength. Unfortunately, she was still asleep. Something about the tumultuous emotions, reliving several of my most traumatic memories, and seeing Donyelle in a pool of her own blood in her shop... I became completely undone. I cried, laying my head on the edge of her hospital bed, slowly moving my hand to interlock with her soft still one. I was just planning to rest, but the strain of the day took hold of my whole body, and before I knew it, dreams of the perfect wedding filled my mind.

Chapter 5
A FAILED SEDUCTION ... OR IS IT?

Donyelle's POV:

Oh bollocks. I know that beeping. I'm in a freaking hospital... what a mess I made. And all because of jealousy. Envy. Anger. Bitterness - okay, all the negative emotions, really. How frustrating! I willed my eyes to open, and was shocked to see Flynn was not only in the room, which I guess shouldn't have been such a surprise, but he was asleep, clasping my hand like it was his lifeline. I didn't move, not wanting to wake him. This was a peak opportunity to get to examine such perfect features up close, after all. And Flynn didn't get nearly enough sleep normally, anyway. *He's smiling, a good dream then.* I fought the irrational jealousy and wild desire to be the reason he smiled so peacefully like that.

If I told him everything, would he ever smile for me like this? I wanted to sigh, but I didn't want to wake him, so I went back to my thoughts. *Perhaps... maybe I need to tell him. I'm in a freaking hospital bed because of how much I care about this man. My unspoken feelings are becoming treacherous to my health!* I peered at his long lashes, the gentle curve of his face, the smooth chocolate skin. Very gingerly, I lifted my left hand and hesitantly hovered near his sleeping face. For just a moment, I indulged, feeling his lovely soft face against the pads of my fingers. But when he stirred, just slightly, I withdrew. *What do I even say?* I tried not to move too much as I peered around the room for my phone, but I couldn't see it. There was, however, a small notepad and a pen in view. It was a bit far away, on a stand on the opposite side of the bed Flynn was napping on. But for some reason this felt extremely important. And so, I slowly edged toward the other side, keeping my hand in his as still as possible, not to mention the arm that throbbed just slightly, who knew how many pain killers I was on for that to just barely hurt. It was a tedious process, so slow I was sure at any second Flynn would open his eyes. But he didn't, and eventually I was able to grab both the notebook and the thankfully attached pen. That would have been unbelievably frustrating if I did all that wriggling around just to not get the pen. But as I went to write, I found another difficulty - I was right-handed. And Flynn was clasping my right hand. I struggled to use my left hand to open the notebook, then I began to write. And it was clumsy. The messiest my normally lovely handwriting had ever been. But there was something about putting pen to paper. Everything I normally couldn't voice; I could put there. *Is it the coward's way out? Possibly. But when he opens those mesmerizing eyes of his, how am I supposed to tell him how much less of a woman I really am? I don't want to see his face when he realizes how trashy I have been, and how like-trash I feel. Easily disposable. Dirty. Something no one wants to keep around. Even recyclable; replaceable. It all fits. Perhaps I do feel like trash, the more I think about it. Maybe that's why I'd let countless men use and abuse me, knowing they'd discard me after they got what they wanted. I have to tell him. I don't want Lydia to end up like me; curling into a ball, letting her trauma define and control her, shaping what she thinks about herself, men in general, and the world at large. How am I supposed to show Lydia she can break free of her fears and abuse if I, a fully grown woman, am still struggling with the very same?*

I snuck another peek at the man that had defied all expectations. *He hasn't gotten a thing from me, other than magnificent kisses and enjoying my dazzling company, and yet he has stuck around.*

Simply by that choice alone he's already a rare breed. He deserves far more than I've given. And yet he doesn't demand more. He asks; kindly - always with respect and genuine care. I've rebuffed him time and time again, and yet he still wants to be my friend. Have I ever had a guy that was actually just a friend? No. Never.

I continued to write, pouring out my heart, until my left hand began to cramp, and my right hand began to fall asleep, and yet I kept writing and didn't let go of Flynn's hand. Not for a second.

"Doni? You're awake!" Flynn's voice came as if from far away, I was that fully engrossed in my work. After what was at least several minutes, I heard him repeat, "...Doni?"

I blinked, willing myself out of my intense share session. Or, at least, my intense word-vomit-on-the-paper session. *Why is it so easy to write everything down... but the second I turn toward him, I completely freeze up?*

My eyes went to his; and suddenly I felt an almost overwhelming level of guilt. His eyes were bloodshot, like he'd been crying, quite a lot. He looked exhausted, and highly concerned. I squeezed his hand, and the shock registered, he didn't seem to have noticed in his barely awake state that I was still holding his hand. A tiny curl of his lips made me feel very pleased with myself. Because though it was a small gesture, it had helped him. I didn't know much about his story, but I did know he hated hospitals. And I got the feeling there was an extremely good reason for that. *And yet here he is putting my needs before his mental health. The feelings I'd failed to stuff down for far too long bubbled to the surface, threatening to explode like a Pandora's box. I know I am at the brink of a monumental fork in the road, and I am right there, on the precipice.*

Cordelia is right; I can't continue to keep Flynn on the hook while keeping him at arm's length. I need to either put up or shut up - either spill my heart and my past to him... or make it abundantly clear that we are not meant for each other so he can move on to someone less damaged. I know which choice I should make, but... where is my bravery?

"You're not talking... does your throat hurt?" He asked, looking steadily more concerned. His eyes darted across the room until they lit up. He gently pulled his hand out of mine, and the impact of the loss of his touch was... more than I expected. He stood up, quickly moving toward the nearby counter. He grabbed a bottle of water, opened it, then immediately came right back. Flynn not only clasped my hand again, very softly and deftly intertwining his fingers with my own, but then he lifted the water to my parched lips. I greedily drank. "How much pain are you in? Can I do anything to help you feel more comfortable? Fluff your pillows?" As I eased back, Flynn put the bottle down, then put his left hand behind my head, assisting me until I was against the pillows again. His tone hardened and his eyes sparked with rare anger as he asked, "I never got a real answer - who did this to you?" I opened my mouth, but nothing came out. He waited a beat, then added, "I assure you whoever did this will be dealt with. Before the police take them in, I'll make sure they feel the pain you're experiencing." I moaned, not because of pain, but because I had to explain my stupidity.

Yet he must have taken the sound to be pain related, because as quickly as the anger and hardness had overtaken his bearing, he was back to gentle and infinitely sweet. "Oh Doni; I can't stand you being in pain like this. What can I do?"

That just proves he knows me better than any of my past lovers. Lovers... what odd terminology. Did I love any of the guys I so willingly had given my body to? At the time, I thought I did. But those instances weren't love. Just lust disguised. Each guy was happy to just have my body; it's not like any of them had really wanted more anyway. And at first, that really hurt. I had become extremely introspective as I attempted to discern why I was so easy to leave. Surely there was something about me that my parents had noticed when I was born that put them off, made them decide they were better off without me. And whatever mystery thing had scared off my so-called parents, it was probably the thing causing so many guys to use me and then ghost. Like... dine and dash. But instead of not paying a tab, each one took a sliver of my soul. It wasn't even my heart; I doubt I ever had one to begin with. But my soul, my very being... it had started to rip since that first lad. I can still picture his face. Every face. Each boy filled with pretty words - empty promises. With each new conquest, I paraded about like a peacock acting like I was so proud that I had bedded so many; even the most elusive of men, but in actuality, I was just feeling more and more broken. More alone than ever before. It was like each lad was a thief, pulling at the tatters of my soul, stealing a piece of their own as they walked out, never to return, leaving me less and less of a shell to curl up inside, pretending I was perfectly fine.

That's why it didn't matter how I felt. Flynn deserves a woman that's got her life together. That isn't coated head-to-toe in issues. He has such a fantastic heart; wide as I've ever witnessed; so why would he want my shriveled one? He wouldn't, that's the answer. I talk a good game, I act like I'm so put together, so posh. But just below the surface, not even deep down... I'm nothing. If I have a heart, it doesn't work properly. As for my soul, do I even have any pieces left to give? I threw myself at any man who looked my way; even just being in my vicinity, how do I dare to take those shattered trampled on miss-matched pieces of myself and give them to such a good man, like he doesn't merit a whole soul and a properly functioning heart? So yes; I love Flynn. Of course I do! I had known that even when I'd attempted to seduce Flynn, when he had first told me how much he wanted and needed me to share my life story with him.

*****

It started out the same as every other lad - the urge to conquer. The lust of the flesh - he was so proper fit. And the fact that he was such a fantastic kisser and was fully turned on by me (I'd seen the evidence on many occasions) but yet he instead respected me; even with my reputation just added to his allure. He didn't let me jump his bones. He had softly told me that he instead wanted to learn who I am, what delights and angers me. It had felt like poppycock. Some newfangled way to get me in bed. And yet... it wasn't. Not once did he do anything more than kiss. He had the opportunity so many times. About halfway through our dating relationship, I had begun to feel desperate. I found myself thinking - *he's only still interested and hanging around me because he hasn't had his needs met. He acts differently, but he is still a guy, after all. The true test will be to bed him. If he sticks around after that, well, I may have found my unicorn. Or whatever mystical creature that only shows up in fantasy books.*

With this in mind, I had dolled up. And I mean seriously, I was one hot mama. Thigh high seven-inch stripper boots. Glittery sequins that matched my three-piece lingerie set. One of my sexiest numbers; one I'd never used before. Most guys would be happy to take me in any outfit I was in, I didn't even have to go through the effort of getting glammed up. But Flynn was special. He warranted true effort. My three pieces were soft light purple, lavender really. Embroidered flowers, so delicate and oh-so-sexy covering my ample chest in a spaghetti strap bra-like top. The thin band of lacy purple flowers encircled my hips for the garter belt, hooking into the over-the-top boots. If I didn't fall and break my neck, or snap one of those crazy-tiny heels, I'd look to die for. And only for Flynn, I had made myself wear matching g-string panties. *Nothing says 'I want you' like wearing butt floss, right?* So that day, I was drop-dead sexy. And I got Flynn's pulse racing; it was abundantly obvious that he wanted me. And as I oh-so-slightly pressed myself against his chest, I was sure that I had won. I felt his breath hitch. I heard his moan, guttural, like he was trying with every inch of his being to resist me. But then he had gently shaken his head. He had looked me in the eyes, instead of devouring my body. He hadn't said much, but what little he did utter I still heard in my dreams to this day:

"Trust me Doni; I want you. You're sexy, and you know it. But I want more than sex. It's you I want. Not your body; you." He had eased me back, which would have given him an even better eye-line of my magnificent body on full display... but yet again, his gaze didn't drop. There was so much respect, honor - I'd even go so far as to say reverence, in the depth of his eyes. His touch was so soft, so slow and deliberate, as he hugged me. But it wasn't a bro move. At any moment I expected that he would sweep me off my feet with those muscular arms, and deposit me on the bed... but he simply hugged me. His tone was very husky as he had said, "If I ever have the honor of being your husband, I will do everything in my capability to make sure you feel treasured at all times of the day." He had eased me back as he whispered, "But until then; please don't do this again. I am desperately trying to respect you. Please don't make things harder on me, looking like the most sensual flower I've ever laid eyes on in my life. Please Doni."

I had felt a huge wave of mixed emotions. Most prominent was guilt. *Why am I trying to force the most upstanding guy I know to do something he isn't ready for? I feel like less of a woman having been turned down. And right now; I am feeling the most exposed I've ever felt. But not because of the almost see-through lace. Not even because of the large amount of skin showing. It's because I am petrified. Worse than just about ever, on par with when I'd been old enough to realize most families had some form of parental figures while I... I have no one. It is that far too familiar feeling of abandonment. Rejection. Feeling less-than. Like I wasn't good enough to stick around for. Irrational, as Flynn hasn't left. On the contrary, his words have actually mentioned the future. But how am I to determine whether it is genuine or just yet another lad blowing smoke up my arse if he won't do the deed?*

Flynn had been even sweeter than normal, fishing in his closet. I felt this overwhelming odd feeling of jealousy. *Does Flynn have girl's clothes here? Had he dated in the past? Was it serious? I had never asked, because everything I wanted to know I was aware he would have countered with questions of his own.* But the cold that drenched my body as his back was to my scantily clad form - it was all consuming. Jealousy. Irrational rage. For a woman who may or may not have been in this room.

But then he pulled out a shirt and pants -men's; obviously his own. I had felt like letting out a great sigh of relief. *How embarrassing, letting myself get so worked up, getting jealous and upset over a made-up girl in my head.* I watched as Flynn turned, being careful to keep his eyes on mine, not straying to sneak a peek for a minute. *The lad has willpower; I'll give him that. No one has been able to resist my advances before.* "Allow me." He spoke in a tone of voice that I found irresistible. As Flynn unbuttoned the shirt he'd grabbed for me, raising it above my head and lowering it to my back, he drew close to ease my hands through the sleeves, first the right, then the left. I felt my breath hitch as he began to slowly button the shirt, especially as several times his calloused hands grazed my bare skin. Such tiny touches, barely a second each time, and yet they coursed through me like the sensation was flowing through my very veins. *Oooh! How has the seducer become the seduced? I am not an embarrassed virgin, nor am I a blushing bride. So how am I so transfixed on his fingers, each one so perfectly formed, as he buttons me so agonizingly slowly? What is he doing to me??*

I felt torn between indescribable relief and an insane amount of disappointment when he ran out of buttons. I fought the wild urge to unbutton them, every single circle, just so he could button them again, prolonging our nearness. But that would have been too telling. He would have recognized how much I liked his touch and how badly I wanted him near me. So, I stood stock still, as he grabbed the pants. I fully expected him to give them to me, maybe turn around. He was a gentleman, after all.

To my surprise, neither of those things happened. Instead, he drew close again, impossibly close. I was draped in his t shirt, mostly just my legs exposed. He wrapped his arms around my waist, and even through his t shirt I could swear I felt the heat of his touch. I felt so overcome; I took a step back. Flynn smiled. It wasn't one of triumph, like I was used to seeing out of lads that made me feel momentary pleasure. It was a sweet smile. The likes of which I'd never seen in a bedroom with a man before. I was so awestruck; I forgot to be uncomfortable. The arms still around my waist lifted me up like we were doing a lift of some kind in a dance, and I barely had the time to marvel at how effortlessly I was lifted; especially considering I'm a fairly well-rounded girl with all the best curves, because suddenly I was placed feather-softly on Flynn's bed.

Is he actually giving in? Finally! I closed my eyes, anticipating something savory. But I instead felt his fingers brush my ankles. I shivered, keeping my eyes closed. He lifted my right leg, and I let him take the lead. *This is new; normally I am the one in control. I've never closed my eyes like this before. But then again, none of the other guys had won my trust. Flynn will be a good lover. Passionate I think; thoughtful, focused on my pleasure. Yes, this will be highly enjoyable.* His fingers skimmed my upper leg again, and right as I was about to let out a soft sigh, it stopped in my throat as I felt material covering one leg, and then the other. My eyes fluttered open in astonishment. I tracked as Flynn lowered both my legs, just barely touching my calves as his calloused fingers traced tiny circles in my skin. *Mmm - it feels so good. Is he teasing me? Is this some new kink I'm unaware of? Dress me up in his clothes just to tear them off?*

My answer came a minute later, as Flynn gave me a loving smile. "There; perfect. You are so lovely, Doni." Now his eyes took me in. Not when I was the sexiest I've ever been clad in lace with a sultry gaze, but now, fully covered in his baggy (yet so very comfortable) t shirt and pants. *He seems to adore me more now than when I'd been decked out like a stripper. Is he wrong in the head?* He stood up from his crouched position, leaning down over me. He adjusted my head upwards, positioning his lips close to mine without touching. He whispered, "May I?"

He was so close; I seemed to be having a hard time processing. *May he what?* "Yes. The answer is yes." I whispered, much breathier than my normal confident assured tone. *Oh bollocks. I am coming apart at the seams in front of this man. Why were my reactions to his actions so inconsistent with my normal run-of-the-mill encounters? I am no stranger to sex and seduction! So... what is going on?*

His eyes lowered to my lips, as his fingers played with the waistband of the pants I was currently wearing. I wanted to beg him to rip them off me, but yet again, his actions surprised me; he tied them tighter. *Seriously, there is something wrong with this lad. Extremely wrong.*

My thoughts escaped me as he took my mouth with his. Kisses tended to be good; men most of the time had at least a fair amount of capability. But Flynn... his kiss was different too. Euphoria I was used to; that was pretty much a given. But new feelings came along with that as I allowed his tongue to access my mouth, letting him explore as my hands did the same underneath his shirt, feeling those well-proportioned muscles. I sighed against him, but Flynn wasn't done. And the more we kissed, the more relaxed I became, which was odd. *'Relaxed' is not the word that comes to mind with a kiss.* Oxytocin filled me, but the peace continued to settle as we continued to kiss, especially as he did some surprisingly and delightfully naughty things, like gently grazing and nibbling my bottom lip. Each time his teeth made contact, even though it was extremely gentle, it sent shockwaves throughout my body. *Whoa.* It was such a mind blowing kiss I almost forgot to inhale and exhale. Thankfully I was able to get the needed oxygen in time, because believe me, I wanted this kiss to last as long as humanly possible. And I got my wish; it did last a blissfully long time. And yet while my greedy hands roamed his *very* well defined chest, his hands stayed cupping my face. *Extremely respectful. Only the kiss itself gives a glimmer of what he is truly capable of. From just that kiss alone I am so tempted to actually try. I have dated the guy for quite a while, especially by my standards. Who's to say I can't marry him? Except...* I felt my mood shift as the fear of abandonment flared up. Apparently, Flynn could feel it because he immediately stopped, easing back and then slightly taking his hands away from my face. I debated whether to attempt initiating another kiss and try to get out of my head, but those frustrating fears of being deserted if I actually truly opened up to him... that kept me still. Froze my body, but especially my tongue. I could physically feel pain in my jaw as I tried desperately to form the words. *I love him. I am pretty sure of that. Why is it so impossible to speak it out loud?* I physically couldn't do it; my jaw locked of its own accord.

Flynn's eyes were still a bit hooded from our intense encounter, but as he came back to reality, he gave me a sad sort of smile that made me feel so very much worse. "It's okay Doni. I understand you don't want to talk now..." he trailed off, and I felt this frustration bubbling in my stomach, giving me an acid reflux feeling, even though I hadn't eaten in at least several hours. *That's just the thing! I do want to talk! I quite literally can't! I'm trying! Don't you see that? I'm different with you in ways I've never been with any man, isn't that enough to give me a little wiggle room? A little grace?* I could almost feel the intensity of my inner monologue, so loud and powerful my ears began to ring, but not a sound was uttered. I sat there, on Flynn's bed, mute and frozen. Nothing like the boisterous Donyelle everyone knew and loved. And yet I couldn't do anything to change it. Words were on the tip of my tongue as I tried again. Which words, I don't even know. *Where would I even begin? Would I have to give him my life story? If I began to share; he surely wouldn't be satisfied with little snippets. But that isn't even the problem right now. Why can't I move? What is wrong with my mouth? My throat? It's so dry... did I drink or eat something funny?*

Before I ran through the list of what I'd consumed today, Flynn spoke again. "Regardless of if you share today, in the future, or if you never share anything about you ever Doni; I love you. Please, don't feel any pressure. You don't have to say a thing." He hastened to add.

If I had the capability, I would have retorted, "Good, because I can't anyway!" Because that was the insane truth. It was like my lips, after that phenomenal kiss, had been superglued together. I had never experienced anything like this... it was extremely unsettling. Flynn gave me a look that pierced my heart, then just like that he was gone. As he had left out the door, I hastily got up from the bed, but truthfully, I was still in a daze.

*****

I came back to the present, my right hand touching my lips at the memory, I had been good since then; I hadn't tried to initiate anything. And instead of finding some other guy to fulfill my needs, I decided to take a boy detox. It had made me abundantly despondent. But it had given me time to realize what I did and didn't want and need... and even more, what my heart truly craved.

Flynn was giving me such a look of pure unabashed concern, his eyes fixated on the hand that was touching my lips. I hadn't spoken in so long, I finally said what I'd wished I had shared over a year ago. "I love you." I blurted out, unbidden, from my lips.

The shock on his face... it would have made a good postcard. Drat that Marley isn't here to capture it. Instead of looking relieved or excited, Flynn bolted up from his sitting position, placing his left hand against my forehead, yelling, "Doctor! Something's wrong with Donyelle!"

It would almost be laughable, if it wasn't so sad that my expression of the depth of my feelings for him was so out of the norm that Flynn was terrified for me. *What does that say about me, and how I've handled this relationship? Nothing good, certainly!*

I felt supreme embarrassment as someone in a lab coat rushed into the room. "Donyelle is acting completely out of character. Is it possible that she has some form of brain damage? Would a concussion cause a huge shift in personality?" *He is utterly freaked out. This is simply mortifying!*

The doctor looked at me, and I said, "I don't have brain damage. This was a series of accidents inflicted on me that was due to a broken vase combined with very badly placed and dropped shards of glass. As for Flynn's concerns, if you wouldn't mind giving him and I the room, I can address those."

Flynn looked perplexed, but the Doctor, not Corenlius, some other guy, gave me a once over. While I'm sure he had no clue what was going on, I think he had at least determined it was not medical, and this was out of his purview. "Glad to hear your speech is clear, if either of you need me, I'll be... uh- not here." The Doctor scurried out of the room as Flynn protested,

"Wait! Please! At least run a scan-" but we were suddenly alone. While that Doctor was probably very qualified to handle issues that arise in his field, it was obvious he was extremely uncomfortable with interpersonal conflict.

"Flynn, I need you to sit down and take a breath for me." I said, channeling my inner Caroline.

Again, Flynn's face reflected worry, but he did as I asked, and he took several deep breaths. I smiled, which seemed to even further panic him, his eyes were darting to the button used to alert nurses to an emergency. Despite the throbbing in my arm, I took hold of his hand and eased it to the back of my head. "What are you doing?" He asked.

"I'm proving nothing's wrong with my head. Feel for yourself, no bump, no gash. Here, come closer." He leaned over, so our faces were about an inch away as I continued, "No blood." Flynn still looked unconvinced, his fingers feeling every portion of my scalp, and his unwavering eyes taking me in with a bit less concern, but still a wary gaze.

"You mean... you actually meant that? That... that you love me?" There was a tinge of hope coloring his every word, but fear was in the mix as well.

Oh Flynn, I didn't realize what a number I'd done to you. I've been so caught up in my faults, what I lack, my trauma... I had no clue how confused I'd made you. I touched his soft cheek with my hand, cupping his face as I allowed myself to say what I had never felt safe enough to express before. "Yes. I mean every word. I love you Flynn. Your caring heart. The compassion and strength you convey. More than anything; your patience. I am not an easy woman to love. I like to talk big; say I'm such a delight... but that's me covering decades' worth of insecurities. And something tells me... you are one of the rare few that know that."

Flynn searched my face, his beautiful eyes lighting up in a way I hadn't seen before. "You are a delight to be around." He said with so much assurance, I actually believed it. He leaned into my hand against his face, nuzzling it as he continued, "I love every aspect of you, the sweet and the sassy. Especially the sassy. I know you are riddled with insecurities; but I am too. And I have always believed that you are brave, confident, and hurt. You can be all three, you know." He leaned down further, hovering just above my lips, and I made up the difference. I kissed him with a reckless abandon, but it was a kiss unlike any we'd ever shared before. A kiss of love was a whole different experience. I completely blacked out, normally I was totally and completely in control, and I had so much experience in pleasuring men that it had become second nature, but Flynn was special. I didn't want to plan out what I would do when, I didn't over analyze when I needed to use tongue or how in sync we were. For the first time, I was totally and completely in the moment. It was blissful and such a heady feeling. I was actually the one that pulled back into the pillows, panting a bit.

"You are an incredible kisser. Believe me, we will be doing much more of that in the near future. But today, right now, I want to do something with you that I've never done with any man before." I gave him a cheeky smile as he leaned back slightly, his hands on both sides of my hospital bed. My words had obviously stumped him.

"Uh, what did you have in mind?" He was trying to sound casual, but I could almost hear his wheels turning. *He is obviously wondering what I could possibly want to do that I haven't done with others. And I can't blame him. While I had tried to sound like I was just so free minded and body positive... and there's nothing wrong with that... I tried to use physical intimacy to stave off the loneliness. He is right in being confused that there might be something I didn't share with other men.*

I smiled brighter, not sexual or beguiling, but a genuine smile radiating from my weary soul. Flynn gasped, audibly, looked at me with awe. "You've never smiled like that before."

"You're right. My brightest smile in the past pales in comparison to how I feel in this moment." *This is it, the defining moment.* I reached for the papers where I had unleashed my heart and soul, then hesitated. But finally, it wasn't hesitation due to fear or insecurities. This time, I hesitated because I realized reading from the paper was the coward's way out. And while Flynn would more than likely not make me feel bad for using the pages; he deserved my courage. Especially with everything I've unintentionally put him through over the years. "I wanted... I want to tell you my story. Everything. As a disclaimer, as I'm sure you're aware based off my uh... prickliness - my story isn't unicorns and butterflies. In fact," I felt a whole-body tremble, so I swallowed to try to steady myself. I thought about wimping out. Leaving it at that.

Flynn suddenly leaned down again, kissing my cheek, so feather-light I almost didn't feel it, but the instant his lips grazed my cheek, the trembling subsided completely. It was exactly the kind of gesture I needed to rally my courage. "The point is, my story- my past, you deserve to hear it." He barely moved back, just enough so our eyes were locked on each other. "Since we've known each other quite a while at this point, you've probably pieced together at least some of this. But... I was an unwanted child. Like, from the get-go. I didn't lose my parents because of some big accident, like a house fire or a car crash... I almost feel that it would have been far easier to stomach. I still would have lost my parents, but an accident wouldn't have caused the level of trauma that a choice did. That's the main issue. The reason I'm so beyond messed up: they chose to leave me. I guess I should be grateful they didn't abort... but... leaving your child with a far too old senile dying woman... is that much better?"

I took another deep breath. *He hasn't bolted yet. His eyes don't show the dreaded pity I thought would be in their depths; instead... is that compassion shinning back at me?* I tapped my hands together, fingers to fingers as my nails scraped against each other.

I shrugged helplessly as I admitted, "I haven't done this-" lifting my hands to show the odd gesture, "since I was a young child, a couple years younger than Lydia, in fact. That was something I had been so terrified of- reliving those memories... they have a way of sucking me in, forcing me back to those moments that negatively defined me for my entire life up to this point. I had sworn I would never go back to that little girl I had been. And if I never ruminated on those days, I was never in danger of being trapped in the past. But now I'm exposing that hurt mistreated little girl I've desperately kept hidden for so long."

As I spoke, I felt more pain than my throbbing arm and the pinpricks of discomfort in my toes and knees. The gut-wrenching pain of feeling abandoned. "Far too young, I came to the understanding that my parents... the ones meant to protect, to teach and guide, to shield me from the dangers... had left me - uncaring whether I lived or died." Flynn sucked in a breath, loud and angry. But not at me, thankfully, and even though I knew this, I barely withheld the flinch my body was aching to let out.

"Doni; I - no one deserves that." His voice was choked with emotion, and I felt myself surprisingly smile, just a little, but it was there.

"My Grams- she was the one I was left with. And she... she wasn't in her right mind, but I would say she did try. I did survive; after all. I was a newborn when the so-called 'mom' and 'dad' split. And not like a divorce; that I could have stomached. They stayed married, far as I know, but left me behind."

The shock on Flynn's face was evident. I continued, "Grams had something medically wrong with her; not sure what, we were dirt poor, after all. She was well beyond retired and far as I remember back, we lived off the charity of others. When I couldn't bring in enough as a toddler. Hence why I hate handouts so much nowadays. Anyway, she had... I don't know, dementia, Alzheimer's- it got really bad toward the end. I was like... I don't know; four or so when I started learning I had to fend for myself. Grams forgot about me most days; and when she remembered my existence, she didn't have the capacity to cook or anything. I figured out that fancy people like flowers, so I'd get up before the sun and pick as many as possible, selling and bartering for money or at least for bread and milk. Flowers growing on the back hills weren't worth too much, but I could normally get some stale bread and some milk close to expiration. And that was a livable situation... until Grams passed."

Water was pooling in Flynn's eyes. "I- I don't know what to say. I wish I was more eloquent; to put into words..." Flynn spoke, impossibly softly.

"You're doing fine. Just... keep listening. Promise me not to bolt; that's all I need right now." I assured him, coughing a bit. Flynn immediately grabbed my water, lifting it to my mouth. Eagerly I guzzled until I'd had my fill, as he put the water back down, and I soldiered on. "I was too young; I didn't recognize that Grams had died for... I don't even know how long. At first, I thought it was just how she was; she tended to be very into herself during those episodes of whatever it was, she was so knackered all the time. Then I thought she was having a kip, but after a long time, it became apparent she wasn't just sleeping."

I coughed again, then continued, "Once Caroline discovered that I was well and truly alone, she went to her parents, asking them to take me in. Susan, her mom... she was very heartless at the time. She wasn't willing to take me in, because having me would make it impossible for her and her kids to escape the Langley province, I heard Susan tell her daughter I was an 'inconvenience'. Went so far as to be called an 'undesirable'. Caroline's mom only had a sliver of a conscience at the time. She knew I couldn't stay alone with the corpse of my Grams. So, she called child protective services."

I took a deep steady breath as I looked Flynn over. *So far so good, he hasn't run yet...* "I was forced out of the shack we'd been living in; and put in a home. They called it a foster home... but all they were fostering was lice, malnutrition, and a whole lot of angry kids, most of them far older than me. I was beaten, often by the other kids in the orphanage, for the small morsels I was able to obtain when I was able to sneak out to try selling flowers to the hoity-toities. I was also beaten because I was a sassy pants, and didn't last long in any foster home I was placed in, always ended up stuck back at what the owners deemed a "fine establishment". They did not take kindly to my attitude nor my 'rebellious jezebel spirit'. I must have been... six or seven at the start, and then like... ten or eleven when I couldn't take it anymore. The guy especially had these willow reed rods he fashioned into a whip; it stung. Really bad."

Flynn's fingers curled into fists, and he began to shake with anger, but he continued to listen, so I added, "I ran pretty soon after the whippings began. I found a barn- it wasn't too bad. It was abandoned, so I had a lot of space to myself. It was cold, but it was far better than that place. No one to bully me, no one to piss off. I was yet again alone."

"Caroline found me, and when she did, she tried everything to help. She would sneak me money and food for a couple months even walking that whole way from Langford to Langley to bring it to me since they had moved, until she was caught. Once her family found out what she was doing, Caroline asked her parents so often to help me that I'm sure they must have gotten very annoyed. Because while Caroline is a mild-mannered sweetheart of a person, she can be extremely persistent and unmovable when she sets her mind to something. And Caroline resolved to find a way to help her new best friend. Without Caroline... I would have been well and truly alone. Basically, I owe her my life, but she's never once called in that gigantic favor; hasn't even brought it up. She's that good a person. She and I will always be best friends, even though when she pries into my relationship with you it annoys me. Truth is, she only wants my happiness. I get sour and bitter at times, but she just takes it in stride and loves me regardless. Trust me; I've tried pushing her away, and when I do, she just continues to love me and attempt to find ways to make me smile, but from afar."

I sighed, adding, "But I'm getting sidetracked. I'm not trying to waffle around, soz." After apologizing, I continued, "Susan grew a conscience when eventually the news started running stories about how the orphanage she'd had a hand in sticking me in was shut down due to heavy and intense child abuse and neglect. Susan especially realized she had made the problem worse, so she gave me what she'd made selling Gram's little shack in installments. When I was like… eleven I think; I was able to buy what is now my flower shop. And while Susan may never be my favorite person, I know that the banks wouldn't have worked with an eleven-year-old kid. I'm fully aware that Susan made that happen. And while it was motivated by guilt, it is still highly appreciated. And thankfully Susan also has never brought up the past. She and her daughter may not be alike in a bevy of way, but in this, they are the same."

Flynn was crying, and I was tearing up, but I wasn't finished, I still had quite a lot more to explain.

"The main thing holding me back from you is that I've tried the relationship thing. Without fail, it let me down. And each time I was used, abused, then discarded like trash. I already felt unlovable, the revolving door of men just confirmed it. Something is deeply broken in me. My parents took one look at me and decided I wasn't worth their love or their time. They made me an orphan without actually dying. Grams may have loved me, but she was so out of it most of time it didn't register that I was there, much less that I was her precious granddaughter. The people running that lecherous home surely didn't love me, I was punished far more than most the other kids. The other orphans didn't love me; they didn't even like me. Caroline did, but that seemed to have nothing to do with me and only spoke to the testament of her goodness, she would have treated everyone as kindly with such compassion and tender care. Even though she tells me often she loves me, cares about me, the person, and she will never abandon me… I can't quite believe it. Even though she's spent almost two decades proving her words; so that shows how untrusting I am. And Caroline's mom, the closest

I'd come to a mother figure as a child, had called me undesirable. Plus, the men- I don't like speaking about it... especially with you. I don't want you to think I'm cheap. Or... a slut, or-"

Flynn put two fingers to my lips, asking in anguish, "Please stop Doni, I can't bear to hear you speak about yourself in such derogatory terms. You are not either of those things, or anything else you could come up with. You deserve to be loved as you. What your parents did... they don't deserve the title. Who knows what was so broken in them that they decided they couldn't or wouldn't parent. That only shows how awful they are; that is not a comment on you in any way. You are the most lovable person I know. I have loved you since our first meeting. Not just your body; but your personality, your very essence. The way your eyes light up when you're laughing. The effortless way you put me at ease as we talked amongst ourselves for the first time after the set up by Caroline and with Ryan's assist. Your humor is incredible, laughter contagious, and I had never met, and am pretty certain I will never meet, another like you. You are far too fascinating and beguiling a person to forget, and as long as you want me near; I will never leave. Never ever."

My heart was in my throat. *Ninety-five percent of me believes him and wants to throw my arms around him, even with my recent surgery, and tell him cheekily that I will hold him to his promise. But that other pesky five percent is holding me back.* My fingers traced his jaw as I whispered, "You have no idea how much I long to believe you. I've told you before that you're different from the rest; you haven't cut and run. But unlike the rest, you haven't had your needs met. The pattern of my life is that once a man has what he wants from me; he acts like I don't exist, like ghosting, but to the next level. Not just on social media or texting... in person as well. I am no longer interesting to them. I'm not worth sparing even a glance or having a word spoken. And my fear... my deepest-rooted anxiety is that while you are a very good guy... you haven't followed the typical pattern. A huge part of me really feels like once you and I have sex, I'll lose you. And I'm torn between never wanting to lose you and wanting to know for certain that you will actually stay even after the deed is done. The constant nagging fear has become an obsession..." I trailed off, coloring in embarrassment. But it was too late to back out now. "I uh... I used to drive by your house every night. Just to ensure you didn't have another woman over. I know I sound mental for that... but I resolved to be honest. No matter how you feel about me afterwards, this is me. I do dumb things. I take the piss, I make rash unplanned decisions on a jealous impulse. In fact, I broke the vase that got me into this mess because I was picturing you and Cordelia as a couple. Embarrassing, and frustrating, but true. Anyway, waffling aside; this is me. Take it or leave it; this is who Donyelle Freya Cox truly is."

Flynn's eyes widened as he smiled, "Freya huh? That's lovely. I have something to admit as well. I know about your nightly drives. In fact, I came to not only enjoy them, but it was also the moment I most anticipated in my day. So what - if that makes us both crazy; we're in good company." He grinned, then wiped his tears with his elbow, maneuvering himself to sit on my left-hand side very near me. He ran his fingers up and down my arm, leaving goosebumps in his wake. "I can't begin to express how honored I am that you were this open with me. I vow here and now that after I share my story and spill my traumas, most of which stem from this exact hospital, you can decide whether you feel like I'm the man for you. But I can say without question you are the woman I want to spend life with. And for every trauma you've been through in your life, I want to replace each memory with a good experience, until all you have left is joy and peace." And then I listened. Flynn shared his heart; raw and real, in a way he hadn't before. I heard about his piece of shit father. About him having incredibly similar abandonment issues. The guilt he harbored for how Micah turned out, as Flynn was forced to take on simultaneously the father role, older brother position, and man of the house to the grieving and slowly healing mother that had just had a catastrophic birth and was now a single mother with two children, crying out to God to fix what has been broken and protect her family. Greta rarely prayed for herself, but Flynn said he begged and pleaded with God to heal his mother, and thankfully He answered Flynn's prayers. Eventually Greta and Flynn went to work at the castle, and even dealing with being around the racist insane Henry, they still made it through.

So much happened as Flynn gave his testimony. I felt a pride for my man the likes of which I had never experienced before. The longing I felt for this man... it was like the slivers of my soul that had survived all the inundation of guys had awakened. His soul and mine were connecting in such a magnificently real way, it was dreamlike, and I found myself focusing on the throbbing in my stitched-up arm to remind myself that I was in fact awake and this was actually happening. As he finished up his story, our eyes were still locked with electricity and passion. I used my left hand to wrap around his waist and pull him close so we could share a kiss. After the kiss, Flynn's eyes filled with wonder, saying, "I will happily, and with supreme honor, choose to be by your side the rest of my days, accepting you as you are; my sassy British bombshell with your goddess-like body and perfect retorts to just about any situation. You bring color to my monochrome life, and I can't imagine a better future than being your partner."

Suddenly, with very little warning, he backed out of my embrace. My lip went into a pout at losing his nearness, but his smirk as he moved from the bed and assumed the position of men fully in love... it about stopped my heart. *Handy thing that I'm in the hospital.* Mortifying also, as the beeps on the machine share the increased tempo to the man that was asking for my hand in marriage. But so much more was happening than just that question alone. He was showing me that he would never cut and run. That I was lovable, desirable. That I wasn't trash to throw away after use. Even that five percent that doubted anyone could love me was silent as I gave him the most genuine smile I'd ever given, screaming, "Yes!!! I'll marry you Flynn Levisay!" I paused from my elation, just slightly, "What's your middle name?"

"Moses." He said sheepishly. I grinned, pulling him as close as my hospital bed allowed as I whispered huskily,

"I can't wait to be Mrs. Flynn Moses Levisay."

He gulped, very visibly, as I kissed his Adam's apple. "Oh, you're going to be trouble, aren't you, fiancé of mine." My whole body was thrilled at the sound of my new label. *I never thought I'd get engaged, and now we're officially going to get married!* Flynn slapped a hand to his head as he chuckled. "Almost forgot one of the most important parts! The ring!"

I laughed as he fished in his jacket pocket. "Honestly, I'd completely forgotten. I already said yes, even without it. Maybe you should just sell it and get your money back. I'm sure Caroline or Greta has a simple band we can use."

Flynn stopped fishing in his pocket to again, with a playful smile on his face, touch my forehead as if checking for fever. "If you're going to keep acting like this, I'm going to start thinking you're a clone. Where's the Donyelle that loves sparkly bling?"

"She's right here. But I'm so happy we got to this moment, bugger all matters in this moment." I said truthfully, feeling incandescently happy.

He shrugged with a smirk. "If that's so, I guess you don't need this after all." He held out the ring box, and instantly my attention zeroed in on it. He chuckled. "That's what I thought."

I reached out my hand to take the box, but he knelt down again. "Might as well do this properly." He took my outstretched left hand gently and placed a dazzling rose gold ring on my finger. Everything about it was like it was perfectly designed for me. It just showed how well he knew me. The large incandescent opal in the middle was for my October birthstone, but also my favorite gemstone. And he knew that. The gold the gemstone was in the midst of had been fashioned into a flower- another beautiful touch. Even more lovely, encircling the petals of the flower were two vine patterns, each with small circular amethysts: my favorite color. And it fit like a dream too; it was the best engagement or wedding ring I could have asked for. But with my happiness I felt some sadness as well; *how long has he had that ring? And how much did he spend?* "Do you... like it? I can find something else if you need something larger; it just seemed perfectly... you."

I tilted my head up and gave him a mega-watt smile. "Flynn, this is completely perfect. I was just wondering... have you had this ring to give me... have you had it long?"

He flushed red, and that basically gave me my answer. "I had it designed in France, actually. It's been locked up in my safe ever since."

Wow. Almost a year ago! He knew he wanted to marry me that long ago? And... he said had it designed. He had this ring created just for me?! "No wonder it looks as if it were designed just for me. I am in love with the opal, the flower, vines, the purple- everything!" *So that was what he had locked up in that safe!* I continued reassuringly, "You did incredibly well. To think, if I hadn't been so stubborn and scared, we could have been at this point a year ago." I looked down sadly. But Flynn shook his head.

"I think this is actually God's timing. Truthfully if we had gotten together back then, I would have had an even harder time dealing with my brother's betrayal and the loss of Robbie... I would have tried to balance being in a relationship with you, but it would have been harder to heal if I'd been in a relationship. And not just with you, with anyone, before you start going down a rabbit hole of guilt. I think finding Lydia was really the turning point; seeing how you interacted with her; it opened you up and softened us both in ways that our traumas and past difficulties had not allowed up till this point. At least, that's my take."

"Oh, I agree completely. Lydia reminded me of what I had been trying to bury for too long. That sweet girl helped us more than she could possibly know. Do you think us getting engaged is going to freak her out? I know if it were me in her shoes, I'd be gobsmacked, automatically thinking that I was going to be shipped off or forgotten about if the people who were just beginning to act like pseudo parents decided they wanted to get hitched."

Flynn gave me a look of wonder. "I can tell I'm going to need to defer to your wisdom on this matter - you and Lydia probably have a very similar way of thinking. Perhaps we could try to make her feel more comfortable before we discuss what we're going to do and how that's going to change things for her."

I grinned. "Maybe I can take her shopping. My arm isn't hurting very much. If it stays in a sling, especially after taking pain meds, in theory I should be good enough to do that. I'm not going to be trying on clothes or anything, this will be exclusively for Lydia."

"Yes, I think that's a good idea. Do you feel like we could actually do this? I admit when I was thinking about and describing marriage, not to mention a family in my head, it didn't look as instant as this. However, I really like Lydia. I know we both care about her a lot. It could be a very difficult battle with this wanna-be Mayor. Trying to get custody of her considering we're two strangers... however, we will want to be sure that we can do this. I will do everything in my ability and on my part to ensure that we get Lydia out of her situation. We want her to know beyond doubt that she's safe."

I nodded, "I get what you're saying. I think we are both on the same page that we want to be able to be to Lydia what we never received as kids."

"Exactly. Or, at least what you never had, Greta was an incredible mother, but I did never have that father aspect, and I would love more than anything to be able to give both a mother and a father to that sweet girl, but like I said it's not going to be an easy road. We're going to be up against a *Goliath* of a person and probably just as equipped as *David* seemed to be." Flynn spoke as he played with several of my braids.

I agreed but reminded him, "True but I will remind you Flynn, even though I haven't read the Bible in a while. I've got to admit my faith has been a bit shaken due to how badly I saw myself, but if I recall correctly, David only had... what, a slingshot and some stones - and yet God made it so that Goliath fell. We can take down our Goliath just like David did with God helping us. Knowing that we're protecting a child the way we wish we had been protected."

"Good point Doni. I think that we should most likely pray and make sure that this is something that we can handle. There's already going to be bumps as you and I adjust to being engaged and eventually married, I love the idea of an instant family with Lydia, but I want to make sure we're not taking on too much - more than we can handle. And if that's the case then I need to make sure that we are not going to make our problems Lydia's problems. We want her as untraumatized as possible and she's already been through too much for her age. If we think that we are going to make things worse for her than better... then we need to think about that as well, because she matters the most. Our blossoming love, but her life and her stability are also hugely important, so we just need to make sure that we take that into account." We agreed not to make any rash decisions, especially while in the euphoria of our recent engagement. Eventually I was discharged into Flynn's care, and we were allowed to leave.

Once we went to Greta's kitchen, both Lydia and Greta deluged me with questions and concern. I reiterated what happened, Flynn fended off the other questions, and then I let Flynn drive Lydia and I home... to his house. Looking around the space with different eyes now, I searched the place, now with the knowledge that I would someday soon merge my life with this person. *Will we live here? My place? Somewhere new? And will we actually get custody of Lydia even though she's not related to either of us - we're just above strangers to her.*

Flynn's phone went off. He went to retrieve it from the charger, and I stopped myself from looking at the screen. *I need to trust Flynn. And show him that I trust him. Even if a girl is interested, that doesn't automatically make Flynn a cheater. He has been incredibly faithful in his pursuit of me. It makes zero sense that now that he and I have finally made a commitment, and not even just dating, which is like a step above friends, but fiancé, which is just below husband and wife, that he would fumble now. He's a one-woman girl. I have no doubt. Well... okay, maybe I have a little doubt. But I'm as close to certain as I've ever been trusting in a man.*

Chapter 6
AN EXPLOSIVE 7ᵀᴴ BIRTHDAY

Donyelle's POV:

The next two days Flynn and Lydia took care of me, and I forced myself to allow them to do it. Never in my life had anyone taken care of me like this. When I got sick, I had to care for myself. Well, besides Caroline, who would do anything for me, but this was different. She was my best friend – it was implied that we would do anything for each other. Ahyoka made me soup each time as well, I had a sisterhood with the two of them. But with Flynn and little Lydia, it wasn't like friends. It was like a built-in family, and it made me so happy. I found myself realizing that I could get very used to this. The pain had almost subsided, and I noticed, as Flynn was changing my bandage and Lydia was brushing my hair, that the clothes Caroline had supplied were a bit tight on the little girl. So, I smiled, which caused Flynn to pause his task. "What's that look for?" He asked with an answering smile of his own.

"I'm just happy. You two have done everything for me these past several days, and I'm so grateful. It's been a weird adjustment... but a good one." Flynn had given me the bed, like the gentleman he was, and he'd set up a mattress on the floor in the living room for himself, until we were married, which we hadn't even discussed the date of; we'd been preoccupied focusing on my health, and waiting to see if Sebastian could get us a list of good lawyers that could be useful in such an odd case. Lydia was beginning to get comfortable, small things really, but I noticed. For instance, she was no longer wearing her shoes to bed. I understood why she had; when you're in a flight or fight response constantly, you feel the urge to run at any sudden movement. Having her shoes on had signified that she was ready to run at a moment's notice. So, while it seemed like nothing to the layman; to someone involved in heavy trauma, it was huge that she felt safe enough to take off her shoes last night.

A very good sign that she felt Flynn and I were the kind of people she could be around without fear, or at least with far less fear than she was accustomed to dealing with on a regular basis. She was still hoarding food, when she thought she wasn't being observed, she would tuck some of each meal away into her napkin, hiding it like it was treasure. But I don't even have the full picture of what she's been through, and baby steps were still movement. With time we would prove that we were worthy of her finally feeling completely at ease, possibly for the first time in her life. I remember the first time I truly felt that feeling. It had been so unattainable, trust me; I'd tried. I had felt fleeting moments of true peace and happiness, but just a taste. When I was with Caroline and Ahyoka. When I was surrounded by my flowers in the greenhouse, or I'd selected the perfect assortment of buds to make a majestic display. But when I felt it for the first time in a longer respite – more than just a moment... that was when Flynn and I had first met. Something about him set me so at ease, it was actually kind of terrifying. I know that doesn't really make sense, but what had gone through my mind was this: if I only ever felt truly peaceful around this man, this stranger, when I'd been chasing this feeling for my whole adult life- probably my whole childhood as well... when he inevitably leaves, I surely will never feel that soothing calm again. And I had been greedy for it. I craved his presence. At first, just so I could feel safe. But with time, and not much at that, I began to long to be around him more than just to get a brief respite from the loneliness that ate away at my soul. I wanted to hear his voice. Something about it was like honey: deep, sweet, soothing. I could listen to him for a lifetime and never get bored. But that had been the problem. Every time I was around him, I started to feel more and more attached. And with that knowledge equally brought on paralyzing fear. When I inevitably lose him, it's going to hurt in a way I am not prepared for. I am not equipped to be as devastated as his loss in my life will make me.

And so... I did the absolute worst thing a person could do in my position. I started fights. Each time he tried to gently and kindly pull back the proverbial hood that shielded my insecurities, fears, traumas and lies I believed about myself and others... I pushed him away. Hard. Not physically, but emotionally I lashed out. No doubt I hurt him, confused him. Why was I so free with my affection, with my body, with my sassy suggestions, but I was suddenly tight lipped when it came to my background, my family, my childhood, my fears? The answer was I had been in a prison. A self-made one.

I thought I had created a shelter, a safe space where I could hide away from anyone that meant to do me harm. The one place where I could retreat into myself and shield my junk from the world, only portraying the outward confidence and sexiness I was known for. But that shelter... I didn't realize until Flynn got close that it was actually a cage. A prison. I had been so desperate to hide any negative parts of myself that I had gotten locked in my own insecurities, trapped in fear, believing the lies, not seeing a way out. My refuge had become my doom. And yet I found myself continuing to go back to that cold unfeeling place, because it was familiar. Because it was mine. I had created it, that area in my mind, and I alone chose who could enter. When I'd tried to let Caroline into my shelter, metaphorically, it was like the posts holding back everything I needed so desperately to hide were beginning to shake. I could see that if I let her in... anyone in, all the way, the place I hid would crumble and I would have nowhere to retreat. The thought of having everything out there, someone knowing just how broken and unconfident I truly was... it repulsed me. Yet even more than the repulsion was that ever present fear. The anxiety that had me clinging to the door, not willing to let anyone take my supposed safe place apart.

Thank goodness Flynn took the time with insane patience, to get me to unlock that door. My shelter, my prison, it was no longer there, in my mind. Someone knew absolutely everything. All the garbage I'd been so good at hiding. And yet he was still here, still by my side. Such a man did exist. Without his patience I surely would have stayed a prisoner to my own emotions, a victim of my own abuse. Now I am a survivor; he has no idea how powerful just his presence has been in my life.

"Everything okay? You've been quiet a long time." Flynn asked, his worried eyes searching my own. I took his hand, as he had apparently stopped bandaging sometime while I'd been caught in my head. I leaned down just slightly as I brought our hands to my lips, kissing his skin.

He let out a breath, as Lydia giggled. I flashed her a smile, then focused on Flynn, who was hovering above me, looking emotional. "I was just thinking. You don't know it, but you changed my whole mentality about myself. All these years I was so bitter and sour, angry and sad. I thought myself a victim of my circumstances. And while I was abused, and I do have trauma," my eyes found my pseudo daughter as I finished, willing her to believe my words, "I no longer think myself a victim. I am a survivor. And I am not alone. No one is. Other people have been through similar struggles; endured pain of their own." Lydia's eyes, haunted by her own pain, reflected a ray of hope. Perhaps if I showed her that it was possible to overcome the past, she might learn that lesson and not become as jaded as me. If she can work through her abuse as a child instead of as an adult, she'll hopefully be far more adjusted than I ever was. I tilted my head back to Flynn, he radiated joy as I added, "I love you – both of you. I thought I had built myself safety by hiding away from everyone. I was in confinement, but I fancied myself protected. You shattered the illusion, in the best possible way. Now you know me for who I truly am, and you still love me regardless." I squeezed Flynn's hand, then changed the topic as I stood to my feet. "Now, I'm feeling better. Much. And Lydia desperately needs some well-fitting clothes, plus; it's her birthday! We have to celebrate. Seven years old is a big deal! So, let's go to Langford's main mall."

Lydia actually jumped up and down, seeming very excited by this turn of events. Who knew if she'd ever had a birthday celebrated before- this one would be very special indeed. Flynn didn't look thrilled, but eventually we were in the car and headed that way. With time, we reached the parking lot, and I took a look at myself in the car mirror. *I look silly all bandaged up.*

After a lot of convincing, I was able to get Flynn to sign off on not coming inside with Lydia and I as we explored the mall. He was all set to spend the whole day with us if necessary, but I made it clear that he was not wanted or needed on our girls' trip. I had leaned over close to him from the passenger seat and whispered in my sexiest tone, "Unless you want to see me trying on bras and thongs." I had brushed his heated right cheek, feeling dangerous as Lydia watched us from her booster chair in the back seat, eyes always taking everything in. *I was pretty quiet just then, but you never really know what a child overhears.* Flynn's eyes were so wide, it made me chuckle internally. I had maintained my guise of wide-eyed innocence as Flynn had stuttered out that he'd wait in the car, and to 'take our time'.

And obviously I hadn't actually planned on getting panties or anything, this trip was about Lydia after all. But we were engaged now, finally. That did call for at least one set of lingerie. I wouldn't wear it for him until we are married... I'd tried that once before, and the results had been... *well, steamy comes to mind. But I also vividly remember my promise not to tempt him like that again. And I am a woman of my word. I will just have to trust that after we get married, once we are finally intimate like I've been with so many others... he'll be the first to stay. He is a rare individual. He might. More than anything I hope so.*

Lydia pulled on my jacket, so I turned my unfocused eyes on her. She held yet another hoodie and pair of baggy-looking pants, but she looked happy about it. My arms, already bogged down with seven fairly large bags shifted as I pulled the four bags up onto my forearm so they wouldn't fall, then took the outfit. I smiled, even though I had hoped she would have liked something a bit more girly, at least she was beginning to relax. She will be the one wearing it, after all. "That's lovely too!" I exclaimed, hovering my hand just above her hand. Now that she had gotten my attention, she went back to roaming the store as I trailed beside her.

She stopped in her tracks abruptly, eyes fastened ahead, a little to the right. Her eyes were wide, but she didn't look scared. In awe was more like it. I cocked my head to see what had stirred up such a reaction. But then I saw it - a dress. A dark Christmas green dress with bright gold stars all along the bottom half. *Ah hah! Guess she too can't resist a little sparkle after all.* I moved towards the highest row of hangers where her dress was. As I lowered it and brought it towards her, I noticed how Lydia's eyes tracked the movements of the dress. "I think you made a good choice! Are you ready to check out?" I asked as I added the dress to the outfit in my hand.

Lydia vigorously shook her head. "Dress too pretty for the likes of me." I flinched as if I'd been slapped. *The way that spilled out of her, it's obvious the child is parroting what she's been told. Probably often. Poor thing; imagine hearing that as a kid! Bad enough as an adult... but as a child, who is just beginning to form opinions about herself, discovering her identity... to be talked down to like that, told she's beneath lovely things, not worthy - I better not ever be alone with this psychopath-mayor-wannabe. I'll murder him for sure. Slowly and painfully. The travesties he inflicted on this little girl... the physical, emotional and mental abuse she suffered- and so freaking young- it's bollocks!!*

Obviously, she really wanted it, but she was waging an internal war between the desire she felt and the lies she'd grown up hearing. Knowing this, I crouched down, bringing the dress with me, as I held it up to her. Lydia jumped back, as if the dress was on fire and any contact would scorch. I stayed patient, holding it out regardless. I made sure my tone was the closest mimic I could to Caroline's sweet reassuring voice, while still adding a bit of my flavor. "I think this dress was made for you. It'll bring out the green in your eyes, and with your bright blonde hair you'll look like a Christmas angel. It would do me a big favor if you wouldn't mind letting me get it for you; we have parties to go to, and dressing up all snazzy is a huge part of the fun."

Hesitantly, and slower than a turtle, she inched forward a step, but then she halted, not completely up to the magnificent dress. *She isn't fully convinced; it looks like I need to do more. Hmm.* I gave her a wide smile, which felt a bit foreign on my face. "Honestly," I began, lowering my voice to a whisper, so Lydia leaned forward to catch my words. "I always wanted a daughter. The thought of brushing and braiding her brilliant hair, dolling her up in all the frilliest and most sparkly dresses..." I sighed. *Oops. I'd meant to be convincing Lydia, but every word I just whispered is true. The problem is with my commitment and parent issues... I doubt I am fit to be any kind of mother. I can't even fully wrap my head around being a wife, although the idea is sending a thrill up and down my spine. But... a mother? I am not equipped. My mother is absentee, the closest I have is Greta. And the thought of going to my future husband's mom with my fears and concerns weighs heavily on me. What if Greta hears my fears, realizes how woefully unprepared I am, and talks her son out of marrying me? She knows I have issues, but she doesn't know why. Will I really have to share the worst blemishes on my life's record with my potential mother-in-law?*

Lydia apparently had come closer while I was having a pity party, and suddenly she snatched it from me, holding the hanger in one hand and reverently touching it with her pointer finger with the other. She was so gentle it was as if she thought running a hand across it might ruin the garment. I smiled encouragingly, gently running my hand on the fabric myself. To my surprise, Lydia gave me a returning ghost of a smile. It only lasted about a millisecond, but it was there. And for that brief moment, her whole face had lit up, shining a light on what a beautiful girl she truly was. I straightened, we walked with purpose to the checkout stand, and we had just been given the receipt, when I heard someone say,

"That's Lydia Strawfeld - our future Mayor's daughter!"

I willed myself not to turn around, as Lydia froze instantly. I slid my hand to my phone, trying to be nonchalant, as I texted Flynn 'SOS' or, at least I tried. Auto-correct changed it to 'sauce.' I sent it anyway, hoping Flynn would either know what I had meant, or would text back or something. I whispered, "We need to go Lydia. Not too fast, just walk."

An answering voice stated in surprise, "You're right! He said his darling daughter was missing! There's a reward. Who's that with Lydia? Is she the kidnapper?" My heart just about went into my throat at those words, but I kept it together, as Lydia and I began to walk toward the escalators. But by then a small crowd had gathered, and they were all looking at me like I had committed the gravest of crimes. They had made a semi-circle around us but hadn't fully blocked off the escape yet; however, at our leisurely pace, they surely would. Not even getting a chance to warn Lydia, I swept her into my arms, all the bags weighing me down and making it that much harder to balance, and I ran. I sprinted like I never had before. I heard a full crowd of people yelling, "Kidnapper!" And who knows what else, but I didn't stop. I heard Lydia whimpering, burying her head inside the crook of my left arm as best she could amidst the ridiculous load I was carrying. I saw the flashes as the crowd of people doubled, and I just barely bolted past the ones that seemed intent to stop me. I made it to the escalators, but there were at least six hot on my trail, and the roar of people yelling at me and calling me all manner of nasty names fueled me as I ran down the moving escalator precariously pretending they were stairs. I pushed number two on my speed dial- the first was Caroline, the second answered immediately.

"I'm at the main entrance door, car is on and ready- I see them behind you. Just keep running, don't worry about them."

Flynn knows what's going on. True to his word, he opened the main door, and coached me to run, placing his hand on my back, his other hand on Lydia's buried head. I saw the flashes as a large group approached the entrance. I wanted to put Lydia in the car but also wanted to help Flynn. I rushed Lydia into the car, shaking my arms vigorously so all the bags fell off. I told Lydia, "Buckle up, now. You're okay." She was trembling, but she nodded, moving to obey. No longer encumbered, I moved to surge forward toward the people chasing us, but the scene before me was not what I expected. Instead of Flynn pinned to the ground, screaming out for help as an angry crowd encircled and pummeled him, the ones that had been chasing us were all on the ground, nursing what looked like black eyes – definitely some good shiners, one was curled up clutching his stomach. And Flynn was on the back of a particularly large man who was swinging wildly but didn't seem to have very good aim. My fiancé's hair was disheveled, it looked like he'd taken a few major punches, but he still had plenty of energy. Flynn was fighting with precision- somehow, I'd always pictured Flynn as just the gate guard to the palace. An important job to be sure, but not particularly challenging or physically demanding. But before my eyes I saw a whole different side to the man I loved. He was strong-tough. He moved swiftly, and suddenly the large man he had been on the back of had been flipped over; it seemed almost unreal. Flynn's shirt had torn in the melee, and as a fresh surge of angry protestors advanced and attacked, it was almost like watching a show. A perfectly choreographed fight scene, at least on Flynn's part. Some of the guys, and even a couple girls, attempted to take Flynn down. The men were swiftly sent flying, while Flynn merely avoided the girls' attacks, apparently, he didn't want to hurt them. *Wow. Look at those muscles...*

"Get in the car!!" Flynn shouted, barreling towards me as I had been so stuck ogling him, I'd forgotten about the impending danger.

I felt a very strong arm choking my neck from behind as Flynn's eyes narrowed. *I've* never *seen him so angry.*

"Give us the girl, and I won't hurt this woman." A very deep voice threatened, his arm against my throat tightening. I coughed, struggling against the assailant, but it did literally no good, he didn't budge. Flynn though, he was still moving at lightning speed. His eyes were focused on mine as he very obviously tilted his head down then looked back at me, like I was supposed to get whatever hidden code he had tried to relay. Then suddenly, Flynn leapt into the air, his leg perfectly positioned to kick the guy's head... and possibly mine. So going off the titled head thing, I put my head down, opened my mouth and bit the stranger, hard as I could, on his offending arm. The deep voice behind me screamed out in agony as he loosened his hold on my neck, giving me a split second to crouch to the cement as Flynn's foot made contact with the guy's chest. As the big guy staggered back, Flynn grabbed my arm with one of his, and somehow with just that one arm he pulled me from crouching on the pavement into his very muscular arm (still just one)! as I wrapped my arms around his neck. Immediately he swept me into the car, barely making it to the driver's side before the angry hoard had reached the entrance. At break-neck speed, Flynn got us past the pedestrians, but then we had another problem: three cars were now following us, more to surely follow.

Pulling my phone back to my ear, I touched number one as I exclaimed, "Go to the palace!" Flynn nodded, zigging and zagging through the very busy traffic, we had gone to Langford after all. The second I heard Caroline saying my name, I exclaimed, "No time to explain. We are being chased, coming to you. Tell the guards to open the gate and be ready for company!"

Immediately Caroline told me it would be done, and I hung up. I gnawed my fingernails, a horrid habit I reserved for when things were very out of my control. And right now? It qualified. Flynn looked very determined as one car advanced, must have been going at least eighty, and slammed into the left side of our car like he'd been attempting a pit maneuver. Our car spun uncontrollably, Lydia was screaming, I gritted my teeth, but Flynn still looked in control. Almost immediately he took us out of the tailspin and back towards the palace, but his car was making some fairly scary noises, like it was attempting to overheat. We were about five minutes away still, more than seven cars right behind us, as it began to sputter and shake. The nightmare of our situation became infinitely worse as we heard a hissing noise. Flynn cursed under his breath as steam, or something, began to leak from the hood. He checked his rearview mirror as he said quickly, "Doni, you and Lydia are going to have to run. I'm sorry."

I shook my head, but obviously he wasn't looking in my direction. "I can't leave you to all those cars- they obviously don't care about killing us!"

"We promised to protect Lydia. I'm going to spin the car around and block off the road. As soon as it stops, you grab her, and you run. Please Doni!" His pleading stopped me from arguing further. *Poor Lydia is utterly terrified, and I am too. I just finally got engaged; please don't tell me after all we've been through, I'm going to lose him like this!!*

I said, "We will. I love you!"

Flynn yelled, "Hang on!!" And with that, he cranked the wheel, throttling the gas, far more steam pouring out of the engine. Yet again we were spinning, and then suddenly we were at a standstill.

I hastily unbuckled, threw open my door, clambered to Lydia, who was failing to undo her buckle, it had gotten tangled in her booster seat. Flynn saw this, throwing his pocketknife to me. I immediately started sawing away at the seatbelt as Flynn got out of the car. The cars were just about on top of us, but I got Lydia out. I scooped her up, her face and hair damp with tears. I didn't look behind me, even as Flynn shouted that he loved me. I sprinted toward the palace as I shouted, "I love you Flynn Levisay!!!" I had just made it to where the guards were at alert, ready and waiting for us. I opened my mouth to explain, but suddenly the worst sound I ever heard echoed over to me, and I spun around.

SCREECH metal on metal - a car wreck. I felt my body trembling uncontrollably, and my legs were buckling. I heard Caroline screaming my name, I felt Lydia lifted off of me, Caroline had picked her up, and some guards I didn't know were holding me steady, as a large group of them ran towards my Flynn. *Will he be alive? Will he be recognizable or mangled beyond repair? I know even if I'd stayed, I wouldn't have been able to stop anything... but to abandon him like that... it doesn't seem right.*

My legs gave out, and the guards made noises of surprise, but they didn't let me fall. His car was only a mile or so away from us, so we could hear the noises of an intense scuffle. After a while, a group of people came toward us. The smoke from the car had fogged up the road so it was nearly impossible to see who was approaching. Sweeping my eyes everywhere, I looked at the people around me, the guards moved into defensive stances, they apparently had realized the same thing.

It looked like there were four, maybe five figures coming at us, as the smoke cleared, it revealed that they were all our guards. And one was in really bad shape. He had Flynn's build, his hair, but his head was down, slumped against one of the guys, as the other two near him carried him awkwardly. *If that's Flynn... how bad off is he? Was he hit by a car?! Was he...*

I felt a burst of energy that had me leaping to my feet, startling the two that had been supporting my weight. I booked it toward who I thought might be Flynn. I gasped as soon as I could clearly see who was before me. It was Flynn alright, but not as I had left him. His right ear was gushing blood like a freaking waterfall. His head was rolling around as if he had no control over it. I felt the tears start coming, but made no attempt to hide them as I asked desperately, "How is he? He's not dead..." I couldn't bring myself to ask it as a question. No one answered. They looked so somber. "Somebody- tell me!" I snapped, angry at their silence, but they just continued to rush past me toward the open gate as if I didn't exist.

I was stunned for a second, but then I whirled around and pursued the group. They were rushing him to the Doctor's office, which made sense, though I still felt irritation that they couldn't spare me a couple seconds to dissuade my fears. But whatever, it was what it was. I didn't see Caroline or Lydia, so she must have brought her inside. *I see the wisdom in Caroline's action, but I need to be close to my little chosen family. Flynn and Lydia both need to be okay. I haven't had time to examine her at all, we were hit fairly hard. What if she is badly hurt, and it just isn't as visible as Flynn? Come to think of it, do I have any injuries? No, forget that. I can figure that out later.*

I heard Doctor Corenlius rushing around, but I couldn't make myself open the door. I had reached the waiting room... but the truth was I didn't know if I could bear what was waiting for me inside. *As much as I need to hear that Flynn is okay... if he isn't... I'd rather live in my imagination that we're all perfectly fine, planning our long-awaited wedding.* I collapsed to the ground as my legs yet again failed me. "Someone needs to tell me what Flynn's condition is, or I'm going to explode!" I yelled, wiping my face as I forced myself to my feet.

From far on my right, I heard a soothing male voice. "He's going to live Donyelle. Cornelius said Flynn is in surgery, he's under local anesthesia. He believes he won't lose his right ear completely, but for sure the top, he had a fancy name for it. I really can't remember. Flynn will survive. That's for certain. He's pretty battered and bruised. But he's going to wake up." I was startled, not expecting to actually get an answer, and especially not from Ryan. It makes sense that his wife would have called him, especially since he and my man were best friends. *I bet he doesn't know I'm finally Flynn's fiancée. After so long. Which makes me that much more shook by him being unconscious in a hospital bed in surgery...*

"What about Lydia? How is she? We were in a car accident."

Ryan's face morphed with shock. "Then why are you in the waiting room?"

"Exactly!" I exclaimed with relief. "Finally, someone who gets it! I should be with Flynn, and Lydia! Looking after them. But no one would listen, they just barreled past."

Ryan shook his head slightly. "I actually meant that you should be getting checked out. You have no idea if you have a concussion, a car crash can cause a lot more than a few bumps or bruises."

I denied his logic. "It wasn't even a full car crash for Lydia and me; we just got spun around. I can handle that, but a child should never experience a pit stop, especially a child so little and fragile. Not to mention she has so much trauma she's working through already. I don't want to add a fear of driving to the mix if at all possible."

Ryan did not look dissuaded. "Please wait here. I'll go determine where Cornelius is and have him decide whether you need a checkup." I was all set to protest yet again. After all, I was well known for my comebacks. However, Ryan knew how to combat that. "At the least the doctor can give you better updates on Flynn and Lydia." I scowled, feeling beaten. Ryan flashed me the tiniest of smiles as I sat down in one of the waiting chairs. It reeked of sanitizer. But that makes sense, it was a hospital after all. They would have to combat germs far more than most places.

After who knows how long, the Doctor came through the door, almost pummeling me in the process. He was startled, but didn't make a sound as his wizened face went from surprise to pity. "Ms. Cox. How are you?"

Crap. He had to go and ask that. Mundane as the question was, the waterworks started. He didn't look dismayed, his face didn't change at all, in fact. He reached out and patted me on my shoulder in a friendly way. I heard the door open and close in front of me, but I had closed my eyes to attempt to stop the tears, so I didn't see who approached. I felt other hands on my back, but I didn't attempt to ascertain who they belonged to. I continued to cry, a luxury I so rarely allowed.

Apparently, I have quite a lot of pent-up emotion that needs releasing. I was shaking, badly, but I couldn't even determine where it had originated. Eventually I looked up, four pairs of eyes staring back at me – the Doctor, the King and Queen, a.k.a. my best friend and her husband, and Ahyoka, my other close friend. I was surrounded by very patient people. Kindhearted too. In their position, at least in my head I would have wanted to say, 'Okay, that's enough. Suck it up'. But that's just my personality. I wanted to get past the awkward moments. *If I had a remote for life, I surely would have fast-forwarded scenes such as these in the past. But what I am finally beginning to understand is that these moments stimulate the most growth. Just like a botanist, I have to dead-head the buds that have wilted, making room and providing nutrients for plants to have new growth instead of competing over nutrients between the dead and the living. I have toed that line, dancing between the two for far too long; holding tight to that which is dead in me, not wanting to let go, even though it is obvious I am at a standstill – no more growth will happen until I allow myself to prune that which brought me misery and stunted me.* I allowed them to comfort me, and I allowed myself to be comforted. It was a very odd feeling, but it was much needed at this moment. All the energy had been sapped from my body.

Suddenly, I heard my name, so I whipped around as the Doctor stated, "Flynn's awake, recovering from surgery, he can only have one visitor at this time."

There was no question; I was the one who should see Flynn. Ryan took a half step forward, before Caroline put her hand on her husband's arm with a soft loving look she gave so easily. Ryan's eyes locked on to his wife's then his gaze turned to me as he mouthed 'sorry' sheepishly. *Technically, Ryan has known him a lot longer. And it's not like either of us has had a chance to announce our new engaged status.* I smiled at Ryan, which caused him to quickly take that half step back. Caroline chuckled softly under her breath, and if it weren't for Flynn's condition being unknown, I would have felt the mirth as well. But as it was, how Flynn was faring took up the majority of my mental capacity. Cornelius led me back to Flynn's room, where he looked to be doing about as well as you could expect, certainly more than I had anticipated. He was sitting on his hospital bed, watching the tv, looking morose. Wincing a little he cradled his hand over his bandaged ear with a frown as the tv announced the mayoral candidates' press conference was soon to begin. I came from behind him, his back to me as I bent down and wrapped my arms around his waist.

He jumped with surprise, but when he saw my hands, he didn't even need to look at my face. I could see the loving grin as he stated, "Apparently you're going to have to get used to your fiancé having one-and-a-half ears."

He put his hands over mine, rubbing them as I opened my mouth to respond. I didn't have the chance however, because suddenly a chorus of gasps erupted from somewhere behind us. Apparently, another perk of being royalty was being allowed to break rules, because there stood our best friends. Mouths agape, Caroline's eyes were already misty. She lunged forward to give me the biggest hug, jolting both myself and my fiancé in the process. And Ryan rushed to the front to hug his friend, until Ryan and Caroline had made Flynn and I into a sandwich. Flynn was beaming with delight as Ryan congratulated him, and I felt pride and joy, the likes of which I had never experienced. I was smiling so wide, so unlike me, it was completely unnecessary to speak my heart, but I did it anyways. "I am so happy!" I gushed, in a very unlike-me way. *Apparently love softens a person. Hmm. Interesting. What other little quirks should I be in for with this I wonder?*

"The favorite for Mayor, Senator Ziddim Strawfeld, has just informed the press that he has an urgent matter he must bring to the public's attention. Here he is now." All excitement was leeched from the room as we fastened our eyes on the screen as the fake-perky redhead on the right of the screen broadcast our enemy on the left.

As the camera panned, it showed a man who looked grief stricken, tears glimmering in his eyes and down his cheeks, sorrow dripping from each word. "Friends, today, I am not here as a candidate for Mayor. I am here simply as a father, asking my darling daughter's abductors to please return her safe and unharmed. If anything were to happen to my beloved daughter-" He stopped, and to anyone who didn't know, he looked to be overcome with emotion.

There's something, and I'm not sure I can pinpoint exactly what it is, but it's... off. Insincere, obviously, but there is more to it. He continued, dabbing at his tears with a ridiculous handkerchief he had tucked in his pocket, no doubt in an effort to appear distinguished. It didn't work, and not just because I loathed the man with my entire being. Everything about him just seemed wrong. I wanted to zone out, but then... he showed everyone pictures. Flynn and I and Lydia. And the image they had captured, well – it did look bad. Lydia looked all mussed, hair everywhere. She was sitting in the car, looking scared. I was almost to the car, and I didn't look particularly sweet or kind, the facial expression was afraid, because Flynn had been attacking all those that had pursued us, but my version of fear is angry, upset. Which didn't bode well for our defense. The evil man showed more images, calling attention to Flynn as he attacked those that supposedly were 'trying to reunite father and daughter'. *I'll hand it to the arsehole; he makes a compelling message. Very public. Saying we are keeping him from his very sick troubled young daughter, that he's just a concerned loving father, and he can't fathom why we would be so hateful. He is the worst kind of evil.*

If that weren't bad enough, he opened his mouth again, "So while I plead for the police to take action, I must remind my friends, my constituents - anyone who patrons the flower shop of the abductor Donyelle Cox, Dazzling Dreams, is condoning kidnapping and allowing them to continue to withhold my precious daughter. In fact, to protect my baby girl, I encourage you to boycott her store -make signs; we will picket together every day, if need be, until my Lydia is safe in my arms." He made a show of sniffling, wiping back a fresh abundance of tears. "Please help me; I'm just a father, missing his daughter, his only child. I ask you; who could be so cruel as to rip a child from her loving, doting family?" The screams and jeers of the crowd grew into a roar as Flynn hurriedly turned off the telly.

The rest of the day was a bit of a haze, Flynn and Lydia were discharged, I had already gotten a clean bill of health. I had received what felt like hundreds of phone calls and emails, all threatening to cancel unless I returned the child to her dear parent. I tried to explain the situation each time, until I was ragingly angry at having to speak to what felt like a brick wall. No one wanted to hear my side of the story. No one cared about anything other than me promising Lydia would be brought to her father, which I would *never* do.

Flynn tried to play damage control, so did Ryan, but even with Caroline's sweetness and poise she couldn't calm the angry callers, and that did not bode well for tomorrow. Ryan insisted that Flynn and I both be surrounded by bodyguards, and even though part of me hated having strangers around, I did take a tiny bit of comfort knowing they were close by. I couldn't sleep, it simply wouldn't come, so by the next day it was already starting out in the worst way possible. On top of that, I couldn't eat anything, because my stomach was not thrilled with the events of yesterday. It was like a very angry snake was slithering around inside of me, occasionally striking, causing my stomach to roil. *So very uncomfortable.*

Flynn and I had put on a brave face for little Lydia as we dropped her off to Greta. Flynn had called her late last night, no doubt after he assumed I was asleep. He had been honest about how bad the situation was, and how dangerous it could become if things escalated further. He downplayed the 'accident' - his words - the car ramming into his parked one was anything but accidental. Obviously, he hadn't wanted to worry her more than he had to. But now that it was just him and I... and like seven bodyguards, I was really allowing myself to feel my feelings. And as soon as we had reached the corner of Langley where my shop stood... my heart was just about in my throat at the scene before me. Must have been over four hundred people, all led by that stupid evil Senator who obviously was riling them all up against us. The sea of signs all had one central theme; Flynn and I were scum. And this time not for being residents of Langley, but for being child abductors, child abusers, and groomers. *Gross.* That angry snake was back in my stomach, and it lashed out in full force, causing me to double over in pain. Flynn caught me, worry filling his face as he ordered his coworkers to get us back to the palace. My phone continued to blow up as customer after customer informed me, many in the rudest way imaginable, that they would take their business elsewhere. In the end, I only had two clients who didn't cancel, and one was Caroline – she doesn't count. I groaned, loudly, as I saw the name I dreaded most in this moment pop up on my screen... *this is going to be very bad.* I shuffled in my seat as Flynn's eyes continued to flash with worry and anger at what we were going through due to that liar. I answered the phone after five rings, unable to delay the inevitable any longer.

"Donyelle?" Almost always poised, Cordelia sounded decidedly less-than-happy. *Understandable given the circumstances, though oh-so-frustrating.* "I assume you've heard the press release?"

I covered my phone's speaker as I let out a loud sigh, then I moved the phone back to my face. "I have."

The silence on the other end was deafening. Finally, she spoke again. "While I am going to continue to encourage my clients to look at your lovely designs, it's come to my attention that as things stand, my clients are more concerned about your reputation than your talent. What that means, to put it bluntly, is that we have to cancel all of your contracts with us, effective immediately. Normally that would mean I would have to compensate you for your efforts and how far you have gotten on the installations and bouquets... however article eighteen paragraph four sub section b states that if my clients cancel due to any form of scandal on the part of the contractor, which is you, then we are not held liable for the contract, and it is null and void." Everything was beginning to spin. That press release had essentially made me jobless, and I wasn't even going to be paid for the thousands of dollars I had invested for the materials, not to mention the countless hours, and that was even before I paid the myriad of employees I had to bring on that currently worked in my greenhouse located in Langford. *Why did everyone just believe that arsehole without a single shred of proof??*

I pulled my phone away from my ear, looking at it; dismay and fear paralyzing my tongue, unable to speak a word. Flynn offered his hands, one took the phone gently from my light grasp, the other unbuckled me, pulling my back into his chest as he wrapped his arms around me, putting my phone on speaker. "Who is this, and what is going on?"

Cordelia reiterated what she'd said to me, word for word, as if she had written it out beforehand. I was too dazed to process what she was saying, I was having a hard enough time not hyperventilating at the thought of being bankrupt, all my hard work to get as far as I had come completely undone by evil. Flynn listened patiently, then he said in a matter-of-fact tone, "That's B.S. Cordelia. You know it and I know it. Not only are these claims against Donyelle and me false, but it's completely unacceptable to not only leave her high and dry while also refusing to provide payment for the work she has already done on behalf of your ungrateful clients. They wouldn't even have sketches if it weren't for Donyelle, not to mention everything she's invested since she signed on to work with you. You don't even know if that contract would be held up in court, and you are burning the best possible florist in the kingdom. You know that when she is inevitably found not guilty of these malicious rumors, and believe me she will, you probably won't have a way to coerce her to ever work with you again. You very well know flowers can make-or-break how the wedding looks, as well as how Donyelle's work is nothing short of magic. You are making a mistake. An extremely costly one. I hope you consider that before going to this length. Why not take a week or two until things die down, then reevaluate?"

"Flynn, I always liked you. But I can't take financial losses on something I can't predict. I won't. Please tell Donyelle it's not personal, this is not a form of revenge for you choosing her; it's strictly business, I can promise you that."

Flynn let out a low growl, animalistic, something I had never heard from him before, and I could feel it reverberating through me as he did so. "So be it, Cordelia." Then he lowered the phone down to me, and I shakily pushed the button. Once it was disconnected, I wailed, startling the driver, as we weaved a tiny bit on the road.

I held Flynn's arms around me tightly as if they were my only lifeline. "What am I going to do Flynn?!"

Flynn moved just barely, tilting his head over and to the side so he could meet my despairing eyes. "I will find a way to fix this. Cordelia is not the only option to gain clients. We just need some sort of proof... oh!" He suddenly looked extremely excited as he continued, "You don't have a website! I bet that would attract people from all over!"

Not wanting to temper his excitement, I hesitantly said, "Right... but I don't know the first thing about setting one up. You don't either, right?"

The fire in Flynn's eyes immediately extinguished, as I saw the exact second his hope died. "I will... I will figure out a way." He seemed to be struggling with this newfound loss of hope, as I saw the slightest bit of excitement re-enter his orbs. "There's always a way. I'll be praying for us, and I'll ask Ryan and Caroline to pray too."

I couldn't resist scrunching my nose. *It isn't that I don't believe in God, but I do have a beef with Him. Why give me to such shitty parents? Why make me go through so much junk in my life? Why not protect me from all that? Give me to a couple that would have actually stuck around, perhaps even loved me? What good is praying when He didn't seem to care before?* But I found myself nodding as the car slid into park right inside the castle gates. *Prayer can't hurt. And at least the concept seems to wrench Flynn out of his hopelessness.* He eased me out of his arms, out of the car, then picked me up and carried me to the royal bedroom where Caroline and Ryan lived with the twins. Currently no one was there, but Caroline was going to let her students out early to be there for me. I only knew this because Flynn had whispered it as he tucked me into the massive bed. He whispered something else, something about finding ways to help me, then he was gone, and with him went the light that he possessed, the light that I did not have. The cold aching loneliness engulfed me immediately. *I haven't felt this alone and upset since I was a child, and nothing in me wants to re-live anything regarding that miserable time.* I willed my eyes open, for only then would the nightmares of my past not swallow me alive, but my exhaustion, as the adrenaline of the day had worn off, was all encompassing, and before I knew it my eyes had closed.

Chapter 7
SAVING DAZZLING DREAMS

Flynn's POV:

What am I going to do?? I told her I would find a way. What way could I possibly find?? I perched, hovering against a wall, not fully leaning against it, as I waited for Ryan to finish his meeting with the delegates. *I want to volunteer to make her a fancy website, fully promise that it will bring a fresh influx of customers, but I have no clue how to do that! What is possessing me to want to make such an outrageous promise? Well, I know the exact reason, if I'm being honest with myself. Seeing that despair in her normally confident eyes was heart wrenching. And the thing was, unlike some, I could see that the confidence was often a mask of bravado, but this was one of the insanely rare times where she was completely and totally helpless, desperate, and was too overwhelmed to blanket her feelings with false confidence, a sassy British phrase, or a joke. Of course I had to help. I would do just about anything in that moment to transform her despair to hope and peace. So of course, I will over-promise. And I'll find ways to ensure I don't under-deliver, so who do I know that is tech savvy? Hmm... Scylla. Scylla Seraph. She's obsessed with her laptop. Probably the best place to start.* I asked her to please meet me at the castle, and that I'd make it worth her while.

I leaned back into the wall now that I had a possible real idea. Before too long, I saw her approach, "What do you want?! What was such a big deal that it couldn't be discussed over the phone??" A young woman's voice snapped with a ton of frustration coloring her tone. She looked far older than her eighteen years wearing makeup that enhanced all her features. As she shook with rage, even under that bravado, I knew immediately she wasn't actually that angry. As she knew very well, a trip to the palace meant a ton of tasty treats courtesy of my mom. As she huffed, her mermaid ombre hair moved like a green/blue wave. Micah had always flirted with her growing up, and especially now I could see why. He would have become quite predatorial if he had been here to see her with all this makeup, very tight skinny jeans and a provocative purple shirt. I kept my gaze eye level after the quick cursory glance, I didn't need to look at others when I have Donyelle. Especially dressed as skimpily as she was.

"I want to help my fiancée's business get more traction, I need a good website, and I thought of you." *Keep it short, to the point, and offer her money.*

She grabbed a bunch of long hair and twirled it around her fingers as she sighed, "No duh. Who else is a genius whiz kid? Ugh. Fine. I need three grand up front, two more once the website is created. That of course covers the domain, the website with all connecting features, and a marketing campaign I will use my media influence to send all the plebes in droves to your girl's site." She must have seen my face sag, because she gave me a genuine smile. "On YouTube alone I have forty million subscribers – Facebook has over 70 million friends, far more followers. X, Insta and TikTok are up to just under a billion, and my numbers are always climbing." She took a couple steps forward, until she was very close, as she whispered in my ear, "People can't get enough of my recommendations and how-to videos. So, while you might think it's steep, five grand isn't anywhere near what I could charge." She backed up just slightly as her hazel eyes teased, "Since we are friends, well, sort of, I'm giving you a heavy discount. Even though you're barely sliding through on the friend scale. More like your mom and mine are tight. The things we do for family, right?" She laughed, a surprisingly sweet sound, as she put her hand on my chest. "But seriously, give me a day. And some good pics of her best work. That's all I need, with my fee." I took her hand off my chest with one of my own, as I pondered what had happened to her growing up. *She didn't used to be so... jaded, I guess is the word? Sanctimonious? It has been a while...*

I know she thinks everyone is beneath her, but the fact remains that she is extremely smart for her young age, and she did have a huge -insanely huge- following. Five thousand dollars... that would be all the money I had left after paying Doni's medical bills... everything I had saved for a much-needed new car... plus like five hundred and some change. I'm sure Ryan would lend me the money after I explained the situation, but yikes... However, there's no price to helping Doni get out of this financial hole. "You have a deal. I'll wire the three thousand, and the other two will be ready when you're done. I'll ask a friend about the pictures. Thank you, Scylla."

She let out a laugh. "You sound so old when you say my name, Flynn. And uptight as ever." She noted, motioning to my wrist that had moved her hand off me. "I'll get started. Don't forget to transfer the money and email me the pics." As quickly as she had appeared in a storm of anger, she disappeared from the hall, powerwalking toward my mom's kitchen.

I sagged back against the wall, suddenly feeling very tired. I pulled my phone back out and tapped my bank app, not excited about what I was about to do. I attempted to sign in, frustrated that they were making me do the two forms of logging in now. The username and password were not enough, and I had it tied to an old phone number and email address. It took far too long going down the rabbit hole of possible old passwords when I was a teenager, but eventually I guessed the right combination of my twenty or so old passwords, and I was in. I winced slightly as I sent more than half my life's savings into the account of the computer genius. I reminded myself multiple times that it was for the best of causes - my fiancé. But still, seeing the money draining out like that... it took years to accrue, and only seconds to lose. Such is life.

Ryan sounded like he was wrapping up his meeting, so I moved away from the doors as the group inside poured out. Once everyone had left, I caught up with Ryan and explained the situation as he listened intently to the whole story.

Pulling me into a hug I honestly really needed in this moment, Ryan quickly agreed to paying the last of the balance, even offering, "You paid three grand, it's only right I pay the other two. Before you argue with me, remember that Donyelle is not only my subject, but my wife's close friend. There's no use trying – once Caroline sets her mind to something, that's it. I'm sure Marley could help with pictures, old and new. And as for clearing your names, we'll figure out something. Just try to stop stressing, it's all going to work out. You are my brother, essentially. I won't let you fry for some-one else's misdeeds. That's a promise. All three of you are going to stay out of this blast zone – stay away from the flower shop. Don't react if anyone approaches you. I will get in touch with Seraphina, that's what she's here for. She will figure out the way to spin all this negative press around. She's done it so many times at this point. Admittedly, never against an accusation of child abduction, but she will no doubt know what our next steps should be, and how Caroline and I can help."

I felt better just listening to Ryan as we eased out of the hug, and I felt my left hand begin to tremble. It had only acted like that when dad had been mad at mom or me in the past, but it made a sad sort of sense that it would also affect me now. Ryan tilted his head and asked, "Are you still going to see Micah?"

I blinked, completely forgetting I'd planned on going to see Micah with mom today. She would go without me, like she had the last four times we planned this... but I had promised her I wouldn't reschedule again. The truth was the last three times I hadn't been that busy. I had been working, true, but Ryan would have let me go. I could have switched shifts with any other guard. *Truth is I dread seeing him. Seeing my brother behind bars, it's tough to stomach. It doesn't quite seem believable that he could be so evil. Honestly, I wouldn't have ever believed it if I hadn't witnessed the way he has choking Caroline, the taunting psychopathic voice admitting beyond a shadow of a doubt that he had aligned himself with one of the topmost hated criminals in the kingdom, possibly even the world, though that could be an exaggeration. Maybe.* "I promised Mom. I have not gone since that first time, and I have had every excuse under the sun the last three times mom and I planned these."

Ryan nodded sympathetically, adding, "Not to pile on, but tomorrow is Robbie's birthday, Ariana is going to need us all to support her."

I hung my head, shoulder drooping unintentionally at the reminder. "The next two days are going to be pretty heavy, huh?"

Ryan didn't say anything, he just looked very sad. Mutually solemn, we walked in what felt eerily like a death march toward the dungeon. At least Ryan and my mom would be with me, but still. This was going to suck.

Chapter 8
OPERATION: 'CHEER UP FLYNN'

Donyelle's POV:

I heard voices as I moved from the huge bed. At least two. Flynn was one, an unidentified female was the other. And that... that made my heart beat up tempo. I opened the door as silently as I could, peaking out, but I couldn't see anything. So, I opened the door wide enough to get out, sneaking toward the at least two speakers. I hadn't gotten far, when I saw Flynn and an unknown young woman in a barely-there outfit which clung to her in a way that left nothing to the imagination. I felt rage simmer within me, as I reminded myself: *I know he loves me, and he's not the type to cheat... but man is this testing my ability to trust him so soon...*

I felt a tap on my shoulder, and I just barely muffled my scream. I heard soft giggles behind me, so I whirled around, giving the startler my patented death glare. It would have been more convincing, but as soon as I realized it was Caroline, I couldn't help but soften. She whispered, "Why are you watching Flynn back here? And who's that girl?"

I simmered a bit more as I snapped, "First off, you spied on me too, so don't get that tone with me bird. I don't know who she is. So, hush up." I turned back to see the girl far closer than she used to be, with what appeared to be a hand on my fiancé's chest. Worse yet, it looked like Flynn grabbed it and held it. I let out a tiny yelp as Caroline warned,

"You don't know what that's about. I don't see Flynn doing anything untoward. Don't get in your head. Remember, in just about all those dramas we watch, the foil to even a hint of romance is secrecy. And about eighty percent of the time, it's a misunderstanding that one of the leads, male or female, holds on to and gets bitter about, acting out in jealousy and hurt, and ruins things, at least temporarily, when instead all they had to do was say 'hey, I saw you hanging out with this woman. Would you mind telling me what that's about? I'm feeling a bit jealous and insecure, and while you've never given me a reason not to trust you, I would just like a little reassurance, it seemed to be a bit intimate'."

Well, when she puts it that way... I watched that tiny girl strut away quickly, and I realized that my bird was right. And as Caroline hugged me tightly, before saying she had to set up for her adult reading and writing class, I got back into my head.

Flynn is allowed to have a life outside of me. Just as I am allowed a life outside of him. But for the sake of not driving myself insane, I'll ask in a way that explains it's nothing that he's done, but I need clarification. It's just... it's hard to trust. And he knows that; he actually finally knows my story! That gives me such relief that I don't have to feel like a crazy person for feeling the way I do. I don't want to come across as this super needy clingy girlfriend who doesn't trust and is insanely controlling. Flynn is allowed to have friends. Guys and girls. But... Caroline is right. It is making me feel a type of way that I don't want to feel. And holding something against him and acting different... I was about to try to talk to Flynn, but suddenly, Flynn and Ryan were talking. And unlike when the girl spoke, which had been far too quiet to understand anything, Flynn and Ryan were louder. Hearing how torn up he was about needing to visit his brother, and especially how much he had bonded with Robbie before his untimely passing... it pricked my heart. It made me feel a bit bad for being jealous of his protentional romantic rendezvous with that curvy girl. I should try to help him feel better. Perhaps... my mind started whirling, and before I knew it, I had a plan to attempt to cheer him up, as well as nicely asking him what the deal with that girl had been. *Nice and casual... not jealous or angry... at least, I'm going to really try.*

Knowing I couldn't get access to my flower shop with all those rioters and picketers, I set out on the long drive to Langford, not only to gather a collection of flowers, but also to quickly put my employees' minds at ease, paying out of my own pocket each of their salaries. After paying all nine... I had a measly five-dollar bill in my pocket. Sad, pathetic, a little frayed on one side. Of course, my employees would stick around for another month, now that they were paid. But that only stalled the inevitable if I couldn't get some clients and wedding contracts. But now was not the time to panic about that. I have thirty days exactly until that becomes an issue. A lot can happen in a month. I went from not opening up at all to slowly and painfully divulging the main roots of all my issues. At least the ones I knew about, anyway. And when I did divulge, he showed me that I was his priority, and that he truly treasures my vulnerability. I should do something special for him. Not too special, since I only have like three hundred and five dollars to my name currently, but I could set up a date night or something. That might ease Flynn's burden. Idea firmly in mind, I set about heading toward what was recently considered home. *I wonder when Lydia will be home. And Flynn, for that matter. Well, I'll be quick, before anyone shows up.*

I followed the recipe Greta had texted me when she informed me, I had an hour before Flynn got home, and that she had convinced Flynn that Lydia and Caroline needed time to bond, apparently Lydia had fallen in love with the twin babies and were treating them like living dolls. So, I took chicken out of the fridge, preheated the oven, and began the process of combining the seasonings and such, following everything perfectly, so as not to have a repeat debacle, that might get a small pity chuckle out of Flynn, but he needed a real cheering up, the kind that good food and an even better woman could provide. Once the apartment was filled with the smell of roasting chicken, I set about husking the corn on the cob and prepping the tin foil, plus rolling cookie dough (store bought, but I was very limited on time). By the time Flynn stepped foot in the door, everything was done and there were little strings of cheery flowers everywhere you looked. Flynn smiled, and it was like all that weight and burdens he had brought up the stairs had vanished instantaneously.

"You did all this? I mean, the flowers, obviously you. But - and don't take this the wrong way; did you also make that incredible-smelling food?"

I pursed my lips, but internally reminded myself my mission for the night, so I morphed into a genuine smile as I answered, "Yes. Your mom thankfully wrote a step-by-step guide, and it might be too soon to say so, but I think I did pretty well."

He moved to wrap me in his arms, all thoughts about the possible other woman no longer the forefront of my mind. I let myself bask in his warmth, in the familiar scent of vanilla and honey – he tended to always smell like his mom, especially after such an intense moment, he would have wanted to support his mother, not allowing himself to feel weak like he probably wanted to feel. "Whatever you need to say, whatever you need to do – seeing Micah, and Robbie's birthday being tomorrow; you express yourself however you need to. This is a safe space. Hence the flowers."

He chuckled slightly, as he lifted my chin so our eyes met. "How do you still manage to surprise me after knowing you for so long? It's truly impressive."

I grinned, as I led him by the hand to his seat at our table. I let him talk, everything on his mind. Once we had finished dinner, and I brought the cookies out, I asked, more hesitantly than was my norm, "If you are in a mental space to discuss it, I'd like to ask you something, so it doesn't live rent free in my head and potentially dismantle our new vibrant relationship."

Flynn, whose eyes had been focused entirely on my tray of cookies, snapped all his attention to me, confusion all over his face. "Did I do something?"

I put my hand over his on the table and answered, "I don't know if you did or not. There was a girl with blue hair. She had her hand on your chest, it looked like you were holding her hand, you were talking in the palace. I want to trust you; believe me I do. But remember, I told you about my pattern with men. They tend to leave after they get what they want. And while you and I haven't had sex before... I still worry. So even though it's not really my business... could you just tell me what was going on there?" *I feel like a dumb, jealous girlfriend. Fiancé, whatever.*

He smiled. It was one of those trying-to-hide-it smiles, but it was there, nonetheless. And it really pissed me off. But before I could lay into him, Flynn opened his mouth, which made me close mine. After all, I really wanted to know what he had to say. I was desperate to know, in all honesty. "It was meant to be a surprise. But I should have known you'd figure it out." He took my still-shaking hands in his as he rubbed the tops of each softly with his thumbs. He gave me his entire focus, eye to eye with me, as the smile grew. "I'm really proud of you Doni. You've never just come out and asked me anything like this before. When you were jealous in the past, you let it fester, you didn't talk it out with me like this. You've really grown in your communication skills. Now, first off; I'm not cheating. That girl shouldn't have touched me, and I told her as much as I moved away from her. She's eccentric. And very young. But she's the best in the business when it comes to creating the perfect website for you. Which she's about done with now, I believe."

I stood there, his hands soothing mine, as the trembling ceased. *Not only do I have nothing to worry about, but... he has commissioned a website just for me? That's... I don't know what that is. Amazing. Wonderful. Makes me feel...* I lowered my head to hide the blood-shot shame as I answered, "Great. Now I feel like a complete arsehole."

Flynn let out a chuckle as I felt his hand let go of my right one. I expected him to let go of my left too – complete the abandonment. *Surely, he is done with me now. I'm too dramatic. Too untrusting.*

"Doni, come here." Surprise had me raise my head, as Flynn's gaze showed nothing but love and devotion, his right hand beckoning me closer. I moved into his embrace, as let go of my hands and encircled my waist, whispering into my ear. "You are not an 'arsehole'. You have your moments, but that's just part of what makes you so wonderful in my eyes. I love you as you are. I'm proud to be your fiancé. Always and forever. And I will be ten times prouder when we make it official, and I'm your husband for life. If you say I do, you will not get rid of me. No matter what insecurities we both have, it doesn't matter. We will work through them together. I know asking me was a huge step forward. I'm really happy you told me what was on your mind and heart. Just keep doing that. We'll be the strongest of couples if we both just speak what we are trying to bury. I love you, Donyelle. Every facet of you. That won't change. Because I'm choosing to love you, each and every day."

What is happening?? Am I...? I felt the liquid, slow at first, then pouring down like a gushing waterfall, explode from my eyes, and I was horrified. But Flynn only chose to hug me tighter, completely unbothered as I sobbed. Deep within me, the fears seemed to be pouring out. But this time was different. I felt fear leaving my body. Felt in its place a very new feeling. *Peace.* I relaxed into his arms, felt his chest against mine, ignored the twitches from his nether regions, because unlike any other man, our bond was not prioritized on sex. *I feel safe with this man. Secure. I actually believe that he will stay, unlike the litany of guys that have come before. He loves me as I am. And he will continue to do so until his dying breath. I know I feel the same. I will choose to love this man until I pass. He makes it fairly easy. But even on the most trying of days, I know I can choose to be this man's person. He completes me, he challenges me, endures my sass covering up insecurities and shame.* Eventually, the tears dried, and I felt exhausted. But in the most blissful of ways. Flynn hadn't moved, his face tilted to my ear as he had softly spoken words of love and encouragement throughout the sob-fest. He must have noticed the tears slowing until they stopped completely, because he whispered, in a deep masculine voice, "May I?"

What is he asking permission for? I have no clue. But I did know his voice sent delightful shivers down my entire very-drained body. I said, "You may." *It doesn't matter what he wants at this moment; I trust him. Like no one I've ever trusted before. He knows he has my heart, and I know he will cherish it.* He scooped me into his arms, carrying me like a bride as I tilted my head to cuddle into his chest. His heart was beating very rapidly. I looked up, as he smiled at me, so much adoration and excitement in his gaze. "Why do you look excited Flynn?" I couldn't help but ask. "You aren't one of those lads who needs a lass to act all helpless to get turned on, right?"

He shook his head with a smirk. "No. I just feel that we took a huge step in our relationship today. Not only are we engaged, but you're finally trusting me enough to really let out your emotions and tell me what you're thinking. You have no idea how often I wanted... almost needed to know what was going on in that dazzlingly gorgeous head of yours." He began to walk forward and to the left, as I pondered his words. *They feel more special than the numerous accolades I've heard in the past. Everyone praised my beauty. I am fully aware I am a very attractive woman. But so few try for anything deeper than that. Except for this man. My Flynn. He always did. He went deeper. He isn't afraid to find out the contents of my mind and heart. To hear what I really think and feel.* He approached Caroline's room as I had expected the door guard to greet Flynn and I, letting us in. I was surprised to see that there was no guard, and the door was unlocked. He opened the door, then Flynn deftly moved through the living area and before I could even tell him he could put me down, he had somehow managed to also open the other doors; first to the bedrooms, then to the adjoining guest room. I'd spent far too many nights in that room, so many in fact it had become like a second home. Flynn lowered me softly into the large pile of pillows, pulling up the blankets until they covered my feet to my chin. I felt very cozy.

A thought struck me. Several, actually. "Where's Lydia? How long until the website is done?"

He chuckled, still stooped down. He tapped my nose as he said, "Lydia is with my mom and her suitor. I think the website should be done soon, Marley just needs access to your plants and stuff. I don't know the fancy words. Just the... you know, the stuff that you want on the website. Flowers... uh... standing up things..."

As the man who had captured my heart fumbled for the correct terminology, my heart swelled even more. Wait... "Was today the day you saw your brother?"

A shadow crossed over the previously playful expression. "I did. It went about as badly as you would expect."

Although I'd been just about lifeless before in his arms, now I felt a surge of energy as righteous anger coursed through my veins. I pulled a decidedly ugly face as I thought about that psychopath being anywhere near my man. I flung my arms around Flynn's neck, pulling him into the bed with me. Flynn stiffened, and this time I was the one to reassure him. "I just want to cuddle. Help you get your mind off Micah."

I felt his body relax as he moved to my left side in the bed, a pleased expression making him that much more handsome. "I would like that Doni, thanks." As he settled in, putting his left arm under my head and his right arm over my body under the covers, I backed up into him, but just slightly. *I don't want to give him a boner. This is going to be the first time I am completely wholesome in bed with a man. Ever. And I want to keep this pure. Not trying to seduce Flynn, but to help calm his racing heart, give him comfort, and relax us both.* Flynn let out a sigh, and I absently began to rub his right arm as he traced my stomach. We laid like that for a while in companionable silence. Eventually, when I felt his left hand begin to flex slightly underneath me, I recognized his hand may have fallen asleep, so I shifted positions, turning so I was face-to-face with my sweetheart. His eyes were open, but relaxed. I seem to have accomplished my mission.

Inching a bit closer, I put a hand to his face, stroking his soft skin and his slight beard. "Is that better?"

His lips turned up into a smile, and I found myself far too focused on them. "Far better." He sighed softly. "This was exactly what I needed to get my mind focused on much more pleasant things. Namely, you." That got me. I couldn't contain my desire anymore, but I did want this cuddle session to remain sex-free. *How to walk that line though...*

Flynn whispered in a deep, husky voice that I found incredibly sexy, "I really want to kiss you."

That is more than enough invitation for me. I placed my lips on his, and instead of taking all the initiative, like I had before, I allowed Flynn to set the pace. And it was... heavenly. I matched his pace, so we were perfectly in sync, and I marveled at how much better the experience was when we both put in the same amount of effort. I got lost in the kiss, but instead of worrying about getting him hard, seducing him into the logical next step like every other interaction. This was pleasure in a soft way, pleasant, warm, like sitting near a fireplace. It felt like home. Eventually, we both pulled away, and we cuddled as we faced each other. I nestled into his chest as he ran his fingers along my braids. *This is such a lovely feeling, something I've never experienced. Headier than sex with someone I wasn't even that attracted to, and certainly had never loved. Lust? Sure. Lust had been the defining factor in all aspects of every other intimate encounter. That combined with how much I needed to fill a hole so deep in my heart that no one else knew existed. Well, Caroline and Flynn did. But I doubt others had noticed the cracks in that great wall I had built to protect myself. Metaphorically, of course. Imagine me trying to build a wall. Ha!*

We laid like that, both undoubtedly feeling very relaxed, until Flynn whispered, "I think we should go get Lydia. Because as lovely as that was, now that my mind is off of my brother... it's starting to run wild with what I'd like to do to you. Here and now."

I shivered as images of what that could look like came to mind, but instead of using my body and beguiling voice to make it happen, I shimmied out of the blankets and climbed out of bed. Flynn looked shocked that I had listened, and a part of me was as well. *But this man... I wanted to do things right with him. He was worth more than a cheap meaningless hook up. Far more. And so, I'd do the only thing I actually hadn't done with a man... I'd wait. Until our wedding night. The way Caroline had. It had worked out more than fine for her; she was living as close to a fairytale as a human possibly could. And sure, she's an incredible bright, sweetheart of a lass, but I have positives about me as well. They might run more sassy than sweet, but to each their own. Flynn loved me, what a wonderful thought to hold close to my heart. I think I've finally gotten to the point where I don't need someone to choose me to feel loved... but it certainly doesn't hurt that Flynn has proven time and again he's the staying type. I put him through the ringer. Not because I'm terrible, but those deep-seated insecurities... they controlled my thoughts, my actions, my beliefs about myself. They were so firmly entrenched that they had created this impenetrable barrier around my heart. Like the thorns on the loveliest of roses. And it was time. Time to take a thorn and leaf stripper to those pesky things stopping me from feeling the pleasure, when always before I'd only experienced the pain.* "Let's go hunky man of mine." I got up off the bed, and Flynn's face registered surprise, but also admiration. He obviously could tell how hard that had been to resist the urge to succumb to the sexiest of urges... but it wasn't the time. Nor the place. *If Caroline came home... Ha. I can imagine the look on her face as she would hurriedly rush out. Last time that happened we'd only been making out, on a couch. Not in bed. About to do far more.*

Flynn took my hand, gracefully jumping out of bed in a way that had me looking at him differently. *Has he always been this graceful and charming? Or have I been so focused on his sexy self that I hadn't thought too much about all of his other qualities? Interesting. I wonder what else there is to discover about my lad.*

With that thought, we both exited Caroline's old place (I forgot, she's been married a while now, this is no longer her room, just another beautiful empty place that the homeless of Lehavre is going to live in while Dante renovates those homes, he hasn't finished yet from all those fires by that bitch of an arsonist. Excuse my language. But seriously. She's an arsehole that ruined my first shop, until quite literally only ash and soot remained. I mean... I did get a far grander and luxurious shop custom-designed for me per King Ryan's request... but still. Awful woman). "Flynn, this isn't Caroline's room anymore. Right? I mean... they have their own far larger space for her, Ryan and the twins."

Flynn smirked a little, more mischievous than I was accustomed to, but it sent a thrill down my body. Especially accompanied by his words. "I was wondering when you'd notice that. For now, this room is vacant. Hence why there's no one needed to watch the door and it stays unlocked now. This room might even end up being my mom and her boyfriend's, if they end up getting married."

I opened my mouth a little, registering his words. Cocking my head a little to the side, I asked, "And would that be a positive or a negative in your eyes?"

Flynn gave me a smile. "Positive. It's sweet of you to be worried about me, but I have no attachment to my father. I don't hate the man, but the fact of the matter is that he chose to abandon me. This other guy, he might not ever be my 'father' but he seems to be a great father figure. Obviously, what's most important is how my mom feels 'bout the man. And boy, she loves him. So intensely. And I understand how much two people can love each other, and how it can create the most genuine and lasting of friendships, and then marriages."

I blushed, probably more crimson than I'd ever been before, because it takes a pretty extraordinary blush to register on my cheeks with my gorgeous coloring... but I felt it. The warmth from my cheeks burned right toward my heart. *If there were any thorns remaining as a last-ditch barricade around my heart... they were gone now. The ice queen was no more. I had felt the most pleasant sensation I could experience and nothing could compare. Not even the best wine in the world, combined with the most exotic and comforting of cheeses. That combination had always worked for me in the past. But this love that permeated my very soul, this was so very different than anything I'd ever experienced in my lifetime. Ever. Nothing even came close.* Looking into his eyes, I just had to say something, and nothing could express my feelings better than the most cliché of phrases. "I love you, Flynn."

Again, I had surprised him, but then it was his turn to surprise me. No sooner had those words come off my lips did Flynn pick me up in the air by my legs, right below my butt, hoisting me up so we were face to face, then he leaned in, obviously waiting before initiating, his way of asking for consent. This man was the complete opposite of the hit-it-and-quit-it type I had become so sadly accustomed to. I felt my eyes shining as I immediately devoured him with kisses, intermingling between sweet and soft with rough and desperate. He cupped my booty, I wrapped my arms around his neck, and we made out in the palace hallway. I was completely lost in the moment, and then I opened my eyes for a brief second... and his mom was right there. *Ohhhh joy.*

I whispered, "Flynn, Greta is behind you..." Flynn spun around, his hands still cupping my booty, as he quickly took on a look of bashful sweetness.

"Uh... Hi mom."

Greta tittered at us, then waved her hand. "You two look like you're already married. Not to rush you or anything, but if you do intend on having kids, it'd be nice to have some grandkids in the future."

"I definitely want kids. It'd practically be a sin not to with as much attractiveness as we both bring to the gene pool. If I'd known you were right there I would have been less... well..." *I wasn't known to mince words. But she was basically my mother-in-law at this point. And I was feeling a bit of embarrassment, when I hadn't felt that since my first male interaction... it was a bizarre feeling after so long.*

Greta's smile widened even more as she supplied, "Enthusiastic?" Flynn choked on a laugh, and Greta tsked. "Flynn my boy, don't let dear Donyelle handle this on her own." Then she directed her comments to us both, as Flynn finally seemed to regain control of his body as he eased me to the ground. "I happen to think love is the most special of all, and seeing you both fully in love with each other after this long while, seeing how you both gravitated toward each other even during the lowest points... I see you two as having the foundation necessary to be the kind of nurturing loving couple that my sweetheart and I are. And you even got engaged! Now, I think I can guess the answer, but are you thinking of having a short or long engagement?"

Flynn and I locked eyes for a second, both smiling at each other like lovestruck fools, then turned to his mom and answered as if with one voice, "Short." We locked eyes in surprise, laughing.

Greta laughed. "Oh goodness. Already speaking at the same time and everything. I'm so happy for you both; it's as if you are already married. What about little Lydia?"

Flynn looked to be deferring to me, so I spoke passionately. "Flynn and I haven't discussed it. If it were only my decision, I would want to adopt her. I don't know if it's even possible... certainly not easy, especially with a wanna-be mayor against us, yet when I look in her eyes... she mirrors the pain I used to feel. I have this longing feeling to provide her the stability and loving parents she so desperately craves. Better than who I am though. I want Flynn and I to be the kind of parents for Lydia that I had craved for as a child... and still wish for to this day."

Greta's eyes were welling up with tears as she rushed toward me, smothering me in her love. I could feel it radiating off her in waves, the same feeling I got when Caroline was around. "You dear, dear child. I am so very... I don't want to say sorry. That's what everyone says when they don't know what else to say. You deserve parents who adore you. Who helps you understand what's right and wrong, who would comfort you when you are hurt and challenge you when you needed guidance. If it's alright with you, I already consider you as a daughter. Not a daughter in law; a daughter. You and my son are blessed by our Lord to have found each other, enduring tribulations and working through the things that try to hold us back. It would be an honor to be a mother-like figure in your life. You are so loved. Not because of anything you did, not even because of who you are. You are loved by our Maker; He created you with a mighty destiny in mind. You don't know how your life touches others, but it does. Everyone has something that contributes. And dear, you have made my firstborn so very happy. Nothing lights up his face like seeing you smile; nothing storms it up like witnessing you cry or be frustrated. Remember to turn first to God, then to each other, and you will have all the pieces necessary to have the kind of marriage... the kind I had envisioned." Her voice turned pained, and I was the one to squeeze her.

"Greta, yes. I just want to say yes. You're the kind of mother I would want. You are supportive, funny, thoughtful. You know how to have fun and be vulnerable. You are strong, going through life as a single mother when someone else's choices made it impossible for you to stay married. You are a role model, and a great friend to me."

We were both a mess now, tears streaming down our faces, ruining the lovely makeup that had been there moments before. Flynn was sobbing quietly beside me, joining our hug until we all cried enough. Flynn whispered, "I must be the most blessed man I know. A mom who's so strong hearted and yet so tender, and a fiancé who brings color and vibrancy to my life, as well as all those around her. I agree with you Doni; I want nothing more than to be Lydia's father. She seems happy in our care, and she would absolutely be far safer with you and I than with that slimeball abusive piece of shit."

I am shocked to hear even that semi mild curse word fall from his lips, as Flynn is usually a very mild-mannered man. But it is obvious that when it comes to something as important as keeping a child safe, he can be trusted to stand up against evil and unrighteous people. There is something so comforting about knowing that he is like a sleeping lion. Docile and sweet while asleep, but when he was roused, for healthy reasons, not due to a bad temper, but against injustice, he would awake and be willing and able to roar and pounce if necessary. He really is my lion. And this side of him just made me love him all the more. Who knew you could love someone with more than your heart? My entire being loved this man. The safety and love I feel with him was astronomical. We pulled back from the hug as Greta smiled happily yet again. She really is one of the loveliest older women I knew. So joyful that the happiness and beauty within basically radiates out of her, enhancing her beauty until she all but shines. Greta sighed a bit wistfully. "Oh, to be young. If I was your age, I'd go right up to my boyfriend, kiss him just as intensely as you were going at it then, and I'd ask him to marry me on the spot."

Flynn gasped, "Mom!!"

But that got me thinking. "Why can't you?" I questioned.

Flynn turned horrified eyes to me as he begged, "Please, don't encourage her!"

I chuckled, but also buckled down. "Greta, there's no time limit on love. And especially with regards to romance. Because you are a little older, you know that much more that there's no time to waste. If you want to propose, what's stopping you?"

Greta clapped her hands together, looking a bit shy. "Nothing, except I'd want it to be very special. I had always fantasized about being the one to ask my love to marry me, but that wasn't what was done back when I was dating. Is that... is that okay nowadays?"

"Who cares if it is or not? It's what you want to do. The worst he can do is say no or tell you he wants to be the one to ask you. As long as your heart is prepared for those possibilities; I say go for it! You spent your life for your kids, and they were very lucky to have that much sacrifice. But it's your turn. Your time! And I just happen to have a fantastically romantic idea for your proposal, if you're serious. Though... drat." I pulled a face as I realized the hindrance to my plan.

Flynn asked, "What's wrong Doni?"

I sighed, putting a hand on Flynn's arm. "I just looked at the video cameras today, there's still a bunch of protestors with nothing else to do but picket my business. And that's where I wanted your mom to have her special moment."

Flynn suddenly hit his forehead with his right hand, the one I wasn't touching, and I jolted by the random act. "Oh my *gosh*! Of course!!! The cameras! That's all we need!!" Both Greta and I looked at Flynn, completely lost. "Right." He said as he sheepishly looked at us. "So, you know how I had those cameras installed? I'm not saying I told you so... but they finally are going to come in handy. We must have a video of Lydia coming to your store. Proof that she was abused before she came near us. That would stop the naysayers and should help our case to win custody of Lydia. Though of course we aren't related in any way... but it should show that there's at the very least suspicion that her biological father is abusive. That and the findings by Doctor Cornelius, plus the website with Marley's pictures of all your hard work... Doni, I think you are going to have an influx of customers here soon!"

I cheered, Greta was shining with pride, but then Flynn's smile drooped. "I forgot... Robbie's death anniversary. I should check on Ariana. She's still so rocked by his sudden passing..."

My hand on my beloved's arm rubbed him up and down slowly as I whispered, "How about I go check on Ariana for you, I'll give her someone to talk to while you get the footage figured out. Then we can talk to Caroline and Ryan's uh... I forgot what her title is, but she handles all media related things. She'll know how to clear our names."

Flynn physically sagged with relief; I could even feel it under my fingertips. *Poor sweet man, trying to handle too many things he didn't have the bandwidth for.* Greta turned somber as well at the mention of our departed friend. Robbie had left such an impression on everyone, it was like we could physically feel his lack of presence, even a full year later. I kissed Flynn chastely on the cheek, Greta's lip twitching into the barest of smiles, as I headed toward where I *hoped* was Ariana's salon. *Better to get this handled now, when I felt so much love and encouragement it wrapped around me like a blanket freshly warmed from a dryer. That was the best way to go into a conversation that was going to cause sadness. All the negative feelings, honestly.* I reached Ariana's salon after many twists and turns, (I seriously got lost there for a good ten or so minutes), and it was all for nothing, because in the end she wasn't even there. There was a note that read:

If anyone cares, I'm at the Emernoque Lagoon. Please don't come to find me unless it's important. Schedule your hair styling another day. -Ariana.

Where in the heck is the Emernoque Lagoon? I pulled out my phone, typing it into google maps. *A full hour and forty minutes away. Lovely. Of course she'd go to the middle of nowhere to grieve. Fine. That must be pretty close to Langford.* I followed the GPS instructions, and in just under an hour and thirty minutes, because I went just above the speed limit the whole way, I found the place. And I saw only two cars were parked in this little place, such a tiny area it barely counted as a true parking lot. Gathering my courage, I followed what looked to be a trail, wondering internally why I even needed to gather courage in the first place. *Why am I a bit uneasy being here? Is it the fact that I've never been, that it seems desolate, or because I'm wondering who had brought that other car up here? Who knows.* I went against my instincts, and I continued, and suddenly I heard a light breathy voice speaking. "He was, you know. I'm glad to hear that you knew how funny he was. We weren't together long... but I just felt... I don't even know how to describe it."

Who is she talking to?

"Magnetism maybe? Curiosity because he was a handsome man, so sure of himself, a little rough around the edges, but a good heart." *Hang on... that's a male voice! Why does that sound so much like Caroline's brother? Surely, he wouldn't be in the middle of nowhere with Ariana...*

"You get me. And him. You always have. That's what's so amazing about you Aaron-" *Holy... that is Aaron! Caroline's brother is with Ariana! Does Caroline know? Does Aaron have a thing for Ariana? If so, how long has this been going on??* "Even though you admitted you like me, you are still willing to talk about him. And let me process his passing. Even when I told you I need more time to heal... you are just – so incredible."

I moved a bit closer, wanting to witness this interesting conversation firsthand. I was shocked to see that this seemingly desolate-looking place from that supposed parking lot had hidden a little slice of heaven back here. It helped of course that the sun was setting, causing the sky to turn a radiant mix of purple, pink, and orange, but the lake was so still, so peaceful, the colors of the sky were mirrored in its shimmering depths. And the snow-covered mountains on the left combined with the darker trees on the right, both on the other side of the lake, while the space was surrounded by the most cheerful flowers; it was nothing short of majestic. *Later, when I am not witnessing a possible love confession, I will have to come admire and take stock of all the numerous flowers this hidden gem possesses. But right now...* Aaron was standing over a kneeling Ariana, he was rubbing her back, her red hair even more luminescent in the rapidly descending sun's light. *They look like an actual post card. One modeled for romance; the sweet kind instead of the harlequin type.*

Aaron had his eyes closed, but he spoke with tenderness, "Thank you Ari. I mean it though. I have nothing but time- I will continue to live my life, but I can stay loyal waiting for you to heal. I just didn't want you to feel pressured. You are allowed to grieve Robbie as long as you need. Grieving is not a linear process. I lost a close friend, and sometimes I feel that ache at his loss over the randomest of things. A song on the radio. A movie we used to quote for inside jokes... The grief of loss never completely goes away. It just... fades. With time it becomes less sharp. Less of an ever-present sting. Eventually it becomes a dull ache. At times you might not even remember or think about him, then something happens that brings it all rushing back, and you might feel like you're right back to where you started. My mom wasn't always the kindest woman, but she gave me a piece of wisdom when she said, 'grief is not linear'. I was so upset when I had felt like I was finally past the throes of pain when Min-Sik had died over five years ago... and then I saw a man who looked similar to my best friend, and I completely lost it. Mom taught me that grief is not a one-time event. It comes and goes, ebbing and flowing like waves. Instead of fighting it, I chose to embrace it, remembering what made Min-Sik such a special friend. All those times he would come play Grand Theft Auto, when we'd rock out doing Guitar Hero. And when we came to this spot. His mom was wealthy, very much so, so even though Henry had been oh so against anyone but white people, he'd allowed Min-Sik's parents to live in Langford. So, I met him when mom had decided Langley wasn't good enough for us. Thankfully though, I met Min-Sik when I was out exploring the town. He invited me into his home, I met his parents Min-Jun, his father, and Min-Hae, his mother. Plus, his adorable tiny baby sister at the time, Min-Ae-cha. I felt so welcomed, so completely like family immediately. It's what set me on the path of missions' work. Plus learning little bits of their language, hearing how the names are different than ours, like the family name is first, then the name that they go by is second- I wanted to spend every minute with them. And so, Min-Sik brought me to this hidden oasis. So few know about it, and I was let into the special little group of people who know about this place's existence. It's where I go when I feel the need to grieve. There's nothing quite like being here. I can almost palpably hear his voice, the laugh that could pull me out of any funk I was in, the quotes – famous movies both in Korean and in English; his accent was wonderfully thick, but he could speak English remarkably well too. His family... I visit them every time I come here." I was in awe of how much Aaron had just spoken. Not that he'd ever been deemed a quiet child, but still, that was a whole 'nother side I was seeing in a guy I'd felt like was an honorary brother for basically my whole life. Ariana turned her angelic head up toward Aaron, giving him a dazzling smile, just in time as Aaron opened his eyes. I heard his breath catch; he was that entranced.

"Thank you, Aaron. Min-Sik sounds like an incredible person. I am honored you chose to share your reflection spot with me. And allowing me a space, your space, to feel my feelings regarding my ex... I don't know what to say. It's just... it's a big gesture. And it's really appreciated." Aaron softly massaged Ariana's scalp as she sighed with contentment, closing her eyes and just soaking in the moon's beam. It was so precious a moment that I felt I should not interrupt it. *I'll just let Flynn know that Ariana is doing okay despite the circumstances.* I slowly and silently pivoted my feet, taking care not to make any sudden movements and staying out of their eyeline, as quiet as I could possibly be. Painstakingly, I finally made it back to my car. Apparently, I didn't have any service in that tranquil place (perhaps that's part of why the place was so tranquil) because my phone practically exploded as fifteen messages and four missed calls suddenly assaulted my phone. *What in the...*

Five texts from Flynn, asking how Ariana was doing, thanking me for volunteering to help his mom propose, another telling me how much he admired me and was so excited to see me as a mother, and then two telling me about the videos- first, he had them, second, call him to set up a time for us all to go to my business, currently surrounded by very angry people waving all kinds of hateful signs. Some were just straight up hate-speech, many were slamming us for abuse and child abduction/endangerment.

A ton of the texts were from Caroline, Ahyoka, Greta, everyone checking on me. But Marely had also reached out, asking when she could take pictures for the website spread. The other voicemails were from Ryan and an unknown number, Seraphina, the royal couple's publicist. She determined after speaking with Flynn and attempting to reach out to me that she was calling an emergency press conference at my place of business in order to show the proof from the security cameras and be able to expose the mayoral candidate for his corruption and deceit. She uses fancier words than I do, but the same message remains. I also noticed a text audio message from an unknown number, and something about it set my hackles up, so I decided not to touch play. *Wait until I'm near Flynn. Use his phone to record it, since it seems to be one of those messages that delete themselves after a short time once the clip is played.* So that's what I did. I called Flynn, putting it on speaker as I discussed what I'd witnessed between Aaron and Ariana without going into depth about their private sweet moment. *Let that be special between the two of them, especially since it seemed like it was only just possibly beginning.* Then he gave me updates about the videos. "It shows everything. In horrifying detail. But Lydia is already covered in bruises and scars, and she already has the gash on her head even... it's awful, it'll turn anyone's stomach... but it's the truth. And it proves that the senator is a liar. And hopefully we can pin it on him, maybe finagle a confession. No matter what though, we can state to the audience that will surely be there that we are willing to fight for full custody of Lydia, and that her safety will always be our first priority. That's been proven as we allowed character defamation and you to lose so much business. But I think we have a really solid case. Sebastian sent me the contact information for the perfect kind of child custody lawyer we need, so if you're serious; we are ready to do this."

"I have never been more serious about anything, that much I am sure of. Let's do it. All of it. Protect Lydia, figure out how to have her be our child, and clear our names. In that order."

I could hear the smile in his voice as he told me, "I love your determined voice. It's extra sexy. Okay- it's as good as done. How far away are you from your shop?"

"Well... about an hour more at this point. We've been talking a lot, but it's a long drive."

"No problem. Let's do this; meet me at the castle please, and we'll all go together. Ryan and Caroline plus Seraphina are coming as well. And Sebastian is flying in, plus Ahyoka, Whitney and Dante plan to come too, Lily and my mom is going to watch Lydia, as well as the twins, Logan and Bobby-Jean."

My heart swelled at how many people were not only willing to - beyond a shadow of a doubt - just believe us, but also were willing to also go to bat for us, coming to the scene of a potentially unsafe situation. *After all, there's a reason none of the kids are coming to this press conference. It could get very messy. Since that pig is willing to hurt his own daughter, especially to the level she is with so many scars and who knows how much pain he inflicted over her young life... he would certainly not flinch to harm any of us. Potentially... he might even try to end our lives.* Ryan had that in mind though, as he instructed his fifty or so guards (a lot more than I'd ever seen before) dressed in regular clothing instead of armor, to blend in with the crowd. To fully surround the mayoral candidate especially, in case things turn ugly. *Thank goodness the King isn't just there for eye candy. Though he is very... but anyway, I'm a happily engaged woman, and Ryan is married to my sister from another mister. Gross. I take that back, even in my mind, that's a phrase I don't need to ever repeat.*

We headed out to the insane fray – the senator in question was up on a podium he seemed to have had erected just for this moment. *But that makes sense, he seemed to be the pompous arrogant arsehole narcissist that would want to be up higher than everyone else. Quite literally looking down on the people around him. Yuck.* He was, as we had expected, trying to fan the flames of discontent in the crowd, making us out to be the worst kind of monsters. I ignored him, moving with Flynn and our group of friends toward the front of his created stage.

His face was half sneer-half snarl as he pointed an accusing finger our way. "There they are- the ones that kidnapped my precious girl. Your Highness, your Majesty; how do you plan to punish your two subjects for taking Lydia from me?!"

A quick glance a little to my left showed that Ryan was furiously clenching his right fist, and Caroline was whispering in his ear, placing her hand on top of his fist as he began to relax it. *I wonder what she said.* Whatever it was, it was effective. Ryan even managed to smile, all trace of his previous anger completely gone, as he spoke. "We are indeed here to right the wrongs done to Lydia. And believe me, the guilty party will pay, dearly."

The senator looked appeased, as if Ryan had agreed to punish us for wrongdoing. *Obviously, he hadn't read between the lines and realized Ryan never stated who he was talking about.* That's clever!

Suddenly the girl that I had been jealous of when I saw her near Flynn moved through the throng of people chanting our downfall and waving their signs. She seemed wholly unbothered by the crowd, other than a quick roll of the eyes. She had in her hands a small laptop and something else. Suddenly, in front of us all, on the outdoor walls of my store, there was projected the feed from my security cameras. And just as suddenly, a pixie-looking person was holding a microphone and speaking above the chaos. "What you are about to see is the truth of what happened to Lydia; watch closely so you know who the culprit is." Now, I know that my cameras didn't capture who hurt Lydia. But it would show that it wasn't Flynn and me.

Many of the reporters that had been viciously against us, a good deal of the crowd as well, froze as they watched the truth unfold before their eyes. It was unmistakable. I had forgotten just how bad Lydia had looked, so run down, coated in both dried crusty dark red old and bright red new, blood. I'd never actually seen this before, and it physically hurt my heart to see the child that had become like a pseudo daughter staggering around, swaying like she was drunk, due to lack of blood, malnutrition and exhaustion. We all watched with bated breath, able to see even more clearly as she came closer to where the cameras were perched. The huge gash in her skull, even some of the cigarette burns and discoloration from bruises showed up in high definition.

Lydia started audibly gasping for air, a little at first, but by the time she was limping past my shop, it was apparent that the labor of breathing and moving was becoming too much. Suddenly, she tripped over her own legs in the recording. A loud collective gasp sounded around the area as we watched with horror as that frail little body collided with my window. Even with that security bar on, somehow, she crashed into it at just the right angle, and because it was tempered glass due to being so close to the stairs and ramp... it shattered into far too many pieces.

Lydia let out a wail that felt like it shattered my eardrums, not to mention it made me feel so incredibly bad. I watched as she shook her head multiple times, flinching and groaning out in animalistic pain, as she surveyed her surroundings in the dimly lit room.

It wasn't too long after this that I heard Flynn and myself on the video monitor. *Is that really what I sound like recorded? Gross! But... so not the point.* The rapt attention of everyone was still on the screen as Lydia seemed to have heard our approach. She grabbed one of the few large pieces of glass that remained, the one she'd been holding when we first encountered her.

It is surreal to see yourself in a different perspective like this. I'm not sure what I thought I looked and sounded like through another's eyes and ears, but I guess this is the closest I've come to that. How odd. I honestly don't remember how we coaxed Lydia to come with us. I felt a tiny chuckle threatening to come out of my throat as I cheerfully told Lydia she could hit Flynn with the hammer if she felt threatened. But for the most part I did an okay job at helping the little girl to feel at ease. And thank goodness for that, because now she was as close to my daughter as I've ever felt about a child. Who knows if I had taken a different approach if things would have been the same or wildly different.

That little girl, the one on the screen clutching anything that made her feel a tiny bit safer back then; she changed me. It was so subtle and so instantaneous I didn't recognize it was happening, but it was a certainty. Something about Lydia had made me act different. More open. More honest with others but also, arguably more importantly, with myself. Not only the first interaction, where I was vulnerable in a way I never had been before, but also with Flynn.

How long had I led Flynn on this not-so-merry goose chase? And yet, it was right there on the screen- his love for me was written across his features, so obvious that perhaps even a blind person would discern it. But only, I notice, when I wasn't looking his direction. The second I had turned toward him, he was back to smiling, sweet, carefree Flynn. And that... that made me feel like he really and truly respected me. He knew, or at least he thought he knew, that the depth of his feelings made me uncomfortable, and while in actuality that wasn't the case; he was rearranging his expression for me. To put me at ease. To soften the pressure of his heart being so set on me.

I will never fall out of love with him. I will choose him forever. I'm certain of that. And finally, I'm not consumed with worrying about being abandoned. Flynn will stay. I'm like... eighty one percent certain. And that's incredibly high odds for me.

Everyone stood there in stunned silence, except the Mayor who was fumbling to turn this around on us. I fully tuned him out though, because apparently Seraphina wasn't done. She stated with confidence, "Now you know how Lydia came to be with Ms. Donyelle Cox and Mr. Flynn Levisay. Now I direct your attention back to the screen one last time, for we have footage of who actually committed what the Senator mentioned as atrocious acts and heinous crimes." And suddenly, Senator Strawfeld blanched. He looked so pale, so shaken. I noticed how he was beginning to attempt to descend his ridiculous podium, but Ryan's plainclothesmen were ready for it, they caught him by his arms and held him still as he protested how important he was and someone must have doctored the footage. Since he was freaking out so easily, those that had been chanting and waving signs were beginning to look uneasy. Finally, they were starting to see the Senator in a new light. Not so assured. The fake bravado was gone, and all he cared about was what was truly in his heart – his own self-preservation. I waited for the clip to be shown, trying to emotionally prepare myself for seeing something that would undoubtedly boil my blood even further until I was like molten lava. And yet... nothing played. And suddenly, the Senator attempted to pull himself together, acting offended. "I knew it! You couldn't even doctor the footage well enough to attempt to pin such a crime on me!"

Sebastian took the microphone Seraphina offered to him wordlessly, as he stated, "Those who know me know I have a particular fondness for kids." *That's for sure. How many orphanages and homes for children with extra-large families had he personally funded at this point? Must be over a dozen at least.* "We don't have footage of Senator Strawfeld abusing Lydia. But I will leave it up to you to determine how his reaction swayed you if he is guilty or not. We do have one more clip to show you, and it's live. We are not going to subject a young child to seeing a potentially suspected abuser, so she is filming at a different location with the King's mother." That was actually a surprise to me, and I was torn between pride for my surrogate daughter and a little anger that I was not included in this discussion to determine if Lydia should speak on her abuse. *She is just a child, after all.*

Yet Lydia looked much older as she came into focus. Lily was sitting beside her, holding a microphone so everyone could hear. Her lovely voice was more solemn than I'd ever heard before. "Lydia, please tell me about your owies."

Lydia looked sad as she said softly, just loud enough for the microphone to catch, "Owies hurt. Here, here, here-" She kept pointing out each one, and my eyes welled up with tears. She started to talk about how her dad hurt her, and I just couldn't handle it. I wanted to cover my ears. Wanted to stick my head somewhere I could hide until she was done recounting everything... and yet this was her story. What she had survived. *How tough is this little one. Forced to never get the childhood every child should be allowed to cherish.* When it was finally over, Senator Strawfeld was taken away. He was cursing us all and shouting at the once adoring crowd to stand up for him, for justice. But no longer were they on his side, as they began to boo in unison, turning all their hate from us to him.

Flynn gave me an adoring look as he asked, "Are you going to open up your business today?"

I shook my head. I told him, "I want to find out how to adopt Lydia. Whatever the steps are, I want to get the process started. The sooner the better!"

Chapter 9
DOUBLE THE SURPRISES

Donyelle's POV:

It's been a little over a week, and a lot has transpired. My business has been absolutely booming. I had to hire on a bunch more help; between the extremely professional and eye-catching website combined with the professionalism it projected, as well as the news report showing everyone how we were falsely accused... well, that caused some very guilty-feeling people to open up their hearts... but especially their wallets. In just a week I had already made more than enough to do what I'd set my mind to the very first time I'd gotten in Flynn's car... and it was going to coincide with the other planned surprise. Greta was finally going to propose to her man. I had everything as ready as it could ever be. I nudged Flynn with my elbow as we stood on my shop's roof taking in my fine work. "If the man still says no, just based off your mother's supreme goodness and the most romantic of locations created expressly for this moment... he's an idiot. And he doesn't deserve her."

Flynn's lips quirked as he answered immediately, "I whole-heartedly agree. You've made nothing short of a masterpiece."

I nodded, happy with his response, happier still when he wrapped his arms around me, trailing kisses up the side of my neck from my collarbone to my scalp. I shivered, amazed at how my body thrilled at even his slight touch, only the very beginning of foreplay. I never thought I'd get this excited over something so simple, sweet even. I was used to the heady pleasure of going all the way... but that momentary ecstasy was almost immediately replaced by that gnawing sense of abandonment. *Flynn brought out something in me I didn't know I possessed. I had a soft side. I craved his tender touch. I thought I had enjoyed it rough, being in charge... but this felt undeniably better. I couldn't fully wrap my head around it, but it was true, and it was wonderful.*

I let out a small moan, which had him sighing, "Mmm. I love that sound." I grinned, thinking him a bit cheesy. *But apparently, I like that. Or I just like him so much that I like it when he does it anyway. Interesting concept.*

I grinned widely, so beyond excited to show him the ultimate surprise. I turned around, which had his eyes widening, obviously wondering if I was going to try to get more intimate. But for once, that was not what was on my mind. I took out my phone, and I saw Flynn's eyes downcast as he tried to hide his disappointment. *Silly man, I'm not prioritizing my phone over you. Just you wait and see!* I sent the text in the group thread, then I pushed my phone back into my *very tight* jean front pocket. I was so happy that even tight jeans couldn't ruin the mood. Especially when I started to hear it.

Flynn perked up immediately. "Whoa, that's the prettiest sound I've heard in my life. That's got to be the Chevy Corvette. I think it's even a Z06 model!! It sounds so new like... 2024, maybe even a 2025!"

He is right, but there is no way I am going to admit it! That would completely ruin the surprise I'd been hatching with Ryan and even Dante for this whole week. I knew what Flynn's secret heart's desire was. He was too sacrificial and thoughtful to splurge on himself unlike how he was about myself and Lydia, but he deserved to be doted on just as much as us. He was the kind of man any woman would be blessed to be partnered with; and I want him to know that. And while material possessions aren't the most important in the world, the fact is he desperately needs a new car. The one he and his mom affectionately dubbed 'Old Faithful' was anything but. It was starting to stall at every intersection, and the noises had grown to such a crescendo it was a complete wonder it hadn't blown up underneath him at this point. Besides, I did my research. Ryan showed me what Flynn had paid to cover my medical bills and to establish the website. And I had a savings tucked away, and especially with the exorbitant number of tips and business that was pouring in from the whole kingdom and beyond who were trying to right their wrongs for picketing my business before... I was wealthier than I'd ever been. *So why not share the wealth with the man only dreams could create? I had plenty left over, even though I will admit the car is spendy. It's sleek, its sexy, but... it's just a car. I don't get car-lust like most guys seem to. However, I do very much want to honor, support, and bless my man. And this is a very special way to do that, something that he won't soon forget.*

I honestly don't get the allure of spending over a hundred thousand dollars on just a vehicle... I could think of so many different things I could do with that money that would feel much more like an investment... more worthwhile. I mean, when you think about it, you don't need something super fancy when all it needs to do is get you from point a to point b. But Flynn... he doesn't prioritize much in this world possessions-wise; so why not bless him with the luxury car he's always wanted?

Just then, Ryan was parking at the base of my shop and Flynn's eyes opened extremely wide. "Ryan bought a Chevrolet Corvette Z06?!" He took off at a sprint toward the door leading downstairs, before stopping in his tracks and turning back toward me, offering his hand. "Sorry Doni, I didn't mean to forget you." His voice and expression were sheepish, but I just chuckled.

"It's fine babe, I know you want to see the car. Go ahead."

I had surprised him, that much was obvious from his expression. He took another second to fully process what I'd said, then he rushed down the stairs as if he was escaping a fire. It was pretty impressive just how agile and quick he truly was. It even turned me on a bit, seeing how passionate he was. *And he still thinks that this car is his best friend's. I can't wait to see when he figures out the car he'd dreamed about for so long (obviously a different year, this was the 2025, the most up-to-date and luxurious model created).* I picked up my own pace, not wanting to miss out on that moment; *it will be seared in my brain forever, I just know it.*

Before too long, I had also reached the bottom, going out the side door. Following the excited sounds, I was quickly able to discover the guys. Flynn and Ryan were inspecting the vehicle, using all kinds of words and phrases that may as well have been Greek but they fully understood and fed of each other's energy. *It's fascinating, watching how two fully grown men, mostly pretty reserved, pretty calm... completely lose it over a shiny sportscar. Sure, it's beautiful. But calling it 'sexy'? Really? It's a car. Simple as that. It's a shiny fancy-looking method of transportation.*

Flynn turned around to me as he gestured for me to come closer. "Doni, you won't believe the interior of this beauty!! Come feel how soft the seats are, soak up the new-car smell."

I grinned, following his lead. I let him and Ryan continue to go on and on about all the features of this spiffy car that I gladly tuned out. *Flynn's happy, that's all that matters. And he was happy without actually knowing it was his yet. Part of me wants to wait until he deduces that for himself, while the other part really wants to blurt it out. I am so bad at secrets, it's not even funny. Caroline could, Ahyoka was the queen of confidences... but me... I feel an instinctual need to share what I know, and that is that much more tempting with the knowledge that Flynn is absolutely going to be blown away. He probably wouldn't be able to utter a word. And the thrill through my body is reminding me that I can't wait much longer. I need to see how he will react.*

"Want to take it for a test drive?" Ryan encouraged, causing a chill of frustration to run through me. But only for a second. Ryan was instrumental in helping me know which make and model to get, after all. Ryan might as well have asked Flynn if he wanted to explore a distant planet.

Flynn's face showed more excitement than a posse of children at Christmas as he asked with awe, "Can I really?!" Ryan grinned and shrugged.

"It's not up to me. You'll have to ask Donyelle."

I leaned into Flynn's back, feeling his superb muscles as I snaked my arms from behind to his chest. He leaned back into me, as he cupped the back of my head. I leaned up just a little to make up for the height difference as I brought my lips close to his ear, hovering just above without actually touching, it was partially damaged, after all. Although I couldn't see his face from my position, I could completely picture his smile shifting to shock and confusion.

I felt his heart rapidly accelerate at my actions, I felt and heard his gasp as he immediately turned astonished eyes to me. "Doni... did you rent this car for me?"

I couldn't help but let out a high-pitched giggle. "You're only partly right. This car is for you – but I didn't rent it. You are now the proud owner of this... whatever it was called. I honestly don't remember. But this is your car now babe. I love you!"

Ryan was smiling beside his friend, clapping his hand on Flynn's back as he was prone to do, congratulating Flynn on getting the car he worked so hard for. Flynn didn't seem to be able to compute. He asked about how much was owed on the car, what the monthly payment was. Ryan answered, "It's paid in full my man. And before you pour all your gratitude on me, all I did was hand the money to the dealership. Your fiancé was the one who pooled together the capital. All in cash too; she is one incredible businesswoman. It's paid outright, no monthly car payment, no debt."

"No... no debt?" Flynn echoed, total disbelief in his tone.

I volunteered, moving over just a little so I could see both Ryan and Flynn, "Well, you'll have to sort out your car insurance. I imagine with something that quick and sleek it'll be a pretty penny. But other than that, you're free and clear."

Flynn shook his head. Multiple times. I thought he was about to argue with me, but then I noticed he was trying to stop the liquid pooling in his tear ducts. "Thank you... that's not nearly enough to just say that. This is the biggest thing you could have possibly done for me. And you didn't have to. You know I love you regardless of if you spend money on me or not. And wow... this must have been a very hefty sum. I'm honored. Humbled, but honored. I just have to ask; are you in a financial place where this car is actually feasible? While I very much want to accept it, and I'll happily pay it back in installments, first we need to make sure that you have more than enough to make ends meet."

I felt the smile overtake my face. "Thanks to you, the whiz kid, and Marley, my business is fully flourishing. The website brings new clientele hourly it seems like. Plus, I'm riding the high of basically everyone in and outside of the kingdom thinking the worst of us, then feeling guilty about it. The best way to assuage their guilt is to buy a lot of things and patron my store. Even with two dozen helpers I am paying to help, keeping up on the workload currently is tricky, but also enjoyable and fulfilling. I could pay for your car at least two times over. Besides-" *I want to tell him this is a wedding gift... but suddenly I'm not feeling quite as carefree. We just got engaged. What if he doesn't want a wedding right away? What if he was dreaming up this gigantic fancy thing, I don't want to ruin his expectations, just because I selfishly don't want to wait!* So, not sure how to phrase the desires of my heart, I finished sort of lamely, "You paid my hospital bills and for my website. So please, just accept it."

Flynn seemed overcome with emotion, gratitude clear on his face, as he turned clockwise to face me, putting his hands to my face, then kissing me, filled with passion and need. I eagerly returned the thank you kiss, until Flynn and I remembered Ryan was there, smiling while looking away. *Oops. Talk about embarrassing!*

Ryan waited until we had disentangled before his easy smile widened. "Glad you guys are happy. Now Flynn, Donyelle, Caroline and I love you. And you know how Caroline loves to match-make.

So, she wanted me to show you this; then you guys can decide what you want to do from there."

Confusion registered on Flynn's face, and mine mirrored his. *This wasn't part of the plan; what did Caroline have up her sleeve?* Ryan pulled out his phone and pushed play, and suddenly Caroline's bright sunny face cheered, "Don, Flynn, you both are such wonderful people. Your love is an inspiration to those that have gone through numerous ups and downs, yet you are now stronger than ever and on the same page." As she paused, I snuck a peek at the King who was holding the phone. His loving smile for even his wife's recording was plain to see. *He really was the one meant for my bestie. And Flynn...* my eyes searched for his next, only to find they were on me, with a slight smirk on his face, obviously noticing I'd not been fully paying attention to the video either. Caroline continued, "Greta mentioned that you had set up the roof of your place for a romantic proposal. Sooo... and I'm just offering this as an option, with no pressure backing it up. You both *could* have a romance induced wedding... right here, right now. But again; no one needs you to say yes. Completely up to you whether you do or don't want that. I just-" Caroline winked in the video, then she continued happily, "I just want you both two be happy. You two and Lydia. Whatever that looks like."

I whispered, not even waiting for the end of the video, "I want to marry you. Now. I secretly wanted to give this car to you as a wedding gift."

Flynn suddenly looked over-the-moon excited, but this time, not about the car. In fact, he completely turned his back on the luxury vehicle to wrap me into a hug and then shocked me by lifting me very high in the hair, almost above his shoulders. *Whoa – my man is* buff. *How did I not know he could do this??* He lowered me slowly, as if he barely registered I was currently in his arms. Once we were nose-to-nose, he still didn't set me down all the way. When he moved his face closer, I eagerly took his lips with mine. *I was always better at show more than tell...* I let my body express how much I loved him, while still keeping things clean enough to not make Ryan jealous. *After all, my lovemaking is top tier. Or... that isn't really the right way to describe it though, is it? What I'd had in the past... that hadn't been actual love. This though; I feel this in every inch of my body, but where I really feel it is my mind. Not my heart, as I had expected. But as we are kissing, feeling myself still levitated off the ground, I know I am safe. Cared for. That this man will be the one that stays. That peace, that certainty, is washing over me like the warmest and most pleasurable wave of ecstasy that has my body, my everything, craving for more.* But yet I forced myself to hold back, and Flynn noticed immediately as he lightly set me down completely. His eyes, normally brown, almost looked cinnamon; lit up with the afterglow of our moment and my confession. He held my hand to his cheek as he asked, "Doni, are you sure? You'd be sacrificing the white wedding, getting to design an elaborate bouquet and whatever else bride-to-be's get. The bachelorette party -will you miss not having that opportunity when we've been married for a decade or two?"

Feeling blissfully happy in a way I simply never had before, I answered with complete honesty. "I was not looking forward to most of what makes up a traditional wedding, to be up front with you. Everyone would notice what I try so hard to hide – that I don't have a dad to walk me down the aisle. You know my... uhm... my colorful past with the lads of this kingdom... if we had a wedding inviting people from the four provinces and even beyond... well, I imagine numerous people in the crowd would smirk at the image of me in a white dress. I don't fit that chastity vow; that ship has long since sailed. I don't have a ton of true friends; just Care and Ahyoka really, so I wasn't thrilled at showing that I don't have a ton of people to stand beside me. But none of that matters more than the fact that I want to marry you. Have you be mine and me be yours. Forever and always. But know this Flynn, and I sincerely don't mean this as a threat or ultimatum; but if you marry me, barring you transforming into an evil monster or a right git, you've got me for life. So be sure that's actually what you want. Do you want to spend the rest of our time doing life together?"

I knew the answer, even without him opening his mouth. *Talented lad, this one. His eyes; the muscles in his face; every twitch of his body- it foretold that there was nothing Flynn wanted more than to not only marry me but to be with me till the end. Not many could say the same! My man is just that incredible.* I put my finger to his lips, as I smiled. "I already got your answer. No going back now." He grinned, his lips moving my finger as he smiled so hard it must have hurt. But yet he didn't wince, didn't seem to feel anything but the ecstasy we shared during that kiss, if his face was any indication.

"Oh good! I do love a wedding, don't you *Oginalii*?" Caroline appeared from behind a placement of flowers I'd designed, fittingly, in the shape of a heart. Just behind her was Ahyoka, and they were both beaming with intense excitement, so radiant in their beauty.

"I certainly do, Caroline. Oh Donyelle; I'm so glad we get to witness this!" Ahyoka, ever the calm and serene one, gushed with happiness while still maintaining an enviable amount of serenity. *Goodness, she is a true vision of beauty and grace. Ah, and my dear Caroline. No one like her in this world. All light, sunshine bubbliness, sometimes a little over-the-top, but a heart big enough to burst, and just as selfless.*

"It does have a certain poetry to it that the one that paired us together would be here for the wedding vows. But tell me Care, what was your plan if we didn't marry today?"

Caroline looked down sheepishly, then tilted her chin, look-ing utterly adorable. Dazzling us with a smile she answered, "Oh, I was like ninety-eight percent sure you both would be all about our plan... but in the very unlikely two percent chance you weren't ready... well, A and I were going to hide behind the flowers until you left."

Flynn burst out laughing, and Caroline took on a wounded ex-pression that was obviously forced. Ryan immediately stated, "Hey!

Don't tease my Queen." And it would have been a lot more believable that Ryan actually meant what he was saying... if he wasn't silently laughing, holding his hand to his mouth immediately after coming to her defense.

Caroline put up a finger to scold her husband, and Ryan quickly pulled her into a side hug. The instant they touched, they melted into each other, as if they had become one person. It was adorable, but like... in a sickening way. "Alright, you two had your moment, now Flynn and I will have ours. But who will do the ceremony? Doesn't it have to be an official of some kind?"

"I believe a King does count as an official. However, to be doubly sure, I became ordained so that I can marry people in my spare time. It'll come in real handy too; all that time I spend in those senior care centers; you wouldn't believe how many grown folks want to get hitched. It's... it's a lot."

Now it was my turn to laugh. Once we got it out of our systems, we witnessed the reason I had created all the flower decor on the roof in the first place. I heard Marko, and even without seeing him, I could hear the smile in his voice, "Greta; my sweet, this is such a lovely surprise. I thought you wanted to buy flowers; but climbing to the roof? What, you want to sneak a kiss beneath the twilight? You know I'll happily oblige!"

I saw Flynn's little grimace, before he grinned. *It can't be easy hearing his mom having a relationship, but also, he probably is extremely happy for her as well. Probably combined with being mildly embarrassed. While he fully supported his mother's possible marriage, hearing about kissing and... other things, well, that would make me feel squeamish too if it were my parents. I imagine. Or maybe not; but my experience is so radically dissimilar. If I saw my parents making out, I think I'd just be thrilled they were in my life at all. But perhaps the excitement of them being there wouldn't outweigh the embarrassment for those that could take having their families around forever for granted. Hmm. Interesting thought.*

I was still in my thoughts as Marko and Greta finally came into view. Marko, ever the gentleman, was holding Greta's hand, escorting her up the stairs. Greta was in the lead, as Marko liked to ensure happened, and his eyes were only for her... until he noticed the small audience. "Oh; hello everyone! I don't know what you saw or heard... but I'm not ashamed of a moment of it! Not a gosh dang moment. Greta is the finest woman this side of the world, and I don't care who knows it!"

Flynn smiled genuinely at his potential stepfather. "I think that's all a son could hope for. My mom means the world to me; and while my father didn't treat her with the respect and dignity she deserved; I am glad you do, Marko."

Greta's boyfriend shed a tear, something I was starting to realize was more normal than media at large had made it seem. His look of relief was palpable. "That's right good to hear, Flynn. I was fixin' to do something real romantic like... and this seems to be the time and the place. If you folks don't mind, that is."

Greta looked thrilled, saying with a smirk (an expression I don't recall seeing on her face before). "Actually, sweetie, I have something I want to ask you. Will you marry me? Right now?"

"Now? Let's do it!" *He answered the second she asked. No hesitation, no thought, he just knew Greta was his person. I love that! He and Flynn certainly have that in common.*

"*Wait a second...* now? Mom, are you sure you don't want a real engagement? A special wedding worthy of the celebration of you finding a man worthy of your heart?" Flynn seemed worried, but I doubt it's because he was having second thoughts about Marko, or even about having a double wedding. I think he truly wanted to make sure his mom actually wanted to get married here and now.

"Flynn my boy; my dear son; I have never been surer. Caroline filled me in on the possible wedding for you and Donyelle; it was so obvious you'd get married. I want to share in your joy, while reveling in the joy of my own; two couples; four people – My son and my daughter-in-law and my fiancé and myself. What could be more... more. I don't know how to say it; but it's what I want."

Marko and Greta kissed, and I found myself a bit morbidly fascinated by the slew of expressions as Flynn's face ran the gambit.

Disgust to see his mother French kissing. Oh yes, there was tongue. Respect to the old geezer, he seemed to have experience. Joy and happiness intermingled, with a touch of remorse. I imagine there must be a small amount of grief seeing his mother move on. Not that his father wasn't a really shitty person. He was. But losing what could have been. If his father had made better choices. If he'd been a kind loving husband and father. If he'd stayed. But the paths created by our struggles, our traumas, they led us to this point. I am not at the point of thanking my no-good 'parents' who don't deserve even that title for abandoning me, but I do see the strength that had to come from that. However, that also brought on a ton of baggage - I could have been a completely different person. Well, hopefully not completely. I love who I am. I love that Flynn loves me as I am. I might have been able to avoid a bunch of speed bumps on the way to love, could have done without the kissing of so many frogs, so to speak, but this is the path I want to be on. The man I want to marry, here and now.

We let Greta and Marko go first; they were our elders, but also great examples of a sweet Godly romance with mutual respect and teamwork throughout. Both Greta and Flynn got teary-eyed as I produced the flowers that had been such a labor of love. Greta even said, "It's like mom is here with me... these are just... oh thank you, my precious new daughter!" We were all sobbing. Eventually, once we gathered our composure, we listened to them say their vows, and they were so perfect, so heartfelt, I felt a bit of remorse that I wasn't going to be able to top that, or even come close. However, all that faded away. When it was my turn, I produced the colorful flowers Flynn was shocked and moved to receive. It was the perfect start to say my vows! I opened my mouth, and while I'd been a bit nervous that I wouldn't know what to say; exactly what I felt came out. That he was perfectly perfect for me. That he was *so* patient, fantastic at communication, sweet to a fault, thoughtful, and protective. He found ways to ensure that everything that needed to happen always happened. He had been there for me for some of the more intense and most joyful moments of my life. He'd seen the lowest lows, and the best of my vibrant personality as well. He knew what I brought to the table; the wonderful and the... not so wonderful, and he accepted me as I was, wholly and completely. He didn't ask me to change. He didn't demand anything of me. His listening skills were top notch, but he knew how to use his tongue too. (Yes, I had to throw at least a little innuendo in; I am still me, after all). And he loved it; he laughed right in the middle of my big spiel. For the life of me, I couldn't process one word of what Flynn vowed to me. I tried, mightily even. I'm sure his words were moving, flowery and undeniably sweet, but I couldn't register them. I just found myself lost in his eyes, so lost that nothing else mattered, not even what I am sure was a very impressive speech about my attributes. *Hopefully someone had the foresight to film this, because I certainly didn't!*

Thankfully, I didn't miss the part where Ryan told us happily that we could kiss. We had that action down to a science at this point. *I can only fantasize about how wonderful the rest of our intimacy will be. I finally get to legitimately make love! Wait...*

I felt panic rise within me, and I must have showed at least some of that intense feeling in my face, because Flynn pulled me close to him as he whispered, "I am not leaving. I never will."

Is it a good thing or completely annoying that he can pick up on even my slightest cue? I honestly don't know. It's frustrating, but also... a huge relief. With Flynn by my side, I won't have to attempt to manage my very strong emotions on my own. Even the ones that come sporadically, trying to take hold of my body and brain. Those voices in my head, older, a female and a male, my imagining of what strict unloving parents would sound like, those had been silenced since I first told Flynn my darkest shames and fears. For the first time, I am only hearing my own thoughts, and I love this man. I've never loved anyone more. He is my very soul's cry; and now we are finally joined as man and wife. It's the most beautiful occasion ever, and I am not going to let my worries dampen the joy.

Flynn hugged his mom and stepfather, I did the same, also getting a squealing group hug with my girls while Flynn and Ryan embraced. After a little while, Flynn held out his hand, saying, "Shall we?"

My breath hitched in my throat. *This is both exciting and wildly terrifying.* I took his hand, noticeably shaking a bit, as his calm kind eyes took me in. Slowly, we descended the stairs together, and we stopped at his dream car. Yet now he only had eyes for me, all excitement seemed to be derived from us being a married couple, the car that had brought him so much joy seemed to pale in comparison. *How incredible!* I couldn't help but marvel at how much this man loved me. I felt the same, of course, but so few in my life had really shown that... and he had in spades.

As Flynn maneuvered us to the passenger side of his brand-new car, he did something very unexpected. He spun me just a little, so I was facing him. Then suddenly, he advanced on me, as if he couldn't wait even until we were in the car, much less at our home. The closer he got, the more flustered I became, and yet he was not finished. He placed his hands on either side of me, pining me against the car, but I was no helpless victim, and this attention was just what I wanted. *He is so incredibly sexy. Well, two can play at that game!* I teased him, leaning over so my very abundant cleavage was readily available, and I positioned my head so that I could begin to kiss along his collarbone. I felt his desire pulsating, making me feel like I was doing a very good job. I whispered, "We should at least get in the car, shouldn't we?"

Flynn shook his head, desire blazing in his eyes. "You're my wife; I am so in awe of that fact... I don't want to wait. Unless you do?" The question was in his chocolate eyes as well as in his tone, and I found myself shaking my head, mimicking his earlier movement.

"As long as no one is looking, I do like the outdoors. But everyone can see us from their vantage point." I reminded him, though it killed me to do so. *I so badly want to continue to see this lust-and-love filled version of my husband. I can't believe I actually get to call Flynn my husband! Forever! A year ago, I would have balked at even the thought of settling down, being loyal, not experimenting with any other guy, only with one person the rest of my life. And yet so much transpired in this last year. Especially recently, I realized just how precious settling down with the right person truly was.* And so, as Flynn backed up, putting forth his hand, I clasped it, letting him lead me into the forest.

He smiled from beside me as he stated, "Since you're the expert on flowers; you get to pick the spot." I beamed a happy smile at him as we explored the terrain. About a half mile from where we were currently, I saw the perfect blend of saffron and roses. *They literally made a bed of flowers. Very appropriate for a horny couple with a year's worth of tension built up to consummate their very shot-gun marriage.* We spent the next hour in that field, and I was awestruck by how he made my body hum. I don't know if it was some talent of his, or just how very besotted I was at this point, but everything he did, everything I did – it all felt just a bit better than it had ever been. It was heady, beautiful, and so intense but in that same oddly calm sort of way. I found myself being in the moment, for the first time not worrying that my bedmate (or in this case flower mate) would up and leave right after. So, after we were both spent - feeling so many endorphins as if we'd spent half a day in the gym, we collapsed in each other's arms. In the middle of the forest, hair in disarray, makeup smeared, clothes haphazardly put back on in a rush before cuddling (we were outside, after all. Who knows who might find us if we press our luck).

As we cuddled together, Flynn cradling my head on his chest, running his hands through my partially unbraided hair, we began to devise a plan. A way to protect Lydia, to win custody of her. *And goodness knows if it's going to work... but we have to try. That child needs a better family. I don't know if her mom passed, ran away... No clue. But that so-called father is an abusive piece of trash, and he should never be allowed even to be in the same room as Lydia. Ever. So, while having a romantic sexy honeymoon where clothes were optional but very discouraged would be... oh I can just imagine what it would be. But right now, that would have to wait. Once we have Lydia safe and secure, then we can dream up the sexiest romps and have a jolly time of it. But now was not that time.*

Flynn helped me up from the mess we'd made of what had been gorgeous flowers (sorry but not sorry), then we used his fancy schmancy new car, and I gotta admit... I could see the allure. *Sort of. Still ridiculously priced. Still just a car... but a very, very nice one.* We pulled ourselves together so we wouldn't look... well, like we had just had sex. Numerous times. Once we had made ourselves legitimately presentable, we met with the custody lawyer Sebastian had given us the information of. It was overwhelming, hearing her map out just how badly the odds were stacked against us. Neither of us are related to the child, or have any direct or even indirect ties to the child, and certainly not longer than what, weeks? Not even a month? A child this young doesn't normally get to decide which family has her, and that much more people that are basically strangers. We would have to prove that we are stable, mentally and financially, that our schedules allow Lydia to go to school, doctor's appointments, anything and everything that might come up if she were to be granted into our care.

However, though a lot was stacked against us, we had a pretty good case in some respects. Her biological father, if we can prove it, is and was abusive. Lydia was in extremely poor physical health, bordering on close to death when we found her. She is quite obviously visibly terrified of the man. Hopefully that will help us in court... at least a little.

The custody lawyer finished going over the case, then she said, "But we have something that very few families can boast. And that may well work in our favor, possibly even win us the case without a huge hassle and time investment."

"What are you referring to?" Flynn asked, looking as confused as I was.

"The King and Queen. In this kingdom, their words have weight. Having them as your character witnesses... that will speak volumes to the judge. I can't promise it will be enough to turn the tide, but if we could find proof of Lydia's abuse, it would be a slam dunk. We wouldn't even have to have a trial held for custody; the judge would award it to you on the spot. The potential senator is Lydia's only blood relative, not even any distant relations. Hence if he is deemed unfit, provided you both pass the background check, the house inspection, and all the paperwork involved... I would be congratulating you on becoming parents."

I was thrilled and a bit terrified at her words. *I had barely pulled myself together, and now I was really going to attempt to be a mother to a child who had been through the ringer in every sense of the word?* Flynn leaned over, squeezing my hand and whispering for only me to hear, "I think I know what you're thinking, Doni. But even as trauma filled as we might be, we would still be better than that ass."

Flynn had such a gentle demeanor; it was always surprising when he chose to swear or show any amount of anger. *Absolutely! He is so right. Of course, we'd be better than that prat! He's the lowest of the low. And even us fumbling in an attempt to be parents would be far better than an abuser who didn't even love his child. Can't believe I let myself worry about that for even a second.* I squeezed Flynn's hand back, silently thanking him.

We went straight from the custody lawyer to a meeting of the minds with our best friends and their publicist. Seraphina told us we would issue a reward of five thousand dollars, generously funded by the crown, for any irrefutable proof of what happened to Lydia. Phrasing it like that allowed the bio-dad to believe we hadn't deduced what he had done and gave us an advantage.

So, we hit the pavement. We handed out fliers with information on who to contact if they'd witnessed anything. We talked with hundreds of people, not just in Monic, but also the four provinces, and even a bit beyond. The first day taught me that this was going to be an arduous frustrating undertaking. Everyone we talked to sang the evil man's praises. Propped him up on a pedestal with nothing but affirmations of his great character and 'gentle fatherly way about him'. *Gross.* Since it was the exact same sentences, the same words and phrases said by all, it was pretty obvious everyone had been prepped. How they had been bribed was anyone's guess. Perhaps he had something on each townsperson in Monic. Or he was offering a pretty penny to spin his tale. *No matter how he is able to pull the strings; everyone Is performing like marionettes. It's incredibly discouraging. I wonder if we are actually going to save Lydia after all.*

Chapter 10
THE STRATEGISTS:

Donyelle's POV:

Exactly a week and three days later, it finally happened. Someone called, saying their child had found their old cam recorder... and it showed the politician beating his daughter. And from what the distraught woman described; it sounded positively mortifying. Because while this was exactly what we wanted and needed, it was also so incredibly heartbreaking to be reminded of the travesties this tiny child has gone through. I couldn't handle when the footage was brought to us; I had to step out. But not before I heard the most blood-curdling scream I could have ever imagined. The raw terror in that sound echoed with me even after I had moved far enough away that I couldn't hear the torture that recorder had captured. As I reached the palace gardens, normally my happy place, I felt my eyes fill with tears, and this time I gave in to my emotions. I sobbed my heart out at the unfairness of it all. At first, I was crying thinking about little Lydia, but eventually I was letting out everything I've been through in my life.

"Why would a loving God let that poor child go through so much abuse?? I want to believe You are the Lord that Caroline and Ryan love... but if You are... why...? Why would You let my parents abandon me?? A newborn baby! Was I that terrible that I deserved to be left like that?!" I choked on a sob, then I continued yelling at the sky. "Did You abandon me too?! I never felt like You were there, when I was abandoned, when I was abused, when I was homeless and destitute. Why create me then leave me to my own devices when I was far too young to care for myself?? You let me grow through so many tribulations-" I stopped, mid-rant. I hadn't meant to say 'grow' I was going to say 'go'. But saying grow made me see things from a whole different perspective. And as I closed my eyes, I felt that same peaceful calm I had felt kissing my husband. I felt rather than heard God speak to me. And as my eyes were closed, it was as if the Lord showed me a slideshow of the worst moments of my life... and how He came through, morphing each until they were beautiful. I saw how I was abandoned as a baby. But instead of feeling resentment, I felt a surprising amount of compassion as I watched the young kids, my parents, who looked fearful and unsure. My biological mother had me swaddled, it seemed as if she had given birth at home, with only my biological father and my Grams. She didn't look totally out of it like I remembered, but I wouldn't have memories this far back. I couldn't hear what was said, but the body language didn't act like I was some burden, a piece of trash to be discarded. Actually, the lady holding me was being so gentle, she looked in awe, but so terrified. It still doesn't excuse how they never came back, but I could see how scared they were. It wasn't quite as blasé a decision as I had assumed. And Grams... she looked so honored. Her face lit up as her semi-feeble arms reached out to comfort me. The baby version of me started to cry, screaming even, and I saw the anguish in my biological parents' eyes. *They did care about me. At least a little. Perhaps... perhaps they had thought I would be better off with Grams. They had no way of knowing that Grams would develop whatever disease she had that made her forget and eventually die.*

The moving picture before me became brightly dazzling, then suddenly I was in another memory entirely. I saw myself, around

Lydia's current age, when I realized Grams wasn't ever going to wake up. But then I saw Caroline, and I felt her heart; how much she truly cared about me, even as young as we were. She gave younger me a huge hug, Caroline cried - I hadn't seen her do it at the time, but in the memory, I could see her now. She was trying to be brave; to be strong for me. She was filled with so much compassion, so much love for myself. A second later my vision had morphed to Caroline begging her mom to take me in. Susan's face was exhausted, pinched and drawn. "Caroline, how many times do I have to say no?!" Caroline's mother sighed, so deeply she sounded like she had the world's weight on her shoulders. "I understand Donyelle is your friend, and she is a great girl, I get that. I was close with her Grams, before she..." Susan blinked back tears, something I'd never witnessed – *Susan had never shown any kind of emotion around me before. And she was close with my Grams? Since when?*

Susan in my vision, something that was most definitely not in my memory, shrugged, keeping her tears inside as she continued, "King Henry graciously gave your father the job we need; this is our one and only opportunity to escape Langley. If we took in Donyelle... I told you how King Henry is. He would never allow a transplant of a child with her... uh... skin tone. I told you before - she would be considered undesirable."

Young Caroline looked frustrated and sad, "Why does that matter? I don't understand mama. Don is my bestest friend; can we just ask King Henry?"

Susan sighed with exasperation, snapping, "No! And I don't want to hear another word about it! Go to your room; this instant!" Caroline looked so heartbroken, she hung her head, padding off toward the stairs to her room. I thought it would morph, or it would follow Caroline, just like eavesdropping mini-me had... but instead, I watched Susan break down. After she'd cried, she picked up her landline and said, "This is Susan Hart. I know of a child that needs care." She paused for a minute, seemingly listening. "Her name is Donyelle Cox. No, I don't believe she's ever been in school. Uh... I think eight or nine? Something like that? No, no one knows if her parents are alive or dead, they got pregnant very young and entrusted the child with her grandmother, but she has passed on. Me? No, I wish I could... but my circumstances won't allow it. I- yes. If it will ensure that she has a spot, I will pay the monthly fee." *Wait... she paid for me to be in the orphanage?* In disbelief, I watched Susan do a double take. "It's how much?! Goodness. Uh, no. That won't be a problem. Just make sure she's well taken care of. Donyelle's a good girl. A hard worker, and her Grams was a dear friend of mine. I will pay the monthly fee for her schooling and space. Thank you." She hung up, and I saw her sigh, whispering under her breath, but I could still hear her. "How are we going to afford a thousand a month on top of everything else??"

Scene after scene flashed before my eyes; where something happened that I found a very negative moment in my life. And for almost each one, there was a positive moment that delivered me through it. It felt like Jesus was telling me that I had not been abandoned. That even though these awful things happened; due to choices made by others; He was there with me through each one, and it might not have been exactly as I had always assumed. *I wasn't unlovable, like I had forever believed, but I was actually very loved. Bad things happened to me, and around me, but I was shielded from a lot of it, and nine times out of ten, someone or something happened that helped me get to where I am now. Married to the man I love wholeheartedly. Fighting to save a child who had been through similar circumstances. Financially secure, my business is booming, I've got fantastic friends. Couldn't ask for more.*

I found myself opening my eyes, and I was back in the garden. The slideshow of images had vanished, but the peace and joy those moments had brought with my brand-new perspective remained. *Now, more than ever, I am determined to adopt Lydia; I will do what I can to better her situation, like others did for me.*

Epilogue:
ONE YEAR LATER

Donyelle's POV:

Can't believe we have been married a year! Our official anniversary! And it's been just over nine months since Lydia has become our adopted daughter! It was a lot of red tape, a lot of meetings, paperwork, and planning, but Dante has finally finished our newly renovated home, so it's time to decorate and furnish the place. Lydia can't wait to have a larger bedroom that she'll be able to make completely her own. Greta and Marko have completely accepted Lydia as their grandchild, doting on her to the point of spoiling my daughter with so much love! That isn't surprising of course, Marko and Greta are a match made in heaven, and everyone who meets Lydia falls in love with her immediately.

As we were going through IKEA, I found myself gravitating toward the baby furniture. Flynn came up behind me, nuzzling me with his nose against the right side of my neck as he asked, "Trying to tell me something?" He was joking, in his sweet way, but the fact was that I was showing a few symptoms of what *could* be pregnancy. *It's just... I don't know for sure. My breasts are sore, but sometimes that happens when my time of the month is near. I am late, but I have never been particularly frequent. I feel sick to my stomach at times, but it could have been something I ate. I don't want to get too* *excited, just to be let down. After all, I had been on birth control for so many years, I believe it takes a good long while before it's completely out of your system. And I never got tested to find out how fertile I am. So why get Flynn's hopes up, and possibly either excite or freak out our daughter for no reason?*

I decided to answer, "How would you feel if we ever did get pregnant?" *I know the answer, of course. We both get so excited when I take a pregnancy test when I am even possibly late... and we get just as let down when it inevitably tests negative.*

I could feel Flynn's smile against my skin, and his heartbeat quickened, feeling it pound against my right shoulder. "I would be thrilled. You are already a wonderful mother, and I love our family. Adding another child to the mix would just double the love. But don't feel like you have to. I am perfectly content loving you and Lydia."

I felt a large smile blossom on my face. *There he goes again, giving the best possible answer he could. Exactly what I wanted to hear. Truth is, I really want to be pregnant. Hope and pray that I am. I've been trying to be more at ease with just letting God have His way in my life, our relationship has been so much stronger, and that inner peace has become just about a daily feeling. So nice to finally feel secure in myself and those around me. Not constantly waiting for the other shoe to drop. Not waking up cringing, feeling like someone might leave, or something might go terribly wrong. I wasn't cursed after all, not really. And now I can empathize with Lydia and that whole group of children I mentor.*

Over the past six months, Caroline, Ahyoka, and I had been going to a home for girls created by women who actually care about children that don't have a home, good food, and loving education. Caroline handles the education part of it, the home was created by Dante (that guy sure does keep busy, he's got a whole team now). Myself and Lydia bring meals direct from Greta each week, planned and set up to be nutritious but also delicious. The home is run by seven of the kindest women out of the several dozen we interviewed, and it had been going so well. I have cameras set up in all the main areas, and I have encouraged the children to tell me anything that happens; really good or extremely bad. I haven't had one bad report; not even close. It seems my pet project is going swimmingly. And Lydia loves when we go; she looks forward to it, because she has befriended the girls there. They all get to play together with myself and my friends. It's the perfect set up, and Flynn is beyond supportive of the girls' home, of my flower business, and of my happiness in general. *Yes, life is beautiful. Having a baby of my own... it would just be the cherry on top.*

I turned slightly, as I changed my mind, and whispered into my handsome husband's ear, "I'm not sure... but I think we should buy a pregnancy test."

Flynn's face positively radiated with excitement, and I couldn't bring myself to remind him that we were just going to find out. Nothing was for sure, of course. But the anticipation was palpable, for both of us. Thankfully, Lydia was off in her own little world, completely entranced with selecting exactly what furniture she needed to make her room unique and special. So, I went and paid for the test... and I made my way into the bathroom. *Yes, I know it's unconventional to handle something so important in a public bathroom... but I can't help it. I have to know. And that drive home, even though it was only like fifteen or so minutes from our new place... it would kill me. The curiosity, trying not to freak out. If I wasn't, would I be ready for yet another dashed hope, yet another month passed? We'd been trying, not fully actively, but certainly staying very, very intimate, and I certainly wasn't on birth control. But without protection, up until this point I hadn't proved to be very fertile. So, what made this time any different? I'd felt gross before, gotten all excited, and then found out it was just a stomach bug or the flu.* While I set the timer on my iPhone, I washed my hands and tried to quiet my mind. I left the test on the counter, next to me, but far enough away I would have to crane my neck to the left to peek. I texted Flynn, asking him to meet me in the ladies' bathroom. *An odd request, to be sure. However, my husband is intelligent, and he will connect the dots, realize how import-ant this is.*

Rrrrr -ahhh -rrrrr. The most annoying alarm on my phone went off, so I pushed stop. Then I waited. It felt like a full day, I so badly wanted to look. Just a tiny peek; I could find out if it was good news or bad, know how to react and how to comfort or celebrate with Flynn. *But... no. That wouldn't be right. This is something we always shared together. I am just finding myself more and more impatient with every passing month.* Flynn burst through the door, and just as al-ways before, he swept me gracefully into his arms, hugging me tight. I knew what he was going to say before he even opened his mouth, after all, he'd been saying it for eleven months already. "I love you, Doni. You are the best wife and mother. Nothing changes that, no matter what." And just like every other time, I believed his words, to my very core. He had proven he was the staying and not straying type. I couldn't have asked for a more devoted man, a gentler yet pas-sionate lover. He had this almost magical way with Lydia that made me forget we hadn't raised her from the very beginning. Normally I smiled, said, 'you too babe' or something similar. *But this time... I don't know. It's different for some reason.* I felt my heart swell with emotion as I kissed him soundly. He was a little surprised, as this de-viated from our regular monthly routine, but it wasn't an unwelcome one, of course. He kissed me back, our tongues dancing in delightful, synchronized rhythm from off and on about two years of practice. *Goodness - he is a talented man!*

Once I'd had my fill, I leaned back while saying, "You are in-credible Flynn. Absolutely incredible. You are the kind of father I wish I had. Lydia is a whole different young woman now because of your kindness and affection. Monic even has you down as the favor-ite to win the Senator position after that prat ended up in jail. Good riddance to him. But you are so much more than I ever thought. I apologize that at any point I thought you were just a gate guard. There's nothing wrong with that job, first off, but you are so full of hidden depths. This past year especially, getting to delve into your psyche, learn what makes you tick, experiencing life with you, that has been... all I could ever ask for. So regardless of if we are going to have a baby or not, remember that."

His eyes mirrored the wonder I felt for my man; our feelings so reciprocal even being married a year. "I love you, my Doni. Now let's hurry up and check out this test and get out of here; I really don't think being here as long as we have is very appropriate. Any ladies may deem me a pervert."

I laughed, responding as I flicked his nose, "Impossible. They'd just think I was very, very lucky."

We closed our eyes, counted to three, then opened them. And... there were the two little lines. *Is this real? Could it be?!* I stated, "Before we get too excited, we should see Cornelius." Flynn nodded. We had long since dropped the 'Doctor' title. After all, he had married Lily, Ryan's mother, about three months ago. He was essentially family at this point. But thankfully, he still made frequent house calls, and this was one of those times. I pushed his contact, put it on speakerphone, and waited. I heard Cornelius answer, "Hello, this is Dr. Cornelius, what is this regarding?"

I heard a women's giggle in the background. Cornelius hushed with a laugh, "Honey, I'm on the phone!"

"And yet it still gets me every time. Dr. Cornelius. So official. So important." It was Lily, teasing and so much love in every decibel of her voice.

Flynn and I shared a smirk. We were known for our banter as well. It was cute to see Lily, an older woman, having real fun and enjoying the pleasure of real love. "Right, well, much as we'd like to leave you two love birds alone, Flynn and I need your services."

I heard a cough as Lily said, "Whoops. Hi Donyelle and Flynn! Don't mind me!"

We chuckled, and Cornelius asked as business-like as possible, "What seems to be the trouble?"

Flynn waved at me to answer, so I waited for a dramatic moment, then answered, "I just took a pregnancy test, and it's positive."

"EEEEEE!!! You're pregnant!!!! Congratulations the two of you! Oh, another boy or girl!!!" Lily's excited yelps were so very loud, I turned the phone off speaker until she was done.

Flynn whispered, "Thanks, sweetie."

I kissed his cheek in response. We set the time for the appointment in the next half hour, so we quickly went back out onto the store floor, me hurriedly stuffing the pregnancy test in my pocket. *Remind me to wash this jacket. Or burn it. If I am pregnant though, I'll probably save it as a keepsake- the outfit I was wearing when I found out I was going to be a mother for the second time. Oh... that's something else Flynn and I will have to discuss.* Before we reached Lydia, who was happily chatting away with our mutual friend who owned this IKEA, I whispered, "If we are pregnant, we need to talk about it with Lydia in a way that doesn't freak her out."

Flynn nodded solemnly, though his eyes were twinkling with barely contained enthusiasm. I smiled as we reached Lydia, as she was gushing, "-and then I'd put that nightstand over on the right side, right here." She had a picture handy, showing off her room as she apparently had been talking it through with Celestina, the owner.

"I can't wait to see everything all decorated!" I piped in, causing Lydia to turn to face us. *Each time I look at her, it is still a bit jarring. She's just so happy, so animated, such a lover of life now; it's hard to reconcile the memories of when she'd been scared of her own shadow, shallow gaunt cheeks, eyes haunted by fear and pain.*

"Mom! Dad! You have to see this; Miss Cel said I could fit fifteen things in my new room; they are all my favorites!"

I just love hearing 'mom'. Imagine having two children calling for me; how full would my life feel! I crouched down, Flynn right beside me. "How exciting!! Fifteen of your favorites! Please tell us all about it!"

Eagerly our daughter explained everything, as we listened patiently, or as patiently as you can while really wanting to rush out to the fancy car (still in pristine condition too) and head to the Doctor's. Once she'd finished her diatribe, we bought everything on our lists, gave all the combined lists to Celestina so we wouldn't have to wait in a line or try to pack anything in that car. "Thanks for your purchases! We should have all three loads delivered within the next 2-3 hours. I'll make your delivery top priority, you are some of my best customers, after all!" We quickly group-hugged, then rushed to the palace, still had about ten minutes to spare when we dropped Lydia off to Greta and Marko. Flynn had texted as soon as we set the appointment, asking if they could watch her for a bit, and of course, they said yes. It was very rare that they said no, unless it fell on one of their date nights.

"Lydia! Get in here sweetheart! Your Grandpa and I were just getting ready to make cookies!"

Lydia excitedly screeched, "Cookies!! Bye mom, bye dad!" She barreled into Flynn's mom and stepfather's arms, but I wasn't jealous; it was a very good thing that she felt so comfortable with Greta and Marko. *They are wonderful grandparents!* We blew kisses to our rambunctious daughter, then hand-in-hand, we walked toward Cornelius' office. He and Lily had a lovely home on the far side of the castle, but his office was still conveniently located close to the garden and Caroline's old suite. We walked inside the waiting room, and the perpetually cheery nurse greeted us. There were a couple people waiting around, people I didn't recognize actually, but my name was called first. Corenlius greeted us with his signature hug (he had really come out of his shell since professing his love for Lily, his former patient that he had always had feelings for; but that's a story for another time).

He told me that he needed to get labs and urine to test my hCG levels, and unlike Caroline, I wasn't scared of them, so I barely even flinched. *I just imagine it's a mosquito, annoying and pesky, but not particularly scary.* I was shown where the bathroom was located, so I excused myself to pee alone. I tried not to let myself get caught up in my swirling mixed emotions, but it was hard not to. I whispered to my stomach, feeling kind of silly. "Can you hear me in there? If you can... I love you. Whoever you are. And I really hope that you're growing in my tummy right now." I caught my pee in the cup, looking at it as I wondered what secrets my slightly yellow liquid would reveal. "Please God, I want to be pregnant. So badly. You know that is the desire of my heart. Amen." As I cleaned the medical cup with a paper towel, I let myself imagine what it would be like. *Growing larger, feeling a tiny human living inside me. The occasional kick, possibly developing slightly odd cravings. Childbirth... let's skip over childbirth. That wouldn't be fun. Every single mother I talked to, even Caroline, who just about spouts rainbows and sunshine wherever she goes... even Caroline confided in me how unbearably painful it was to give birth. But she did always reassure me how worth it the experience truly was. Whether it was worth it or not was beside the point. If I was pregnant, I was having this child. Unless Christ calls my baby home early; he or she would be loved, well looked after, nurtured... well, Caroline would help with the nurturing. Besides, Rigel is turning out okay, for a young toddler, with Flynn and I as godparents. And of course Lydia is a whole different child, in the best way possible. We can do this!*

Feeling courageous, I gave the cup to Cornelius as he left, then I sidled up to Flynn. We cuddled together, my head on his shoulder, my hands around his waist, his arms around mine, gently rubbing circles on my bare skin. I shivered, with anticipation, but also, Flynn's touch seemed to illicit that reaction. *One touch, and my body is ready to go. But now is not the time.* Though my lips twitched at the thought.

Flynn's teasing voice cut through my reverie. "What are you thinking about, naughty girl of mine?"

"I may have been fantasizing about you and I getting it on, right here, right now."

Flynn's one and a half ears (yes, I am a terrible wife who teases him about his ears occasionally) turned red, quickly followed by his cheeks, as he whispered, "Doni! Don't make me hard! Cornelius could come back any moment!"

I winked at him, "That's part of the fun, isn't it?" I heard my man groan, kissing me so deeply I felt like I was being swallowed, and while that wasn't an abnormal experience when we were to-gether, it was heightened with the possibility of us being preg-nant. *I mean sure, I'd be the one carrying the baby in my womb, but just like every other part of our marriage, I have full confidence Flynn would continue to be my teammate throughout any pregnancy as well!*

The creak of the door signaled we needed to end our tryst, so we quickly pulled apart, me only slightly resting against Flynn's shoulder, looking like the picture of innocence. Dr. Cornelius came inside with a smirk that was very uncharacteristic. "What's that look for?" I asked, too curious to keep my gob shut.

"Oh, just that you both aren't fooling me. I am a Doctor. I'm trained to pick up on the most minute of details."

"What details exactly? Just so I know for next time." Flynn asked with a bit of a cocky nod in my direction. *If any other guy looked at me or talked like Flynn just did, I would be repulsed, but with Flynn... what can I say; it's adorable. Hot, even.*

"Donyelle's right center braid is now located on the left. You are both panting, which tends to mean your heart beats are irregu-lar. Both patients' eyes are glazed, and your lips are a bit bruised/swollen. All signs that you were mid-make out when I entered. I would worry it was more than that, but nothing would suggest you had hurriedly dressed as well."

Ooop. Talk about embarrassing! I quickly asked, "So uh, those results? We're ready, as soon as you are."

Doctor Cornelius gave us both a knowing look, then he smiled. "You are pregnant Donyelle; I assume this is a very good thing?"

Flynn shouted his excitement as I squealed, jumping up from our sitting position, then up and down with our sudden influx of excited yet nervous energy. We group-hugged the unsuspecting Doctor, then all cheered together. "We have to tell Care and Ryan!" I exclaimed. As Flynn and I rushed towards the door. All of a sud-den, my husband stopped in his tracks though, making me ask wor-riedly, "What's wrong? Are you okay?"

Flynn nodded, saying, "I just realized that we shouldn't be running. Exerting yourself is probably not good for the baby."

I frowned, then smiled a little. "Sweetie, we don't need to worry about that until possibly... the third trimester. So just calm down."

He grinned, unabashed, but we ran at a bit slower pace than we had before. Before too long we reached the royal suite, Flynn asked the guard to announce us, but I was not willing to wait. I texted Caroline.

Get your butt out here!

Seconds later, I could hear Caroline's musical laugh, and then she opened the door. "Only you Don. Please come in. Ryan and I were just trying to enjoy a very rare baby-free moment. But that's okay; we're always happy to see you."

"Speak for yourself!" Ryan shouted from the other room. "I want alone time with my lovely wife! Come back tomorrow!" Flynn chuckled, and Ryan called out again, "I'm kidding! Sort of. Come on in."

I said, "We'll make this quick. Flynn; go ahead and do the honors."

He was pleasantly surprised, but quickly said, "My beautiful, incredible effervescent wife... is pregnant!!"

Caroline rushed toward me with a hug, as Ryan congratulated us both, it was a very sweet moment. Ryan said teasingly, "Now if you don't mind, you both should go get that sweet daughter of yours, and if you haven't told her yet, share the good news... because Caroline and I want to attempt making another baby of our own."

Caroline playfully slapped Ryan's arm as she chided, "Tater Tot!"

Flynn and I laughed, and I put my hands up, a gesture of surrender I normally didn't use. Flynn and I left right as Ryan had swept Caroline into his arms and said lovingly, "Back to bed with you!" Caroline laughed, leaning up to kiss her husband, so Flynn and I quickly vacated the premises. We hurriedly went toward Flynn's parents' home as I asked,

"Do you think Lydia will be worried about her place in the family when we tell her about the baby?"

Flynn frowned; forehead drawn as he gave me a pensive look. "I hadn't really considered that. Would you have?"

I pondered his question, then nodded definitively. "Absolutely I would have. But Lydia isn't me. And we are attempting to be great parents, which obviously I didn't get the privilege of experiencing." He cupped my face with his hand, saying,

"I love you, Doni."

"And I love you too. Let's go give our daughter the extremely good news. I think we should tell her separately, then tell your parents a little later. What do you think?"

Flynn nodded. "Lydia deserves to have a conversation with us without anyone else around. Our opportunity to show her she's still our priority, and that doesn't change, even with a new baby on the way."

We thanked Greta and Marko, then we took Lydia back to our new place. Since it was currently unfurnished, we sat down on the bare floor. Lydia stated wisely, "What's going on? You actin' funny."

Here it goes. I need to help Lydia feel cherished and dissuade her fears about being displaced or merely being just a replacement child... how do I handle this delicately... "Do you know what being pregnant means?"

Lydia nodded solemnly. "Baby goes in a mommy's tummy."

"Right, so what your daddy and I wanted to tell you is that I have a baby in my tummy. I'm pregnant." I waited, checking to see what her reaction was. Strangely enough, she just nodded again. She stood up, moving towards the door.

I asked her, "Lydia, what are you doing?"

Lydia looked back at us with tears in her eyes, looking very forlorn. "I understand. I will go. Thank you for... thank you." She sounded resigned, and that haunted older-than-she-should-be look cast a shadow over her lovely eight-year-old face.

Oh my gosh no! She thinks we are telling her to leave!! I opened my mouth, but Flynn beat me to it. "You are our child; nothing will ever change that. All this means is that our family is growing even more. There is just going to be one more girl or boy to love. You will not be forgotten; we will never give you up. I'm afraid you're stuck with us now." Flynn said with a loving look only a father could give.

Lydia hesitated, a hand hovering above the doorknob. I couldn't help but try to joke to cut the tension as I stood up, walking towards my adopted daughter. "Speak for yourself Hun, I am nothing less than a delight to be around at all times." I was teasing, but I quickly sobered as I kneeled down beside Lydia, holding out my hand to my daughter. Hesitantly, she took it, and my hand dwarfed hers. "All banter aside; you are our precious first daughter. And you always will be. Your father and I will always love you. In fact, we have a mission for you, if you'll accept it."

She looked intrigued, while a quick peek at my husband revealed my words had made him a bit nervous. I flashed my handsome lad a bemused look before smiling brightly at my daughter. "What's the mission, Mama?" *Oh, my heart! I will never tire of that label. Never as long as I live!*

I patted her hand as I said, "Your father and I need you to be our big helper. Playing and teaching your sibling, helping him or her learn right from wrong, and most importantly for your sibling to know they are very, very loved. Extremely. Can you do that?" I gave her a big hug before she replied, hopefully helping her see our love wasn't based off her performance or answer. I whispered, "We love you, Lydia. You will always be our daughter. Always, love."

"Oh yes, Mama! I'll be the bestest helper *ever*!" Flynn moved closer, wrapping his arms around me from behind; truthfully one of my favorite sensations, as he nuzzled my neck. Then, he moved closer to our daughter, squatting down and adding to the group hug. Looking around this unfurnished home, I saw my family. The bright potential of the future shone around us, and just like the house we were about to design, our future had limitless possibilities.

SNEAK PEAK OF BOOK 3 VOLUME 2-4

Thank you for reading Volume 1 in *Lehavre's Untold Stories*– The Romance of the Abandoned. I hope you enjoyed it; and that you'll keep an eye out for Volume 2 – Ahyoka and Sebastian's story. I appreciate you!

Continue the journey as we see how Ahyoka and Sebastian try to maneuver their relationship as he attempts to direct his first movie while he balances appeasing the elders and Ahyoka's tight-knit community, while struggling with the language barrier. How will Ahyoka fare when Sebastian wants to show her his world? All this and more will be explored in *Lehavre's Untold Stories* Volume 2!

Curious how Ariana is handling her grief? Is she dealing with it and trying to look forward, or will she attempt to bury her feelings and stay stuck where she is? Check in with Rita and Giovanni; see how the couple work together to attempt to help everyone in the four provinces and beyond. See if Giovanni and Rita's love can go the distance in Volume 3!

What about Dante and Whitney? After forcing himself to be robotic for so long, how will he adjust in his dating life? Will Whitney stick along for the ride, or will she tire of her Hercules? Witness how a new family either is knit together or unravels in the last installment of *Lehavre's Untold Stories* Volume 4!

British Slang Definitions:

Ace. Great
Affectionate jokes
Bagsy. To reserve or claim
Banter. Affectionate jokes
Barmy. Eccentric or crazy
Beastly. Very unpleasant
Bird. Girl
Blimey. Expression of surprise
Bloke. Guy
Bloody. Expletive or used for emphasis.
Bodge. To do something hastily or clumsily
Bollocks. Expression of disbelief
Bonkers. Wild
Bruv. Male friend or brother
Bugger all. Nothing at all
Buzzin'. Happy or excited
Cheeky Chappy. Likable/mischievous man
Cheers. To say goodbye or thank someone
Chin wag. Conversation
Chuffed/chuffed to bits. Very pleased or proud
Chunder. To vomit
Crisps. Chips
Daft. Silly, foolish, or eccentric
Dead. Another way to say 'very'
Doddery. Unsteady
dodgy. Untrustworthy, suspicious or unreliable
Dosh. money
Faff. To waste time or dither
Fam. Referring to family or a close friend
Fancy. Showing desire for someone or something
Gander. To look around
Gob. Mouth

Gobsmacked. Expression of shock
Grand. Fantastic
Grass up. Telling the authorities about someone
Innit. Isn't it?
Jiffy. Short period
Kip. Short nap
Knackered. Very tired
Knob. Annoying person
Lad. Boy
Lass. Girl
Leg it. To run away
Loo. Toilet
Lost the plot. Irrational, acting ridiculous/angry
Lush. Nice or great
Mate. Buddy, a friend
Melt. Coward or wimp
Mental. Crazy
Miffed. Upset or irritable
Minging. Extremely unpleasant or unattractive
Minted. Extremely wealthy
Mug. Fool or stupid person, a person's face
Naff. Cheap-looking or tasteless
Nick. Stealing
Nicked. To be arrested
Nippy. Chilly or cold
Numpty. Idiot or fool (joke or aggressive)
nutter. A crazy person
Off your trolley. Crazy
Pear-shaped. Gone wrong
Peng. Attractive/appealing
Pissed off. Annoyed
Poppycock. Nonsense
Proper. Very, correct, etc.
Quid. Slang for pounds

Rubbish. Trash, nonsense
Sack off. Avoid or stop doing something, get rid of or abandon someone
Scrummy. Delicious
Shag. Referring to sexual intercourse in a callous way
Shiner. Black eye
Skint. Being without money
Slag off. Criticizing
Sod off. Leave/go away
Soz. Abbreviation for sorry
Snazzy. Stylish/impressive
Snog. Kissing passionately/French kiss
Stroppy. Bad-tempered
Taking the piss. To joke or mock uncouth. Lacking good manners, sophistication, or grace
Telly. Television
Tosser. Idiot
Waffle. Ramble
Wanker. Rude term saying someone is annoying or foolish
Wangle. Using trickery or persuasion to manipulate
Wazzock. Fool or idiot
Winding up. Annoying
Wonky. Unstable or not working properly
Zonked. Exhausted

Cherokee Definition:

Oginalii. Friend

www.ingramcontent.com/pod-product-compliance
Lightning Source LLC
Chambersburg PA
CBHW071837020726
47502CB00004B/1397